GAME, SET, and DEATH

ABOUT THE AUTHOR

Game, set, and death is the second novel of Phil Hall, but the first to feature his daring duo of dysfunctional detectives. A second story is in development.

He has previously contributed film reviews to a University magazine and a chapter to an anthology. He attended K.E.G.S. in Chelmsford and studied Economics at UEA, Norwich before embarking on a career in marketing – the perfect grounding for writing. Phil lives in Surrey with his wife and daughter.

His first book was a domestic thriller called Dream House; you can find more details on the website www.philhallauthor.com or dive straight in and buy it from Amazon.

GAME, SET, and DEATH

Someone in the Surrey Hills is not playing by the rules

By
PHIL HALL

DISCLAIMER

All characters and events in this publication, other than those clearly in the public domain, are fictitious and any resemblance to real persons, living or dead is purely coincidental.

Published details: Amazon

Published June 2022.

Print Edition

For

Margaret and Eddie

And

For Russell (Chapter 7 is for you.)

GAME, SET and DEATH

By
PHIL HALL

ONE

A SUDDEN SQUALL of wind ripped down the lane and sent a discarded cider bottle hurtling into a hedge like the final pin splattered into the end pit by a bowling ball. Seconds later it returned to whip up a couple of chocolate wrappers, held them captive in a frenzied dance before it tired of the fun and dumped them on an unsuspecting lawn. Although it was mid-June the weather behaved as if it was late November with sharp gusts racing across the lane as early summer masqueraded as Halloween. Detective Inspector Scott Bee manoeuvred his ageing Mercedes into the narrow lane, rolled over a sleeping policeman and bumped his head; it did nothing to improve his mood. He shouldn't be here, he shouldn't be on duty on a Friday morning, he hadn't had a day off in 10 days. He pulled into a small clearing, parked up and opened the rear door of his car and lifted his overcoat from the back seat. He looked up to the heavens as the wind abruptly stopped its game with the hedgerow and switched its attention to the washing line in the garden of the last house on Green Lane. He scowled, wrapped the coat around his shoulders, snatched a second look upwards, decided against buttoning his coat and muttered something about climate change and the unpredictability of the English weather.

A familiar pained expression took residence on his drawn

face as he looked around for someone to tell him why he had been forced to abandon his early morning run. He should have been jogging along Reigate's middle-class avenues where respectable people would be enjoying muesli in their John Lewis breakfast bowls. In this town no one needed to scurry around in the early hours cleaning floors to earn a crust. It didn't seem right that he should be the only person up and about. With no people to catch his attention his eyes fell on a battered yellow Volvo estate, one of the original mark ones. A tank of the highway. He spotted a N sticker in the back window and smiled at the idea of a Swedish car under Norwegian colours, barely a century since the Norwegians themselves had revoked Swedish rule. His mind drifted back to the waterfront at Stockholm and a smile attempted to cross his face but was abruptly brought to order. This was work, and unpleasant work to boot, based on the short message he had received twenty minutes earlier.

He slipped his car keys into his pocket, pulled out his black covid facemask and stepped across the broken tarmac that marked out a makeshift overflow carpark for the sports clubs that occupied the end of the lane. A cricket club, a bowls green, a rugby pavilion, and the tennis club – a sporting oasis tucked away in a picturesque cul-de-sac. Despite his passion for sport, this was an area of Reigate that he didn't know. It was the running and football clubs that consumed Bee's time when he wasn't investigating murders. Although he was slipping gracefully towards his forties, his fitness regime ensured no one ever believed he could be thirty-nine. He kept his wiry black hair short to assist the subterfuge. Bee didn't have a problem with his age, but one of his few pleasures was ghosting past younger runners on the regular Saturday park run, not that he'd done much of that for the last 15 months since the country had been in lockdown.

He walked on through a pebbled car park until his reverie was broken by a police officer breezing into view and walking towards him.

"What's the situation?" he asked.

"We have a murder victim on court number one Inspector Bee," she said.

They stepped close to exchange pleasantries and then recalled the protocol for social distancing and stepped back a yard while exchanging smiles behind their facemasks.

"Okay, thanks, it's Bartlett, isn't it?"

"Yes sir, thank you sir."

Bee allowed himself a smile and an inward pat on the back. He was terrible with names but knew that the personal touch made all the difference. The chief superintendent had given him this feedback at his delayed annual appraisal last week and Bee was determined to put it into practice. The words 'you're the best detective in the county but you need to bring people with you' still resonated in his head. But there wasn't much chance of him forgetting Jess Bartlett or those beautiful flowing chestnut locks.

"What else can you tell me? Have SOCO been alerted? Anyone else on the scene?"

Bartlett reeled from the barrage of questions, "not much I'm afraid sir."

She looked down at her notebook. "The body was found a little before 8:00am this morning, when a couple of club members arrived to play tennis. They called it in to the station, but as you know we are a bit short of personnel at the moment, what with covid and all that. Sergeant Wilkins sent me down here to secure the site and wait for you. I've been here for about thirty minutes, but you're the first to arrive. Peter, Sergeant Wilkins, said we might have to wait for a forensic team as one team is busy with that crash on the M25 and three people are still self-isolating."

Bee acknowledged the news with a nod and a gruff kick at the lose stones in the car park, then remembered his appraisal and apologised profusely.

"What happened to the two tennis players?"

"As soon as I told them they couldn't play, they went home."

Bee swung his head up and glared directly at Bartlett.

"Not before I took their contact details," she intercepted his wrath.

Bee recognised her catch with a smile. "Excellent. Let's take a look at the crime scene."

Bartlett led the way towards a dilapidated wooden gate which she had wrapped in yellow police tape, Bee remembered his manners in time and lifted it for her to pass underneath.

"You've done well securing the site."

"It wasn't difficult; the tennis club sits at the end of this cul-de-sac so there's not a lot of passing traffic. Ordinarily this gate would be left open and everyone visiting the club would gain access from this road. Besides I'm a member here so I feel responsible, I guess you could say I've got a foot in both camps."

"You knew the two players who found the body?"

"I recognised their faces, and I think one is called Bill but that's about it."

"How about the victim?"

"They said it was Russell, the head coach here, and that seems reasonable, but I hope they're mistaken, he's a lovely man I can't think why anyone would want to kill him. But the only car left in the car park is that red Nissan and Bill said it belonged to Russell." Bartlett turned and pointed to the bottom of the car park where a solitary red Nissan Leaf was parked on the left-hand side.

"Better put some tape around that and keep it for the forensic boys; you never know what might show up."

Bee digested this information as they crunched across the shingle car park of the tennis club. On their right were four clay courts, set parallel to one another, as they approached Bee noticed a hand sanitiser dispenser fixed to a telegraph pole, instinctively he pressed the lever but no soap dropped into his palm. He shrugged, people were already assuming covid was beaten, he didn't share their enthusiasm and pushed his hand into his coat pocket to retrieve his own mini bottle of sanitiser. At the end of the line was a narrow pathway which led passed the fourth court and towards a single tier brick clubhouse which looked as if it was built at the same time as the gate.

Bee mumbled as he thought he ought to make conversation with Bartlett but couldn't think of anything to say. His mind was focused on the puzzle that lay ahead of him. Bartlett picked up on his muttering and turned towards him. "Did you say something?"

"No, not really." Bee kept his head down and allowed the uncomfortable moment to float over his head. A few more steps and they arrived at a grass court; the first of four which aligned with the clay courts they had walked around.

Slumped against the net in the centre of the first court was a body; a man in tennis clothing with a knife jutting out of his chest.

Jess Bartlett gasped and pulled her hand to her mouth. She stopped in her tracks. Bee glanced despairingly at her.

"Is it the head coach you mentioned?"

She nodded, "I think so, I was hoping I was mistaken but seeing him again, it's Russell." She blinked her eyes quickly to hold back the tears.

Bee was itching to take a closer look at the victim, but recognised that Bartlett needed some support, he helped her towards a wooden bench and sat her down. "Is this your first dead body?"

Bartlett nodded, still unable to speak.

Bee placed his hand on her shoulder. "The first one's never easy, – none of them are, but over time you'll develop a degree of immunity."

Bee turned and looked back at the body he was longing to examine. "Take deep breaths, sit for a few minutes, you'll be fine. I'm going to take a closer look and then chase up the station."

When he returned, Bee was on the phone and getting agitated. "What am I supposed to do without any forensic support? This needs to be a priority."

Jess Bartlett composed herself. She swallowed hard and stood up quickly, straightened her skirt and faced Bee. "What do you want me to do first sir?" Jess touched her face as she spoke.

Bee shifted his weight from foot to foot and pursed his lips. He wasn't used to being first on the scene. "We have to wait for the forensic team to examine the body, so our first priority is to preserve the scene. You've made an excellent start with that gate; can you get back to it and keep everyone out. Forensics should be here within the hour, I've hijacked a team from Sussex, I'm going to snoop around the building here, and see if there are any cameras around."

"I'll be surprised if there's one here, I think the club is planning to renovate the clubhouse; they have been collecting money for months."

"Interesting. One other thing. The victim doesn't have a tennis racquet anywhere near him, so I presume he wasn't playing tennis here. Unless you or one of the early players removed it."

"No, I haven't touched it and I don't think the others did."

"That poses the question of why a tennis coach comes on to a court without a racquet. It's the primary tool of his trade, I'd expect it to go everywhere with him, like a teacher and a piece of chalk. So either he came onto court not expecting to play, or perhaps the killer took it with him as a memento."

"Taking a racquet as a memento, – that would be sick."

"Most of the killers I've encountered don't think in the same way as the rest of us."

Both Bee and Bartlett paused to contemplate the mentality of a killer, then Bartlett turned away and started to make her way back to the gate.

Bee called out to her, "Thinking about the set up here; can you tell me how the games work? Is there a booking system for the courts; how does a member get to play?"

Bartlett turned back her brown curls cut a sharp contrast against the green hedge behind, her face turned up inquisitively towards Bee. There was a redness around her eyes, that if she could have seen she would have tried to hide. She cleared her throat before replying.

"The club runs a computerised booking scheme on its website; essentially it works on a first come basis."

"Right, I'll need a list of those holding bookings for last night, do you know who might have access to that."

Bartlett shook her head, if she thought about it she might be able to work it out, but right now she wanted to get away from the detective inspector and let her tears escape. She started to step away backwards. But Bee wasn't done.

"One other thing, there's supposed to be a new DS arriving today to alleviate our resource problem, although unless he's any good, he'll probably add to the problem. DS McTierney from Norfolk; he's already late but if he shows up, send him over."

"Is that to replace Chase?"

"Yes, but let's not tell the new boy."

Bartlett nodded, turned, and walked off heavy-footed to take position on the cordon leaving Bee to wander around the clubhouse and grass courts. Next to the tennis club was the bowls club and Bee noticed an unlocked gate between the two. So the car park wasn't the only access to the tennis court. As Bartlett's footsteps faded their sound was replaced by the harsh machine-gun chatter of a magpie, Bee looked around to find the culprit, hoping to see a pair but it was a solitary bird. It was one of those mornings.

TWO

HE SAT TAPPING his fingers on the leather steering wheel of his Jaguar XF car. His radio programme had repeated the news about the major crash on the clockwise M25 for the fifth time that morning. Sitting in the third lane of four on the jammed but motionless carriageway Ron McTierney didn't need to know that 'traffic should avoid the area or risk being delayed for several hours.' He looked across at the driver of the black BMW in the outside lane; he had already given up with the traffic and was engrossed in something on his mobile. McTierney named him Lewis as he felt convinced he would race away into the distance as soon as the traffic police lifted the restrictions. To his left sat a young blonde, smart pink blouse, probably no more than thirty, a far more interesting prospect than Lewis. He figured she would be a product manager on her way to an important meeting, he christened her Sarah, and gave her a portfolio of crisps and bar snacks. Another thirty seconds passed and Sarah had been promoted to group marketing director and fallen helplessly in love with this budding detective. Three children soon followed and a large house in the country courtesy of Sarah's generous parents who adored their charming son-in-law. All at once Sarah turned and looked at him; scowled at the intrusion and his fantasy relationship evaporated into the ether.

McTierney averted his gaze and stared forward. He cursed his bad luck; he'd left Norwich early, keen to make a good impression, but regretted the full English breakfast he had taken at Thurrock services. It was going to cost him more than the £18 he had paid.

The radio reminded him again to avoid the southern stretch of the M25. He shouted at the announcer and ran his fingers through his long blonde hair, this was not going to impress his new colleagues at all and certainly not his new boss, DI Bee, who was known across the force as a disagreeable old sod at the best of times. But the other side of his reputation told people that he was fair minded, diligent and an exceptional detective, who would probably make chief constable if he could improve his politics. It was these traits that had sold the position to McTierney. He didn't mind the occasional spell of demanding work, so long as he could enjoy himself along the way and he delighted with the idea of someone not playing politics at work. Not that he had a lot of choice; he knew he had to get out of Norwich and escape the machinations of the seductive Angela.

THREE

WHILE HIS PROSPECTIVE partner against crime sat motionless twenty miles away, Bee started the door-to-door enquiries that he had hoped to delegate to his new subordinate. It wasn't that he didn't appreciate basic policework, he knew how important it could be, but at this particular moment he didn't feel this was likely to produce any results. But until the SOCO team arrived he couldn't do much else. He had walked around the perimeter of the tennis courts and established a number of possible access points; either across the rugby pitches which sat behind and to the south of the tennis club, or through the bowls club, but both of those offered pedestrian access only. If the assailant had used a car he must have driven down the path now guarded by Bartlett.

He walked back up Green Lane, passed his own car, and stopped at the first of the half dozen houses that adorned the road. He stood on the step outside their porch and turned back to the tennis club; it wasn't a perfect view by any means, the detached property employed a high hedge along their border to yield some privacy from sports enthusiasts using the lane. This in turn preventing the house watching the action on the courts; clearly not a tennis fan he deduced. He adjusted his facemask and stood contemplating why anyone would buy a house so close to a tennis facility if they didn't embrace the sport. When the front door opened, he found himself face to face with a young blonde woman dressed in black jogging pants and a lurid pink long-sleeved top. On the end of her arm was a golden Labrador puppy. All three parties seemed surprised but the dog reacted first and barked at Bee. He stepped back a pace and fumbled into his inside jacket pocket and retrieved a police identification card.

"Sorry to bother you madam, but I'm investigating an incident at the Reigate Priory Tennis Club last night."

The woman stepped back from the door in alarm.

"Don't worry I'm fully vaccinated. Can I ask if you were here last night and if you heard anything unusual?"

The woman bent down and calmed the puppy but jerked her head back at the suggestion of something untoward in her neighbourhood. "An incident here! Are you sure? Nothing ever happens here, that's why we chose it."

"I'm afraid so madam. So if I can ask you if you saw or heard anything last night."

"No nothing." The woman's face suggested her mind was elsewhere.

"Was everyone at home?"

"Yes, there's just the four of us. These days it's not easy to go anywhere or do anything, so we stayed in, had a meal, the kids had a DVD before we put them to bed around 8pm and then my husband and I watched a movie before bed."

"Is there normally much activity associated with the tennis club in the evenings?"

"Nothing that disturbs us; you get more noise from the cricket club. My husband says that's because they have the bigger bar, but I've never been to either."

Bee nodded, he hadn't expected much but you never knew what might have been seen, sometimes you got lucky. "Thanks for your time, I'll let you continue with your dog walk."

He stepped aside and allowed the woman to pass and followed her back down the path. Bee wasn't surprised by the lack of results, a young family had better things to do than stare out of the window each evening. He crossed the lane and approached the last house on the other side, this was on the same side as the tennis courts and had a much clearer view of the clubhouse; if any building was to deliver him an eyewitness report it would be this one. But again the result was negative; all he was doing was stirring up concern in the neighbourhood that something warranting police interest had occurred in their vicinity in the last 24 hours. He was spending more time re-assuring the locals than discovering what had happened.

He walked away from the last house, little wiser than he had been sixty minutes earlier. He looked down as his leather-bound notepad; three comments: not much noise; their floodlights normally turned off around 10pm and triple underlined, to reflect the number of times he'd heard it; no one had seen anything suspicious. He pressed his lips tight into a grimace, his default expression, allowed a heavy sigh to escape, slipped the notebook back into his pocket and turned back towards the police cordon. As he approached the barrier two cars pulled up behind him; he didn't recognise either. He signalled to Bartlett to take the precocious sports car and bent down to speak to the driver of the first car, a white Renault Megane. It was the pathologist from Horsham station, Dr Kelly, who'd been asked to cover their staff shortages. Bee suggested he park on the side and he would accompany him down to the scene. A sense of relief ran across his shoulders but it was short-lived as the moment was broken by the conversation springing from the other car.

"Hi, I'm Ron; a DS on loan to the Surrey police from the Norfolk constabulary."

"Morning."

"None of the officers in Norfolk are as beautiful as you. I think I'll stay here."

Bartlett's mouth fell open as she stepped back from the car.

"Sorry it's genetic, I inherited it from my mother, she kissed the blarney stone."

Bartlett composed herself and lent back towards the car obscuring part of the conversation.

"… looking for DI Bee, unfortunately I'm rather late due to a crash on the motorway, don't imagine that's going to suit the old goat; is he here?"

Jess Bartlett rocked back from the car and Bee could sense her blushing even though he couldn't see her face.

"I'll take this," he announced and marched around to the driver's door.

"I'm the detective inspector you're seeking. Not the old goat." He stared into the driver's face looking for a trace of embarrassment, but there was none. Instead he found a happy smile.

"DS Ron McTierney, pleased to make your acquaintance, sorry about the late arrival, you've probably heard about the drama up on the 25. Shall I park over there and you can update me on what you've discovered so far."

Bee stood open-mouthed, astonished by the unbridled

confidence of the man, and nodded his reply. Two minutes later he found himself as the meat in the sandwich as the three new amigos walked across the carpark and back to the murder scene.

Bee tried to accept the world as it was and avoid making early judgements about people; he found it imperative to keep an open mind about potential criminals until he had evidence. But this morning he was ready to rip up that theory; Don Kelly, the pathologist from Horsham was pleasant and charming and in total contrast to his new DS who seemed to have been shipped in direct from hell. Kelly was respectful and professional, whereas DS Satan was brash and arrogant.

The two detectives stood around the body while Kelly pulled on his latex gloves and knelt next to the body.

"Seen many of these? asked McTierney?

"A few," said Kelly.

"First thoughts?"

Kelly twisted his head up to look at McTierney, paused and said, "He's dead."

McTierney raised his hands in mock surrender. Bee turned his head away and smiled. Kelly moved to the other side of the body and busied himself checking the victims eyes and ears, he stood up and seemed surprised that McTierney was still watching.

"When will you be able to give us a report?"

"I like afternoon tea, real tea from a teapot, so let's meet after that, say 4pm at the Reigate station," and motioned the DS away with his fingers.

Watching the exchange, Bee had taken an instant like to the pathologist and was quick to agree. "Sounds good Dr

Kelly, we'll see you at four."

Bee and McTierney left the pathologist with the body and walked back towards the clubhouse and stopped by the bench.

"Let's follow up on this abandoned car in the car park," Bee pointed at the red car, "Bartlett believes it belongs to the coach who is most likely to be the victim."

McTierney nodded.

"We should pay him a visit."

"Safe to say he wasn't playing tennis when he was killed then," said McTierney.

"Hmm, what did you say?" Bee was deep in thought.

"He didn't have a racquet and there were no balls anywhere to be seen."

"Play a lot of tennis do you?"

"None, but I play enough sport to know that you need the equipment."

"Maybe the killer took those items to make us think there hadn't been a game. His clothing is not out of keeping with a game of tennis."

"No, but he wasn't playing tennis when he was killed, no one brings a knife onto a tennis court. It's not a good place to kill someone, much too open."

A smile started to break across the face of DS McTierney but it was abruptly halted by a scowl from Bee. He viewed his new partner suspiciously; "Sounds like you enjoy jumping to conclusions. That might work in Norfolk but here I prefer a thorough approach to our work. Wild assumptions might cut corners in the field but they won't cut any mustard in the courtroom. Have you considered that maybe the victim was expecting to play tennis but his opponent had other ideas, and that this was how our killer lured him to his death?"

Bee raised his left eyebrow, but McTierney looked stony faced back at him. Bee continued; "these days it's common for a tennis player to use a sports holdall to carry his racquet, maybe even a spare, a tube of balls and perhaps some water. If our killer had adopted that approach it would be easy to conceal a knife."

"Could be. I like to get a feeling of the murder scene," said McTierney stretching his arms wide and surveying the courts.

"Let's ensure we keep an open-mind, I don't like jumping to conclusions. Let's see what the forensics tell us. I see you're not writing anything down."

"No, I have a near photographic memory, but I will record the key details later. As I said I like to absorb the crime scene." He took a deep breath and McTierney's eyes followed a route from the body back down the path and out to the car park, "and the killer departs with both bags but leaves the knife behind."

This time his smile made it all the way across his face.

Bee wasn't smiling, "possibly, but we're starting to play your game of assumptions again. Let's see what the forensic team can discover this afternoon. And for the sake of those working the case without a photographic memory, kindly record all the evidence you find on our group file."

Bee motioned for them to continue their walk back to their cars, the narrow path ensured they did so in single file and Bee remembered his appraisal plan of action. Once they reached the car park, he quickened his step and caught up with McTierney.

"I apologise if I was a little abrupt back there. It's been a trying morning. I wasn't meant to be working today but the station is overstretched with several officers off with covid. You'd know that having been dragged down from Norfolk."

"Yes I'd worked that one out for myself, but nobody dragged me here. I was looking for a change so this was a good opportunity."

"Been there long?"

"Ten years or so, the first eight were fine, but now I've got itchy feet."

"Good, we're going to need some support here so perhaps this is your chance to shine."

By now they had walked up to the cordon and briefed Bartlett on their plan. She had been joined by two other officers who she had set to work turning back tennis club members who were arriving for their Friday games. She opened the gate to allow Bee and McTierney to pass and was about to log their departure in her crime scene log when Dr Kelly came scampering up to them.

"I thought you should know that I've completed a preliminary search of the body. I'd estimate the time of death to be midnight give or take a few hours.

"Thanks doctor."

"I know you gentlemen like to know those sort of details. Additionally I can tell you that the victim appears to be Russell Dawson based on the wallet I found in his back pocket."

"Anything missing from the wallet?"

"Nothing obvious, his credit card is there and forty pounds in cash."

"So we can rule out robbery," concluded Bee.

FOUR

THE STATION GAVE Bee an address for Russell Dawson in Richmond, "Shall we take your car?, asked Bee.

McTierney nodded and pressed the unlock button. Bee opened the rear door and carefully laid his coat across the back seat, taking time to survey the inside for any clues about his new DS, a black sports holdall was his meagre reward. He slipped into the passenger seat and rubbed his hand over the soft leather seat. McTierney started the engine and ACDC roared out of the music system; Bee winced and cut the volume without asking, then remembered he was in someone else's car and turned to McTierney. "We wouldn't be able to talk with that."

McTierney punched the address into his satnav and the journey began in silence. After the first mile McTierney broke the stillness, "Bono and the Edge walk into a bar. The barman turns to them and says not U2 again!"

Bee stared back at his new partner. "I don't think that's appropriate given the circumstances, do you?"

McTierney shrugged and turned his attention to the Friday morning traffic which was suffering a hangover from the earlier motorway chaos and meant that the thirty-mile journey took close on two hours. McTierney parked his car in Paxton Close and surveyed the community; two rows of smart mock Georgian fronted town houses each with white wooden framed windows and expensive cars sitting on the driveways. "Pleasant part of the world."

Bee nodded. "I think Richmond Park is behind that fence, I've been running there; it's delightful down by the river." He peered through the windscreen and pointed across the road. "Looks like it's the one with the red door over there. I'll lead the conversation this morning. Why don't you listen and take notes?" The two men equipped themselves with facemasks.

A young blonde woman dressed in a casual pale-blue sweatshirt opened the door and Bee could instantly tell she was worried. Before anyone could say anything, she guessed the news.

"Oh no, tell me it's not Russell. What's happened?" her eyes frantically darted from one to the other.

"Could we come in for a moment?" whispered Bee. He showed his police card and the woman fell away from the door letting them pass. They turned to the right and found themselves in a long lounge-diner, two young children were playing on the floor at the far end. They looked up briefly but returned to their game.

The woman sat down on the sofa but never took her eyes off Bee. The men followed suit, McTierney on the sofa and Bee in an individual chair, Bee cleared his throat and began. "We are investigating a death and have reason to believe that the victim might be Russell Dawson, I assume you are his wife, can you identify yourself?"

The woman slapped her hand across her mouth, the rest of her body froze. She tried to speak but was unable to utter a word. But her eyes communicated all that the lips could not.

Her world was imploding. Scott Bee lowered his gaze. "We haven't formally identified the body yet but there is strong reason to believe it's your husband."

The woman turned her attention to McTierney hoping he would have better news, but his face told her to the contrary, she turned back to Bee but his dark expression gave the same message. Abandoned by both options she pulled her handbag onto her lap as a defence. She started to hunt through it but stopped in mid-search. She looked up and tears filled her eyes. "What do you need?"

"Anything with your name and address will suffice," said Bee. He hated these moments.

The anxiety in the room drifted down to the two small girls who stopped their game and switched their attention to the adults. The oldest of the two lifted herself off the floor and toddled to her mother.

"What's wrong mummy?"

Her mother didn't answer but pulled her daughter close to her in a tight hug. It yielded a couple of moments in which she composed herself.

"Mummy's fine, she's talking to these nice gentlemen, now you go back and play with your sister before she gets lonely."

Tina Dawson resumed her search but her hands were shaking and she struggled to find anything in her bag, eventually she shoved a store loyalty card into Bee's hand.

"I'm sorry, I need something with your name and address."

"Here, take the bag," she thrust the bag onto Bee's lap and buried her face in her hands.

Bee discovered a driving licence, returned the bag, and

relayed their news. Tina Dawson said little, she started a couple of questions but couldn't complete her sentences. Bee was anxious to spare her as much pain as he could so he kept his questions to a minimum, recommended that she get a friend to accompany her to the station in the next few days to support her in assisting the identification of the body and decided to head back to the station.

As they walked back to the car, the first drops of rain fell from the sky. They ran the last few yards and slumped into the comfort of McTierney's car, "I hope it's not raining in Reigate, or if it is I hope the forensic team has a tent over our victim." Within seconds the raindrops transformed into a deluge with the water bouncing up off the car.

"That's what we get for polluting the skies," muttered Bee as he peered up through the windscreen trying to work out where the weather was coming from. The timpani of the rain drowned out his comment and McTierney let it pass, hoping it wasn't important before making his own contribution.

"I'll let the worst of this pass before setting off; these storms usually pass quickly. So what did you make of Dawson's wife?"

"She's a strong lady, but clearly this loss is going to hit her hard. That family is going to go through hell. We need to nail the bastard that has done this. Life will never be the same for those poor children."

"Does make you wonder, why Dawson travelled so far to play tennis every day when his house is in the middle of tennis land."

Bee was about to answer but his reply was interrupted by his mobile bleeping with a message. He listened to the voicemail and McTierney watched his facial expressions change from puzzlement through concern and arrive at excitement.

"Good news?"

"The forensic boys have made some progress, let's get back to the station as quick as we can."

BACK IN REIGATE, the rain was still hammering down and Bee and McTierney had to run across the carpark into the police station. They found Kelly in the laboratory hidden away in the basement of the old Edwardian building that had once been a school but now housed the local constabulary.

"Afternoon Kelly, how has your day progressed?"

"I'm still trying to dry out; I've never seen such rain. We managed to erect a tent over the immediate crime scene but the rain has destroyed any peripheral evidence that we might have found on the court."

"That's unfortunate, but I can't say I'm surprised. But what do we know?"

"Quite a lot, and I think some things that will surprise you." The pathologist picked up his clipboard and ran his finger down the top sheet. He tapped the middle of the page. "Yes let's start with the method. Not stabbed through the heart with a kitchen knife as it would first appear."

The detectives exchanged glances and McTierney opened his mouth to speak, but Bee raised his finger. "Let's here the evidence before we jump to a conclusion."

Kelly continued "I didn't notice it at the scene but once I had the body back here, it was readily evident. Our victim died from a blow to the head; blunt force trauma, as we choose to call it. There's some matted blood in the hair, some of which has been cut away suggesting the killer was trying to disguise the real cause of death."

"Interesting," Bee pulled his plectrum from the pocket and twiddled it around the fingers of his right hand.

McTierney was more direct. "Why disguise the cause of death? Perhaps the original crime scene would implicate the killer."

"Maybe, but let's hear the rest of Kelly's report before we start analysing it."

Kelly nodded his appreciation to Bee and continued. "There are 5 other significant points for us to digest. Let's start with the time of death which I would estimate as between 10pm and 2am Thursday night come Friday morning. Secondly blood: there's not much at the scene, and all that I can find, came from our victim. More than that, you'd expect a stab wound to the heart to result in much greater blood loss than is evident."

Bee jerked his head back. "Are you saying someone has removed blood from the scene?"

"Possibly, without meaning to step on your toes, it could be that blood spurted out over the assailant and he or she left covered in blood."

Bee scowled at the idea.

Kelly continued, "number three is a significant missing item; there are no car keys on the body; hence my assumption that the killer took the car keys and used the car, that red Nissan to move the body. But as we stand we haven't yet swabbed the car, not having the keys made it a little more difficult so it remains in the club car park.

"That could be a mistake?" McTierney was itching to discuss the facts, but Bee raised his hand, allowing Kelly to complete his evidential quintet.

"Two to go," said Kelly observing McTierney over his glasses. "Regrettably there is no usable DNA at the scene; the body has been left overnight and what with dew contamination and what have you, we'll struggle to find anything, but I'll look. Lastly we have the victim's wallet. It's over there on the desk. Nothing appears to have been taken and there are no useful fingerprints."

"No phone I presume," said Bee.

"No, that would have been helpful, but unless it's in the car, we don't have it."

"You said the wallet was in the back pocket of his shorts?"

"It was."

"Not what you'd expect from someone playing tennis?" McTierney was back on the starting grid.

"No," Bee interjected, "but I think we can dispense with the idea that our victim was playing tennis when he met his death. You've said that you think the victim is the coach; this Russell Dawson."

"The wallet suggests it's Russell Dawson, but we don't yet have a formal identification. I was hoping you might produce a next of kin to confirm this."

"That might have to wait until a day or so, his partner will need some support when she comes to see the body. Let's work on the basis that it is Dawson; we should be able to get a club member to validate that tomorrow in lieu of a full identification next week. In the meantime, thank you Kelly, your examination has been insightful, unless you have anything else to contribute, we'll let you get back off to Horsham. McTierney and I can talk through your findings and we'll contact you if we have any further questions."

Kelly nodded towards Bee, collected his papers, and headed for the door.

At last McTierney was off the leash; "Key question for me is why move the body. It's extremely risky, plus the killer has chosen not to take the simple option of dumping the body in the woods. If the perpetrator had to move it because of where the death occurred it complicates matters considerably to bring the body back to the tennis club."

"Indeed but I think it gives us a few insights into the murder. First of which is that perhaps this wasn't a murder, at least not one with much planning."

McTierney nodded his approval at Bee's rationale, and then added his own ace. "It would also suggest that the murder didn't happen too far from here; if only because the killer had to make his way back on foot."

"Unless he had an accomplice of course." As Bee made the point his pained expression returned to his face. It was an uncomfortable thought and curtailed their conversation.

The short silence derailed their analysis and Bee decided to call it a day.

"Let's sleep on what we know and have a fresh look in the morning. I presume the station has arranged some accommodation for you."

"I have a room at The Cranleigh Hotel, apparently it's close to the town centre."

"It is. Not the smartest place in town, but you'll be close to everything. If you take me back to collect my car, I'll show you where it is."

"Thanks."

The two men walked towards the door.

"By the way if you're not doing anything this evening, we could get a meal together and get to know each other a little."

"That's kind of you, but I already have a date for to-night."

"A date? Wow, that's fast work. Who is the lucky lady?"

"It's Jess Bartlett."

Bee stopped in his tracks and turned back; his demeanour had changed.

"What? She's half your age! When did this happen? You've hardly seen her all day and now you have a date with her?"

"Not stepping on anyone's toes am I?" asked McTierney pointedly.

"No. It's more that, I thought you'd come down here to start again and focus on your police career and you're not in the team for more than two minutes and you're on a date."

"I wouldn't say it's a major date; she offered to show me around town tonight and I invited her to dinner as a thank you."

"Don't even think about putting that through on expens-es, the chief watches every penny. To be honest I'm amazed he's stumped up to pay for you and the pathologist, both on the same day."

"Don't worry, I'll pay for the meal myself."

Bee started to calm down and dropped eye contact with McTierney.

"I don't like romances amongst the team; it doesn't suit police work. People's priorities change: things can get messy and vital details missed."

"I'll keep that in mind."

"Good, let's go collect my car from the tennis club. Could be a long session tomorrow. We'll start at 8:00am!"

FIVE

AT 7:50AM BEE, dressed in his standard issue of tight black Levi's, brown shoes and casual burgundy shirt was outside the tennis clubhouse pacing left and right across the short terrace. He muttered to himself about timekeeping and his own mistake of leaving Bartlett to secure the keys. As he turned for the fifth circuit he rolled back his sleeve and looked at his watch, it was one minute to the hour. He pursued his lips and rehearsed the ticking off he would soon deliver, but his thought process was broken by the sound of footsteps running over the shingle path that led around the tennis courts. He looked up to see Jess Bartlett coming into view; she was wearing grey jeans, with a white cotton shirt, not tucked in and a black waistcoat. She looked like anything but an undercover police officer. His anger receded, but only for a matter of seconds until he noticed McTierney close behind her. He hoped their joint arrival was co-incidental but tried to put the topic out of his mind.

"Morning sir," said Bartlett.

"Morning Bartlett, and good morning McTierney, how are you this day?"

"Not bad at all, Bee," beamed McTierney.

Bee wanted to ignore the undue happiness in McTierney's voice but it punctured his thoughts. "What's making you so chipper this morning?"

"I always try to be happy, there's no point in being miserable, there's enough trouble in the world without adding any."

Bee grunted at response and thought that he'd had his saccharin intake for the next month all in one go, but McTierney hadn't finished.

"Look at the day," McTierney turned and spread his arm across the horizon, "the weather is fabulous, and we have wall to wall football to watch for the next four weeks as the European Championship gets underway."

Bee couldn't fault McTierney's evaluation, despite the early hour, the sunshine was strong. The sun was giving notice that it would deliver a spectacularly warm weather day, no breeze, and no humidity either. The skies were clear, it was the type of day when people would look outside at breakfast time and say, I can or I will. But still Bee couldn't share his enthusiasm.

"Don't forget we have a murder to solve. Let's hope you're as happy when we finished interviewing all the club members today. Perhaps Bartlett can take us through the agenda for the day."

Jess Bartlett had set up interviews with all the club members who had court bookings for the evening of the killing, together with the committee members and the cleaner, who happened to work on a Thursday. She unlocked the clubhouse and ushered them to a table at the back where they could conduct the interviews, before excusing herself to follow up on Dawson's laptop.

The clubhouse was functional but tired, essentially a large shed with two changing rooms at the rear and a kitchen counter come bar on the left and some general seating with one large wooden table on the right. The furniture was second or third hand, eclectic if you were charitable. Whenever a member had replaced their own furniture the original item had found its way to the clubhouse, where the club had gratefully accepted it. The walls were adorned by wooden plaques listing club champions of the last thirty years, commemorative photos, and handwritten competition trees. It was much the same as hundreds of amateur sports clubs across the country.

McTierney took a seat at the table while Bee read through the notices, but he hadn't got far before a man put his face around the door.

"Inspector Bee?" said the man.

"Yes, Detective Inspector Bee and this is my colleague Detective Sergeant McTierney, thanks for coming along today, please come in and take a seat, we have some questions for you."

"Certainly, it's John Graham, I'm the Club Captain. This is such an awful business. I can't believe anyone would want to kill Russell."

"With your help we hope to wrap it up quickly and let you get your club back to normal."

"Thank you. Yes the timing is terrible, we've only been open for a couple of weeks once lockdown started to ease and now this." Graham waved at the courts outside the clubhouse. "But you must do what you must do inspector."

Bee smiled weakly and started the interview, "How long have you known Russell Dawson?"

"Several years, ten or more, I would say. Russell has been our principal coach for all of that time. To be honest I'm not sure the place would function without him."

"So he's integral to all that happens in the club?"

"Absolutely." Graham poured honey over his answer, "he runs the coaching school, he administers the competitions, sits on the club committee, and even sells a few racquets. He's on site 5, sometimes 6 days a week; I imagine he knows more people in the club than I do."

Bee tilted his head towards Graham looking for confirmation.

Graham nodded, "it wouldn't surprise me. He will meet all the new members and since we started coming out of the covid restrictions we've had a surge of new members."

"How many members do you have?"

"I checked this morning, thinking you might ask, it's 617, an all-time high."

"Does everyone have access to the site anytime of the day?"

"You can see our situation; there's no secure perimeter. Not only can members walk around anytime, so can Joe Public. It's not a thoroughfare, but if someone wants to walk up to the clubhouse there's nothing to stop them."

"Security is not high on your agenda."

"Not especially, it's difficult to make quick changes in a club like this. It's the funding; members want to see where their money is spent. Investing in better security is not sexy."

"I can imagine. What about the clubhouse?"

"We aim to have a committee member here to close up the clubhouse and lock the door every night. I believe that works, but any member is entitled to have a key so …"

Bee nodded. "I see you have a CCTV camera covering the door, could we see the footage from Thursday evening?"

"That won't be possible." Graham hung his head. "We installed the camera a few years ago after a burglary. The insurance company offered us a sizeable discount on the premium if we did so. They didn't stipulate that we had to retain the film; I think it runs on an eight-hour cycle, so all we have will be yesterday evening."

Bee sighed heavily and reverted to his standard questions.

"Can you think of anyone who would wish ill towards Dawson and might have a motive for wanting him dead."

"Good Lord, no. He was a very popular figure in the club. I can't even think of anyone who didn't positively like him."

"When did you last see him alive?"

"It was on Thursday evening; we'd had a first team match against Dorking; it was played out there on the grass. Russell had brought a new player, Dave, into the team and we'd won. We don't often beat Dorking so everyone was feeling good about the result."

"What time was that?"

"The game started at 6pm, and we finished a little after 8pm. Then we had some pizzas delivered – it's customary for the home team to entertain the visitors although no one ever stays long, especially in these covid days. That would have finished around 9pm, maybe half past." Graham furrowed his brow and looked out of the window. "Yes that would be about right, it's a short drive home and when I arrived, my wife was watching the BBC news and they were reporting the covid numbers so it was early in the show."

"Was Russell still here when you left?"

"Yes he was."

"What was his mood?"

"He seemed okay, quite pleased that we'd won. He's rarely if ever in a bad mood, at least I can't recall the last time I saw him upset". Graham paused as if remembering an incident.

"Except it appears that you have remembered such an occasion."

Graham blushed and lost the smoothness of his delivery. "There was one time when I saw him upset."

"Go on."

"It was at the last committee meeting; one we had here. The first time we've met in person for months, you know with all the covid stuff it's been difficult to manage these things."

Bee nodded, "yes, but let's focus on what upset Dawson."

Graham shuffled in his seat and composed himself.

"It was in the debate over tennis coaching. Russell has expanded his coaching programme and some of the committee thought it was going too far, taking over the club, so there was some push back against his plans and he was asked, or rather, told to reduce the number of coaching hours."

"Dawson didn't like this?"

"I won't say he didn't like it so much as he didn't understand it. You see the coaching programme represents a major revenue stream for the club."

"The club needs money?"

"Yes."

"I can sympathise with Dawson, what was the issue with his plan."

"I think some committee members felt he was getting a bit too big for his boots; that this club was becoming his own personal club and that he needed to be brought down a peg or two. Reminded that it's everyone's club, not Russell's club."

"I see."

"I hasten to add that I don't share that view."

"Presumably a decision like that will have been noted in the minutes."

"I believe so."

"Could you get us a copy of those minutes please."

"Certainly, I'll forward them to Jess, they're electronic."

"That's fine. By the way when did this take place?"

"It was three weeks ago, the second Tuesday of the month – that's when they are scheduled."

The pattern was set for the next dozen interviews and it left Bee wondering if there had been some degree of collusion amongst the members. Everybody recognised Russell's pivotal role in the club, everybody liked him, and nobody could think of anyone who would want to harm a hair on his head. Nobody said anything different until Ann Dent sat at the table. She was the woman who cleaned the clubhouse on a weekly basis, taking two hours on a Thursday morning. She too held Russell in the highest esteem, since he was the only club member who spoke to her, but where she differed to the pack was in what she had overheard.

"Tell me again, slowly and with as much detail as possible," said Bee.

"It's like I said, Russell had a terrible row with someone that morning. He was standing here by the cloakroom door and getting right agitated." Ann pointed to a wooden painted door that separated the cloakrooms from the main area of the clubhouse. "He said something and walked away as if to go outside but then turned round and went back and repeated it. His face was red, he looked angry and I've never seen him angry."

"What did he say?"

"I'm not quite sure; I was standing there by the dish-washer, I'd put it on two seconds before and it makes a terrible racket when it starts, time they got a new one really, but they won't spend the money."

"But you're sure that Russell was speaking to someone."

"Yes, I heard the voice but I couldn't see his face."

Bee raised his eyebrow, "Could he have been getting changed ready to play tennis?"

"Possibly, but I didn't see his face. Once I'd put the dishwasher on, that's my last job and I couldn't hang about because my Jim was coming to pick me up."

"Do you have any idea who could have been the other voice?"

"No, but I'm sure it was a man; it was too deep for a woman."

"Okay, thanks Mrs Dent, that'll be all for today."

Bee waited for her to leave the clubhouse and turned back to McTierney. "I don't like it, it all feels a bit too sweet, a bit rehearsed; everybody is saying the same thing."

"If we believe everything we're heard today then this Dawson bloke must have been some kind of saint. Nobody is that nice."

"They're not; we've not asked the right question to the right person yet. These sports clubs often gather a reputation for forming a clique and I think that's what we encountered here. Let's see if we can find some members who are not in the teams or on the committee."

"The player who was dropped from the first team might be good place to start."

"Excellent idea. There's a team sheet over there on the noticeboard, compare the last two sheets and let's see who has been demoted."

"I'm on it."

"Before you do that, any other thoughts?"

"The one thing that crossed my mind as I was reading the list of club members when you were interviewing was the number of women here. They make up 70% of the club."

"Your point?"

"Two things; firstly we've interviewed more men than women this morning, so that's not representative of the club composition." Bee nodded. "Then you have all these ladies running around the courts in short skirts."

"So?"

"It's the sex angle. Lots of swishing skirts and beautiful young legs, men with raging testosterone levels. I bet there are a few illicit matches going on here after dark, it's a secluded location. Love, sex, jealousy, they're always good motives for murder."

"All you need to do is throw in some financial discrepancy or fraud in the club accounts and you've got the set." Bee said it as a throwaway line, but McTierney shrugged his shoulders and smiled.

Bee changed his tone, "No, you're right we should cast an eye over the money. It sounds like Dawson's coaching programme was a major revenue earner, so with that gone or destabilised for a while, that might impact a few plans here. Can I leave that with you?"

"Sure."

"Right let's see what Bartlett has uncovered, I asked her to go through Dawson's phone and laptop."

It was after lunch when the three detectives sat down together in the tennis club. Bartlett produced three typed sheets from her case and placed one in front of each person.

"Where are we on our game, set and murder?" asked McTierney.

Bee frowned at him and changed the tone, "this looks professional," he said kindly.

"I hope so, sir, there is some interesting information here."

"Let's have your top three then Bartlett," said McTierney.

"Don't lead the witness, sergeant, let's see what she has to present."

As it transpired Jess Bartlett had uncovered four important facts. Had McTierney been allowed a number one it would have been a note in Dawson's diary for a 10pm meeting on the night of his death. But there was no name or venue against the time.

Collecting the silver medal was Bartlett's analysis of Dawson's recent internet searches; it appeared that he had been investigating the possibility of switching clubs and moving to a new group in Kingston closer to his home. In addition to the searches there was some correspondence from a Jacob Mills about a potential role for Dawson and even a joining bonus.

Squeezing onto the podium was an entry on Dawson's to-do list which featured somebody called Wheeler, who appeared to be a ticket agent. Dawson had written himself a note to tackle Wheeler about rogue Wimbledon tickets and a further note to report Wheeler to the Lawn Tennis Association.

Completing the set was Bartlett's appraisal of Dawson' business venture. Since the spring he had taken on a role as a sales agent for Wilson tennis equipment and was proving to be successful. His sales revenue had topped £1,250 for each of the last three months and he had received a letter of recognition from Wilson's area manager and an invitation to a celebrity event in the forthcoming month.

"Based on what you've seen today, how would you describe our victim?"

"Neat and efficient sir; the only unopened mail items in his inbox arrived after his death. It seems he opened and filed everything as and when it arrived."

"Wow, which of us does that?" Bee looked impressed, both McTierney and Bartlett looked at their hands unable to compete with the example Dawson had set.

Bee took up the gauntlet. "There's some excellent work here. It looks like we have four avenues to explore; nailing down who Dawson met on Thursday night and where. I'll chase up the traffic cameras in the town. Then there's this alternative club idea, perhaps Bartlett, you could follow up on that and maybe speak to his wife again, we need her to come down to the station and identify the body. She might appreciate a softer touch."

"I'll look at the ticket tout angle and also Dawson's business venture and build a picture of who might be losing the sales that Dawson was gaining." McTierney was straight on topic.

"There's one other task for you Bartlett; can you ask around some of your club colleagues, preferably the ladies and find out what the casual membership thought of Russell and the committee. Everyone we spoke to this morning, seems to have been fed their lines. I had the feeling we were being sold a story and I don't like it. I'd like a different viewpoint."

"Will do sir."

"Good, now let's lock up this place and return to the station, we need to set up an operations room there for Monday."

Back at the station Bee led the way for McTierney upstairs to his office overlooking the staff car park at the rear of the building. Bee's office was immaculate not a file on the desk or a stray sheet of paper to be seen. The light from the window cast a sharp shadow across the room dividing it into two halves. The air was stale no one had been in the room all day and the sun had been beating down on the window cooking everything within. Bee opened the door and walked around the back of his desk, oblivious to the temperature and musty air, he motioned to McTierney to take a seat. There was a red light flashing on the phone; Bee pressed play and immediately the room was filled with Kelly's lugubrious tone.

"Good afternoon Bee, sorry to leave a message here, but I neglected to collect your mobile number. Anyway, I thought you should know that I've finished the post-mortem; I can confirm that Dawson died from a blow to the head, not the stab wound. One other thing you may find interesting; there are no marks on his knuckles or hands to suggest that he was in a fight, and there's no DNA under his fingernails. Hence I would say he was taken by surprise, didn't know what hit him and died within a matter of seconds, perhaps sixty at the most."

Bee flicked his plectrum into the air, caught it and sucked

his teeth. "Poor chap."

Bartlett knocked on the door of Bee's office and Bee could see through the glass panel that she was champing at the bit to share some news. He beckoned her in.

"We're close to stopping for the day; McTierney wants to watch some of the football tonight."

"Sorry to interrupt, but I thought you'd want to know this. The forensic team has brought the car back to the station, opened the door and in their preliminary search they have found some drugs in the glove compartment."

"What? Dawson was on drugs? That doesn't fit for a top-level sportsperson."

"Maybe not; but that's what they've found. They're in the lab now and there was two grand in twenty-pound notes."

Bee and McTierney jumped out of their chairs and headed down the stairs to the forensic lab.

"Thought you'd come running when you heard the news." Carol Bishop stood in the centre of the lab. She wore her bottle blonde hair scraped back into a tight bun, her clothes and shoes were taken from the comfortable rack in M and S. She was everything you'd want in a detective, smart, curious, and thought outside the box, but harboured little ambition. She worked hard and followed orders but rarely put her head above the parapet, but during her 7 years in the drugs team at Reigate station she'd earned a positive reputation. She'd worked with Bee on many cases and enjoyed his respect.

"This is straight out of left field. Nothing about this guy suggests he would be into drugs."

"No? Well his car was carrying a substantial cargo." Bishop held up a couple of transparent thin plastic bags.

"Two hundred white ecstasy pills in here, and a quarter of a kilo of amphetamine powder in this one."

"Eees and whizz," said McTierney, "that's a street value of five grand."

"That quantity would make him a dealer," added Bee, "but it doesn't fit."

"Lots of young people around the tennis club; plenty of money in this town. Could be a big market for a short-term stimulant," mused McTierney.

"That's a grim analysis," said Bishop, "but I can't fault it."

SIX

SCOTT BEE SPENT his Saturday evening in the comfort of his own home. It was an off the beaten track converted stone farmhouse; his nearest neighbour was the farmer himself, not that Scott saw much of him. The house was Scott's sanctuary away from the strife of his job and had been so for 6 years. The place had an ancient rough exterior of sharp angular stones but the interior was soft and gentle, not unlike the inhabitant. It boasted a contemporary kitchen, a plush master bedroom and eclectic furniture scattered throughout, and was one of the few places in the world where Scott felt comfortable, he seldom entertained.

The kitchen overlooked a west-facing garden so that early evening Scott could feel the sunshine through the tall French windows that adorned the long rear wall. He opened the fridge to select a meal; all the food in the chiller was stacked orderly according to the latest food hygiene regulations; cooked meats separate from fresh and all the yogurts standing in use-by date order. This evening Scott selected a duck breast from the third shelf and scored the skin, he sprinkled it with salt and ground pepper and set it to cook in a skillet, while he focused on his accompanying sauce. It was this aspect that he felt made the meal; he liked to experiment with the ingredients and tonight he replaced his favoured oranges with the last two apricots sitting in his fruit bowl.

He opened a bottle of Argentinian Malbec and sat down at the kitchen island to savour his latest creation; a mouthful of wine, a slice of duck and a slurp of sauce; he let the flavours do battle over his tastebuds. Not bad he deduced. Easier to understand than his latest case. Why would someone want to kill the man who was the heartbeat of the tennis club? Probably not a tennis player, he mused. The case intrigued him and followed him everywhere he went. He found himself pondering the rationale of a murderer who takes the risk of moving a body, as he was staring out of the kitchen window with his hands in the washing up bowl and hot water pouring from the single tap. He cursed as the water temperature reached boiling point and dropped the plate he had in his hands.

He moved to his lounge and settled himself in his worn brown leather reclining chair and turned to the sudoku page at the back of The Times; ordinarily fifteen minutes would suffice, but twenty minutes later he had added only 6 numbers and a messy doodle on the side of the page. This couldn't continue. When Scott found himself in a rut he had a rock-solid escape mechanism, his electric guitar. One of the few benefits from living in a detached farm building was the lack of neighbours, especially those who might complain. He climbed the stairs and went into the spare bedroom; his Fender Telecaster model was leaning against the amp; he slung the red strap over his shoulder and plugged in the amp. There was only one song to play in a moment like this; Bruce Springsteen's 'Born to Run'.

Scott had learnt the guitar at school when a group of friends wanted to form a grunge band at the turn of the century. The band lasted seven weeks before crashing on the altar of musical differences which in this case had more to do with their drummer trying to make it with the girlfriend of the bass guitarist. Scott put aside his dream of joining the E Street band and concentrated on playing solo guitar riffs and grooves. He had a good ear for music and soon developed his own repertoire of classic songs that would allow him to escape the real-world.

FOUR MILES AWAY in a different world Ron and Jess were getting ready for a night on the town; neither had spoken a word about the case. They had walked from the station through the town towards the Cranleigh Hotel. They passed the busker outside Marks and Spencer playing 'Life on Mars' but stopped in the Red Lion for a quick drink, and 'to see what the score was' on the football being played that afternoon. Covid had transformed the definition of a quick drink; before you could cross the threshold, there was a pub barcode to scan, hand sanitiser to apply and a plethora of warning signs to digest. Once inside a pint was only available by table service, facemasks were required to get to a table and tables had a capacity limit of six. McTierney flashed his badge to secure a table and some fast service.

The European Championship was barely out of first gear but already controversy was taking centre stage. When they arrived the game had been halted after one of the Danish players had collapsed on the pitch. Ron's quick drink had slipped into extra time and had allowed him a second pint, before Jess insisted on getting some food. They grabbed a couple of sandwiches from the food counter in the local M & S and sauntered back to the hotel. They showered, changed, and Ron watched as Jess sprayed some perfume on to her hairbrush and pulled it through her long curls. Ron inhaled deeply, "that's a glorious scent."

"Cherry bark and almonds," she said anticipating his question.

"I knew that" he smiled, as she elbowed him in the ribs.

Looking refreshed they stepped back out onto Reigate High Street. Their evening was filled with frothy ale, fried food, football, frolics, fornication, and fun. For Ron it was fabulous and Jess enjoyed herself too. It was close to midnight as she sat on the end of Ron's hotel bed while he occupied the bathroom and thought about the whirlwind of the last two days. Life seemed easy with Ron; he followed a simple principle – whichever option would yield the most happiness.

Life had not been easy for Jess; happiness was a distant relative in her twenty-one years. The unexpected child of a single mother; her formative years had been a challenge. It was hard not to feel different when all her classmates had dads, some even had two – which seemed totally unfair. Whenever she had asked her mother about her own, her reply was always the same; 'your father and I were not compatible; he wasn't able to change and I wasn't able to compromise. But he was a good man, he adored you and gave you your long legs and tenacious spirit'. That had been bearable for most of her life but 21 months ago her mother had died in a car accident and since then Jess had felt more alone than ever. Until now, when this unlikely knight without a chivalrous bone in his body had leapt onto the scene and taught her to laugh and smile again. It didn't make sense to her, but she was enjoying the ride too much to try to comprehend what was occurring.

RON SAT ON the toilet in the hotel bathroom and looked around for something to read; he knew he would be occupied for several minutes. The Cranleigh didn't provide magazines in their washrooms and he resorted to his mobile phone. He had a couple of texts from friends he had left behind in Norwich. The one from Adrian caught his eye. It suggested that Ron must have found a female companion as no one in Norfolk had heard from him for nearly a week.

Ron smiled; he'd had many brief relationships. He knew that he was reasonably good-looking, but he never supposed himself exceptionally attractive. But he had often been told that he had something that made women interested in him. An old girlfriend had told him that he radiated self-confidence and security at the same time, that he had an ability to make women feel at ease. Going to bed with him was not threatening or complicated, but it might be erotically enjoyable. And that according to Ron was exactly how it should be. Ron had a trail of broken hearts behind him, akin to the yellow brick road, or in Ron's case the pink tear-stained road.

SCOTT STRETCHED ACROSS to silence his radio alarm and bounced out of bed. Two minutes later he was in the kitchen making himself one of his regular breakfast smoothies, a base of Greek yoghurt and sliced banana topped up with lemongrass oil, acai extract, a sprinkling of vitamin C, folate and fibre, a spoonful of oats for slow-release fuel, ginger, a squirt of honey and some chopped kale. It was a few minutes after 8am; the sun was high in the sky and birdsong ruled the countryside. Scott lifted his Eagles concert t-shirt and beat out the tune to 'Born to Run' across his abs and pondered his route. He felt good; it would be the eight miler this morning. He slipped his key under the ornamental hedgehog that guarded the back door and set off down the track towards the nearest village. His initial route took him across five acres of farmland infused by the crisp morning air, he turned at the cornfield picked up the scent of wild berries and headed east. He followed the scent of fresh strawberries until he arrived at Lacey's Farm where the odour of decomposing compost mixed with newly made pig manure prompted Scott to put in a fast half mile. His sprint brought him onto a minor road, where a tractor greeted him with the smell of diesel fumes. He switched track and headed for the next village where the grass was being mown at the second house; his nose had hit the jackpot, and he relaxed and jogged home invigorated. He showered, made himself a pot of coffee with his new machine and put in a call to an old colleague from the Norfolk constabulary.

RON STIRRED AND glanced across at the digital clock sitting next to the bed; it read 9:45am. Could it be that late? Perhaps. He rolled back to watch Jess sleeping; she was at peace, gently blowing air through her lips but so gently Ron could barely hear it. He smiled to himself; he had landed on his feet here. Time and again he had found himself with a damsel in distress, but Jess was different; she was strong and independent; she didn't need Ron, but she wanted him and that made him want her all the more. He leant over and kissed her softly on her forehead. He hadn't intended to wake her, but she stirred and opened one eye.

She smiled up at him "What time is it?"

"Just before ten."

"Perfect, no need to rush then." She rolled over.

"No, but we ought to move," Ron cuddled up behind her. "No one knows you're here so we can't have breakfast here."

"I don't want breakfast."

Ron pulled her closer.

"But I don't want that either, well not yet. Tell me something about you that I would never guess."

Ron wriggled himself up on his elbows to address the challenge. "Okay I know the word for beer in 20 languages and I hope to visit all the countries to put my vocabulary to the test."

Jess's interest was piqued but she resisted the temptation to move. "How long did they take you to learn?"

"Not long, one lazy bank holiday afternoon. I can teach you now. It's easy." Ron prodded her tenderly in the small of her back, but Jess didn't move. Unpreturbed he carried on. "In Europe there are four main words for beer. Strictly speaking, ale is used in the North, so ol is the word in Scandinavia, so that's four countries. It's beer in the West, so that's beer in England, and bier in Holland and Germany and biere in France and Italy. Cerveza in the South, which comes from the Gaulish word for beer, so we have cerveza in Spain and cerveja in Portugal, and then pivo in the East, covering Czech, Russia, Hungary, Croatia, Poland and even Azerbaijan. Pivo derives from the old word for barley, which should amount to seventeen. Eighteen is bier that's Afrikaans, nearly there, nineteen is bia that's Thai and to complete the list in Australia they say amber nectar. And here's a bonus for listening, beer is not mentioned in the Bible, Jesus prefers wine."

Jess rolled over and starred back at Ron in amazement, then clapped her hands briskly. "Amazing! But you'll need to learn the phrase 'can I have' in all those languages."

"No way. 'Beer!' is an imperative. It doesn't require anything else."

"I guess it didn't last night."

"Your turn."

Jess eased herself up until she was sitting against the headboard and pulled the bedsheet up over her breasts.

"I'm the world's worst gardener, a few weeks before covid kicked in, I was staying with a couple of friends who went away for a week's skiing to Italy and they left me in charge of their garden and flowers and so forth. But when they were away; the lawn dried up and turned brown and I managed to kill an indoor cactus. A cactus which can survive in the harshest climates of scorching heat and barren terrain couldn't last more than 6 days with me in Surrey."

Ron laughed, "that bodes the question what type of micro-climate do you sleep in?"

"Like this, nothing weird."

Ron pulled her close and kissed her. "Here's something else, with you I'm on cloud ten!"

"Don't you mean cloud nine?"

"No it's better than that. Cloud ten definitely. I love your smile. It's so beguiling I want to drink it."

"Huh, you and you're drinking, you'd drink mustard if it came in a pint glass."

Ron feigned a look of hurt but bounced back. "I once read the biography of the man who invented the elevator; he started at the bottom and worked his way up."

Jess laughed.

"See there's that smile again. Wonderful."

Jess kissed him but this time there was something else in her eyes, alarm.

"Can I tell you something else?" she whispered.

"Sure."

"I think you're great for me and I'm enjoying being with you, and I can't believe I've only known you for a couple of days, but can we take it slow."

"Of course."

Ron looked up at her waiting for an explanation, but Jess had her face down. Slowly she lifted her eyes to meet his. Her smile had vanished.

"It's just..." she stopped. "It's..."

"You don't need to explain."

"No but I want to. You see I don't have a mum or a dad. I'm alone, I have no one to go to if things turn dark. When my mum died, I promised myself I would take good care of myself and I do that by keeping myself in check."

Ron reached out to take her hands, "I'm sorry."

But Jess pulled back, "No let me finish." She sat up in the bed. "You wanted to know something about me you wouldn't guess, here it is. I never knew my dad, but my mum was my world and she took great care of me. We didn't have it easy but we were okay, we got by, we more than got by. Then 21 months ago I lost her, she was in a car accident, an RTA, she fought her injuries for 6 days but eventually they overwhelmed her and she passed away. Now there's just me."

Jess took a deep breath and dived into part two.

"Sure I have some good friends but in reality I'm flying solo and I'm scared of being abandoned again, not that my mum abandoned me in a bad way, but the result is the same; 21 years old and both mum and dad are gone forever. I don't want to get close to someone and risk losing them. I don't think I could take it."

A coldness filled the room and chased away the laughter than had been there two minutes ago.

Ron spoke gently, "I understand. I haven't endured your struggles, but I get what you're saying. I'm in no rush. We'll go as fast or as slow as you wish, but we'll go together."

Jess looked up at him and smiled again and he wrapped her in his arms.

"I'm planning to watch the England game this afternoon. I'd be delighted if you'd watch it with me, but I understand if you want some time alone. Or if you want to visit a garden centre and wipe out half their stock."

She swung a pillow at him and crashed it into his shoulder, he buckled and collapsed on to the bed pulling her with him.

RON STEPPED BACK inside the Red Lion; it was twenty minutes before kick-off but the place was dancing. Red and white England flags and banners adorned every wall. Three televisions were in place in different corners of the bar. Fears of covid infections had been forgotten for two hours and supporters crowded into the bar. Ron took his pint from the bar and squeezed on to the end of a long wooden table and set about making some new friends. Three hours later after England had narrowly won the match, and the pub had heard countless renditions of 'Football's Coming Home', Ron had learnt and forgotten the names of the other ten men who had shared his table. There were a couple of Mark's, a John, a Gary, an Alan and something foreign that sounded like Simone, beyond that he wasn't sure. But all of them were convinced that England were going to win the tournament and that Harry Kane was the best striker in the competition, even though he hadn't scored.

SCOTT DIDN'T BOTHER to watch the England game he was convinced they'd lose.

SEVEN

BEE'S SLEEP WAS fitful on Sunday night and once the sunshine had penetrated his bedroom he abandoned the idea and set off for the station determined to make some progress on the case. Every urban police station must function on a 24-hour basis and the uniformed team operate on an eight-hour three shift pattern that maintains that focus. But those rules don't apply to the CID branch of the business, where the hours vary to suit the severity of the workload. Hence an open murder case meant an increase in the working hours, nonetheless Bee expected to find his floor, the second floor of the building empty. At 6:45am he wasn't disappointed. Later on he would need to call a team briefing to ensure all his ducklings knew their place. But that would involve him reading through all the reports and interviews that had been written up and posted on their team folder on the CID computer. Operation Dropshot was in full swing, at least that was what he hoped to tell the chief when the inevitable demand for progress arrived. Now as he read through the material he wondered if he could make that statement.

Bee settled down at his desk searching through traffic camera footage. A semi-rural town such as Reigate didn't warrant many cameras to monitor the vehicles, the rush hour was a misnomer and could in fact be measured in minutes, nonetheless there were six video feeds to be collected and watched. The first of these covered the main arterial road that fed traffic off the M25 motorway down into the town. Bee examined the tape in the hour up to 10pm in the evening and thirty minutes passed the hour. From what he had learnt of the victim it didn't expect him to be late for this type of meeting, but he wanted to be thorough; but there was no sign of the red Nissan car. Bee wasn't surprised, but to make him feel that he was making progress he ran the tape back to the early morning and felt pleased when he noticed the car coming down the hill at 9:10 am in the morning. Good. This made sense; it represented the rationale route between Dawson's home and the tennis club.

Bee hoped to build on this success but the next four tapes offered nothing. However the fifth captured the red Nissan; at 9:45pm on the Thursday evening the car could be seen travelling around the one-way system in the town. Bee smiled to himself, but the smile quickly turned to a scowl. To get anywhere in the town you had to drive around the one-way system; this wasn't narrowing down the venue by much at all; at best it reduced the options by ten percent. Worse still, the picture of the driver wasn't clear; Bee felt it must be Dawson, but he appreciated that a defence lawyer would argue the opposite.

A disgruntled sigh escaped from his mouth seconds before the chief superintendent knocked on his door and entered all in one movement. It was an action that peeved Bee, but one that he had learned to hide.

"Morning sir, how can I help?"

"What's the latest on this tennis murder case? I have the

press hounding me for a statement and much as I hate to pander to the press, I do recognise the need to re-assure the public."

Before Bee could answer, the chief posed another, simpler question.

"Walk with me to the canteen and we'll grab a coffee at the same time."

The station had recently adopted a Costa Coffee franchise and as a consequence the staff canteen had become a mid-morning meeting point for anyone in the building. When they arrived there was a queue of seven, but the chief was not known for his patience and walked straight to the front and politely, but firmly pushed in. Bee cringed as the chief turned and asked what he would like. Bee scanned the room and thanked the heavens that there was a table free in the corner; they wouldn't have to expel anyone. But the chief led the way back up the stairs talking as he walked.

"Thank goodness for the football yesterday, did you see it? Good job England won, that should keep the public and the press happy for a couple of days. Did you know this is the first murder in the town for three years?"

"No, I didn't sir, but Reigate isn't a violent place, you should mention that in your statement."

"Thank you, I will, now I've scheduled a statement for 3pm; can you provide me with an update by say 2pm?"

"Certainly sir."

"Good, my office at 2."

Bee took his coffee back to his office and juggled the case highlights in his head. It didn't take long; there were lots of maybes, a few interesting side lines, precious few facts, and no leads. He hated having to speculate, the press had an irritating habit of throwing quotes back at you, particularly when they had proved to be awry. But in truth he had little to say; he had no compunction about throwing a set of platitudes to the media but the chief would expect more. He grimaced at the prospect but he would need to consult McTierney and listen to one of his barmy theories. Where was the damn man?

BEE CAUGHT UP with McTierney outside the Super Sports shop in the High Street.

"You can take the lead here; I want a few minutes with you afterwards; the chief is looking for an update before he addresses the press this afternoon."

"Sure."

McTierney entered the shop and flashed his badge at the man behind the counter. "I'd like to ask you a few questions about the business if I may?"

"Sorry mate, too busy today, come back tomorrow," answered the man.

Bee wondered how McTierney would handle this push back. His DS didn't bat an eyelid but smiled pleasantly at the man and played his ace. "I'm in a good mood this morning, so I'll offer you a choice. We're investigating a murder case, so either you co-operate now or we'll do this down at the station."

The expression on the man's face changed in an instant; McTierney had won and celebrated his win with a beaming smile. Bee turned away to look at the stock in the shop and concluded that McTierney enjoyed these little power struggles and seemed to like winning.

"In that case, I'll get the boss for you; she knows more about the business, I help out three days a week."

The man disappeared up a set of stairs leaving McTierney and Bee alone in the store. Bee's eyes scanned the room searching for something amiss. He wasn't sure what he was looking for, or perhaps it was something not there. He couldn't put his finger on it, but there was something wrong. His thoughts were broken by the sound of the owner clomping down the wooden staircase. Seconds later a middle-aged woman appeared in front of them. She had a shock of blonde hair held back by a hairband and bright red lipstick and was wearing a white satin blouse above black trousers.

"What can I do for you gentlemen? Oh it's you Ron, I didn't know you were a copper."

Bee swung his head around from the selection of cricket bats he had been admiring and stared at his partner. How could this woman know McTierney when he'd only been in the town for three days? The answer was quickly revealed.

"Hi Janice, yes a copper, in fact a detective sergeant to be precise."

Janice's face switched from friend to business-woman in a flash.

"We're here investigating the murder of Russell Dawson sometime around midnight on Thursday last."

"It wasn't me; I was in bed long before midnight."

"Can anyone vouch for that?"

"No I was alone."

McTierney changed tack. "Can I ask you about your business. We know that Mr Dawson had started a tennis business of his own, selling racquets, balls, and equipment, that sort of stuff. That must have been unwelcome for you, as he became your direct competitor. You must be the only sports shop in the town."

"How much do you take in a month?" Bee jumped into the conversation.

Janice stepped back and raised her hands in front of her. "One at a time gentlemen please." A smile danced on her lips. "I can't give you my best if you both demand my attention at the same time, now how about I prioritise by rank ... you won't mind will you Ron."

"Of course," said McTierney but the look on his face didn't match the words.

Janice paused and weighed up an answer before staring back at Bee. "Enough to pay the rent and little more."

"Can you put a figure on it?"

"Not really, not had a proper month for more than a year now."

Feeling she had dealt with Bee, Janice turned back to McTierney.

"Now, as I was saying, we're an excellent sports shop covering many more sports than tennis. The best in the area if I do say so myself." She giggled at her own words.

McTierney allowed a pause to hang in the air, and Janice fell into it.

"We used to do a lot of business together; Russell would recommend us to all his new members and we would supply him with a free racquet whenever he needed one. It was a good partnership until he got greedy."

McTierney tilted his head and Janice continued.

"He must have come up with the idea during the lock-down.

"Has your business suffered?"

"What business hasn't suffered lately, this covid stuff is going to kill more people through the shutting down of everything than it ever will from the disease. A sports business is all about people getting together and playing games, and there ain't be much of that lately. Then he comes along and takes a swipe at the tennis game. Summer's all about tennis and cricket and there ain't much cricket about at the moment."

"Evidently not. So you and Dawson had words about his new venture."

"You bet we did. I told him what I thought of his new game. Told him it was easy selling a few racquets but could he offer the full package of the shoes, and the kit and the after sales service and all that."

"So he started with racquets, then?"

Janice sniffed. "Yeah he did. Think it was me that give him the idea to take on the whole range. Should've kept me mouth shut. There's good money to be made on the shoes alone."

McTierney paused to scribble some of the comments in his notebook and Janice had a moment to reflect on what she had said. "But that don't mean I killed him. You have to believe that. He was a good man. Been a bit of a bastard over the last few weeks but that was covid making him do that. No, I'm sorry he's gone. I shall go to his funeral if I'm allowed and make my peace with him."

"Okay, thank you Janice, we'll be in touch if there's anything further."

As they stepped out of the shop Bee started his own investigation.

"How does she know your name?"

McTierney was taken back by the question, "I met her in the pub a couple of nights ago, when I was off-duty."

"You're spending a lot of time in the pub these days. I trust you're social distancing?"

"Of course, but what else am I going to do? There's not much to do in the hotel. I'm not going to live as a monk. Is this relevant?"

Bee grumbled something unintelligible, turned away in the direction of the station and let the subject drop.

"Good interview," muttered Bee as they walked back towards the station, and then in a brighter tone. "I've figured out what was troubling me in the store. There's no tennis equipment. Not a racquet, or a ball or anything. It leads me to conclude that Dawson must have taken the whole of the market in the town."

"Perhaps he did."

"That would surely make a sizeable hole in the business for Janice."

"Enough to warrant a murder?"

"Perhaps." Bee pursed his lips, "People kill for bizarre reasons. If it's your livelihood, and your world maybe that's a lot to lose." He stopped and looked up and down the street. "I accept that she has motive and opportunity, but I'm not convinced she's the killer."

"No me neither. Is it worth running a background check?"

"Don't think so, not at this stage."

The pair of detectives started to walk back along the High Street, heading East towards the police station there were few pedestrians for them to dodge.

McTierney looked up at the blue sky, "I get the impression Reigate is one of those places where you think it should be sunny every day and only nice things are allowed to happen."

"If that's so, we've had a few thunderstorms of late."

"Perhaps, but I look around and see pots of money and many wonderful things; okay times are tough at the moment but this looks like a happy town to me."

Bee stopped and looked over the end of his glasses at his DS.

McTierney continued; "Honest there's nothing like this in Norwich; not the money, or the sunshine or the happiness – but it's a calmer place, no subterfuge."

As he spoke they reached a T-Junction which represented the edge of the town centre and was controlled by a set of traffic lights on the conjunction of two A roads. The lights had just changed as they arrived and a white VW started to pull away in the same direction as they were walking but had to slam its brakes on as a bright red Range Rover screeched around the corner from the opposite direction and raced away up the Croydon Road.

"Whoo. That's bloody dangerous!" yelled Bee.

"If only there was a traffic cop here to nail him; that could've been serious."

"Never one around when you need them."

"If I had my car with me, I'd be after him. B009. If I see that around town, I'll nick him."

Bee shook his head; "Whatever, let's step it up, I need to catch up with Bartlett before I brief the super."

BARTLETT HAD BEEN more successful than her superior; perhaps the judgement to allow a lighter female touch had worked or maybe Tina Dawson had benefitted from the extra two days to come to terms with her husband's demise. Either way Bartlett returned to the station with a smile on her face and a bounce in her step. She slipped into the canteen to grab a sandwich as Bee stood in front of the counter dismayed by the lack of choice.

"Hope you're not looking for something to eat, most things have gone; there's a bowl of cauliflower cheese and that's about it."

"No I fancied a baguette but that's always optimistic after 1pm."

"How about a quick stroll into town; there's a new delicatessen opened which might be worth checking. My treat, and you can tell me what happened with Tina Dawson."

As they walked the quarter mile into the centre of Reigate, Bartlett recounted her conversation with Dawson's widow. She had three nuggets of information to justify her free lunch. Firstly Tina Dawson had confirmed that the body was that of her husband. Secondly she stated proudly that Dawson had been wooed by an alternative tennis club, although it was early days. Jacob Mills was reluctant to talk about it, but Tina had been more open. Evidently Russell had been invited to play at Kingston and there had been some discussion around his remuneration, and even a joining bonus of twenty thousand pounds. She wasn't convinced that it would happen, but she knew he was upset with events at the Reigate Priory club and was giving serious thought to a change.

Bee meet the news with his usual pained expression, but he changed it once he saw the smile slip from Bartlett's face. "Interesting but we'll file that under inconclusive. What about the other item?"

The final piece of news extracted a better reaction. It transpired that Russell Dawson was a half decent tennis player who once graced the British top 3. His big moment had arrived in 2002 when he had played Roger Federer on court number one at Wimbledon. Although he had been positioned to be the plucky first round British cannon fodder for the Swiss, he had in fact taken the first set and a shock was on the cards until it started to rain. Cliff Richard had stepped up and entertained the crowd singing 'Summer Holiday'. When they resumed Russell won a couple of games, but his moment was gone and he ended up getting wet and getting beaten.

Bee nodded approvingly; "Doesn't assist the investigation, but nice to know that he's met the great man."

"I don't know about that. I think he just heard him sing."

"Not Cliff Richard – Roger Federer!"

"Oh, yes."

"Come on, let's see what's on offer in this shop."

AT 1:55PM BEE stood outside the chief's office and looked down at his single sheet of paper. He knew it wasn't enough. You can't crack a murder case in two days with covid

decimating your staff and a new kid in town, who spends more time chasing your DC than he does chasing the criminals. But that was making excuses and Bee hated making excuses. He was about to scribble out one of the comments he had written when Chief Superintendent Beck pulled the door open.

"Come in Bee, what have you got?"

The chief took the paper from him, rather than wait for Bee to pass it over, but then started a different conversation.

"I see this new sergeant of yours is staying at a hotel in town. Is that necessary?"

"I don't think it's reasonable to expect him to travel back to Norfolk each day sir."

Beck grunted, "Hmm, let's keep the expenses to a minimum; we're also getting billed for that pathologist chap. Is he any good?

"Yes, Kelly looks impressive. Thorough, detailed, professional. If we had the chance I'd keep him."

"Right." Beck was scanning the page he had taken from Bee.

"Is that it? No real leads, no apparent motive, a disguised cause of death, a saintly victim with no enemies and a bag of drugs in his car."

"It's early days sir."

"So it would seem. I can keep the press at bay today, most of them are getting worked up over the football, but they will want something more substantial soon or they'll print something ghastly. Keep me posted on developments and don't disappoint me Bee."

"Yes sir."

Bee marched back down the stairs to his office with a

renewed sense of purpose. He returned to his computer and decided to attack the problem from the other end. If Kelly was right then the body had been moved after death and most likely the body had been moved in Russell's own car. Consequently there should be some footage of the car driving through the town later that evening or after midnight. This was back in needle and haystack territory; it could be any camera anywhere in the town. Green Lane was much too small to warrant a camera; but it led from Park Lane and that had only two exits; one of which was the main High Street in the town. That had a camera and was the place to start. When the video loop finally showed Bee's own Mercedes approaching the traffic lights at the junction of the High Street and Park Lane Bee realised that this avenue was not going to generate a quick lead.

AS IT HAPPENED Chief Superintendent Beck was only partially right; the press did have something else on their mind but it wasn't football. Later that afternoon Prime Minister Boris Johnson announced a delay to the much-anticipated Freedom Day. The country had been expecting the wholesale lifting of covid restrictions to come on June 21st but due to the growing number of covid cases this was to be delayed to July 19th. Johnson was at pains to state that 'the pandemic is not over, and the public should remain cautious'.

EIGHT

As much as McTierney would have liked to focus on the forthcoming football championship he had work to do and lots of it. Interviews to conduct, background searches to complete and notes to record on the police internal system; all interspersed with meals in a canteen that he was starting to despise. As a new recruit he hadn't yet been assigned a departmental number and couldn't use the photocopier. It was one of a few office grumbles he had, chief amongst them was the lack of his own office, a privilege he had enjoyed in Norwich, but something that didn't stretch to the lower ranks in Surrey. More troubling was the growing pressure of the case, but that's what happens when you're 5 days into a murder inquiry and yet to identify a high-quality suspect.

McTierney had set aside Wednesday to follow up on the ticket agent lead, although he was fascinated by the world of touts he wasn't sure where to begin; – it wasn't the type of problem you encountered in Norfolk. He decided to start with the Lawn Tennis Association although he didn't expect it to embrace the idea that any tickets from their showpiece event could possibly end up in the hands of criminals. This was one of the elements of police work that appealed to McTierney; he could wave his police badge and ask anyone any question he desired. It was the perfect passport to stick his nose into anything that took his fancy.

He put the phone down from his call with the pompous Neil Jenkins and looked at his notes. Wimbledon tickets were distributed in three ways; a public ballot for LTA members which was always oversubscribed. Jenkins had been at pains to emphasise the lengths the club went to, to ensure an equitable process. Secondly each affiliated club in the country was allocated a small number of tickets for their own distribution, again the LTA official had stressed the idea that tickets were issued to true tennis fans with the idea that only devotees of the game should be permitted to watch the championship. Finally Jenkins had conceded that a select number of tickets were retained by the All-England Club for their long-term supporters, whatever that meant. Underneath the three lines McTierney had created his own, less than complimentary, interpretation of LTA. He was not a fan of tennis, but his nose for detective work had spotted the potential for conflict between Dawson and this ticket agent Wheeler. If he himself, had been a tout looking for tickets to sell, he would have approached some of the small provincial clubs and made them an offer they couldn't refuse. Perhaps that was what had occurred and irritated Dawson. Right now what irritated McTierney was that Dawson had not listed any contact number for Wheeler in his phone or on any file that McTierney could find.

McTierney took a 15-minute break for coffee and chocolate to rejuvenate his flagging spirit, but it wasn't the cocoa or the caffein that changed his demeanour rather a chance meeting on the stairs with Bee who passed him the contact details for an enterprising DS in the Met. Ten minutes later, McTierney was on his way to meet Stuart Page in Lavender

Hill. He stepped out of the station and looked to the skies. It was not as hot as it had been, the temperature had dropped a few degrees and the clouds were gathering. McTierney shrugged, whatever the weather in Reigate he didn't miss the lazy winds of Norfolk which didn't bother to go around you.

McTierney's satnav took him the 20 miles into South London and the home of the Lavender Hill police. Bee's description of a cappuccino station with the white concrete on top of brown bricks had been spot on, but so was his estimation that parking would be a nightmare. Eventually McTierney abandoned his car at Clapham Common and started to walk back. Two hundred metres from his car the weather front that had been inching in from the west arrived in London and brought with it a sudden rain shower. Big raindrops started hitting the pavement and exploding. McTierney pulled up his collar and ran.

At the entrance to the station he shook his head like a sodden Labrador. Detective Sergeant Stuart Page greeted him with a laugh, but the conversation quickly paid dividends for McTierney. Mark Wheeler was known to the Metropolitan Police; he had served time for grievous bodily harm in a situation with similar circumstances to the Dawson case. Additionally he had been cautioned for ticket touting outside Wembley four years before and was suspected of involvement in an armed robbery. Page described him as a nasty piece of work, quick to use his fists and could easily imagine him threatening or killing Dawson over next to nothing. But the one area which didn't ring true for Page was that Wheeler had moved upmarket to Wimbledon tennis tickets. "He's too thick to see that opportunity. Either he has a partner or a new master because he makes dumb mistakes. Not only that, but

I've never known him operate outside of London. Doesn't mean he wouldn't but I'd be surprised."

McTierney smiled ruefully. "I don't know whether this Wheeler is a hot suspect or a complete red-herring."

"I guess you can't afford to dismiss anyone, until you've identified a prime suspect."

McTierney shrugged his shoulders.

"One thing that bothers me," said Page, "is how Wheeler thought he could make any money here."

McTierney turned his head.

"Each tennis club affiliated to the LTA gets only a handful of tickets, so it's not easy to get any scale here."

McTierney nodded and Page continued. "Even if Wheeler threatens, bullies, or does whatever to collect a few tickets from a tennis club, he can't make much money, because none of the clubs have enough tickets."

"Right. He would have to repeat the trick at a dozen or more clubs to make the scam meaningful."

"That's what I'm thinking."

"I'll drop in on a few other tennis clubs and see if he's reprised the con anywhere."

"Good plan."

"Unless of course, there's some history between Dawson and Wheeler and nothing to do with Wimbledon tickets."

Unfortunately Page didn't have an address for Wheeler, but he did furnish McTierney with a recent photo and a story to cement his theory that Wheeler wasn't the sharpest tool in the box. Page recounted the first time they had picked Wheeler up; he was selling tickets to a cup final at Wembley and rather than selling a scarf for an inflated price and throwing in a free ticket; he had become confused and forgotten about the scarf element until the undercover policeman had arrested him.

Back in his car McTierney played back a couple of voice mails he'd picked up in the previous couple of hours. One was from Bartlett; it didn't say much, but McTierney liked listening to her voice and played it back three times, before he moved on to the next one. It also helped him decide what he would do that evening and it had nothing to do with Mark Wheeler.

NINE

McTierney had been walking to work whenever possible as he tried to learn the geography of his new town. He zigzagged around the central streets of Reigate slipping between residential and commercial areas and dodging the battalion of Ocado vans that buzzed around the town armed with premium groceries. This particular Friday the weather was bright and he opted for a long walk along the northern side of the town. While his airpods bombarded his ears with rock music, his eyes danced around the housing stock as he found himself on a street where one of the plaques declared the houses had stood since 1893. Even his untrained eye could deduce that there was no longer an original facade to be found. He was in the centre of the commuter area, six rows of housing for aspirational middle-class workers who scuttled off to the nearby train station each morning and scampered across town to Canary Wharf to collect their six figure salaries. Salaries that would be invested in these clean modern properties, mostly semi-detached but so closely bundled together that no one had privacy or a long garden. The upgrades, extensions and renovations had broken the original uniformity of the road but couldn't disguise the community feel to the area. It was nothing like the house he had left behind on the edge of Norwich, less than half the price but with more than twice the land. He had enjoyed his time in that rural arcadia but now it was time to move on. He upped the pace and headed on to the station.

TWO MORE DAYS had slipped by almost unnoticed. A few hours of house-to-house enquiries scheduled to dodge the summer rain showers, endless rounds of paperwork, half a dozen interviews, and ample tedious double checking of statements and without warning the weekend was looming large. This would have been universally welcomed by everyone if Superintendent Beck wasn't stomping up and down the corridor looking for an upside to the investigation that he could offer to the press.

By Friday afternoon the operations room had a distinctive odour; a rare combination of freshly photo-copied reports, stale cups of coffee and bored policemen; – it wasn't likely to be picked up by Dior anytime soon. This was accompanied by the gentle hum of laptops whirring away in the background. By contrast not much was buzzing in McTierney's brain; he stared out of the large office window as the rain rivulets ran down the pain. He watched two patrol cars tango in the tight car park and wished for a collision to create some excitement; he needed to be around people to perform at his best. All he could think of was the upcoming European Championship football match that evening between England and Scotland at Wembley. He had been hoping for a ticket but none of his usual sources had been able to provide the goods. He had more or less resigned himself to watching the game in the pub when his ennui was broken by the appearance of Bartlett. She stepped out of one of the dancing patrol cars and quick-stepped in the rear entrance of the building. Two minutes later she had brought sunshine to the ops room. McTierney's mood lightened appreciably, but lost its sheen when Bee followed her into the room.

"Bartlett has some news to share with us," he said and sat down.

"Most, perhaps all, of my news is gossip rather than evidence," she looked across the table at Bee who twisted in his seat, "but," she held the word until he nodded, "I think we need to consider it. We can investigate some of these avenues more fully in the next few days if we see fit."

"Go on," McTierney relished the half-baked ideas and lent across the table in anticipation.

"Over the last few days I've caught up with a few of the club players that I know. They are all aghast at what has happened; Dawson was loved by many of them. Now all of this is off the record, unofficial stuff. But these are people who have been at the club for many years and seen plenty of change, so I think there perspective might be interesting."

"Yeah, yeah," McTierney rolled his hands anxious to get to the knub.

Bartlett smiled at him and continued, "Number one; less than a week ago, Dawson replaced the former deputy coach with a junior coach Ruth Jones. He fired him for no apparent reason, when everyone considered him to be decent, as a coach, and a player and a club member."

"Interesting," said Bee.

"Could be something untoward between Russell and Ruth," offered McTierney.

"You really do see the best in everyone don't you,"

scoffed Bee.

"This is a dirty business; you don't get murders in toytown; they come along as a result of people pissing each other off. It's not pleasant but that's life," McTierney defended himself with a flourish of his arms and added "or death." Bartlett caught his eye and smirked at the joke but brought herself back to normal when Bee scowled across the table.

Emboldened by Bartlett's response McTierney dived in again. "I think we have to consider the sex angle in this case; you might not like it but a tennis club is full of women and young girls running around in short skirts. It's only to be expected with all that leg on show; it's going to have an effect somewhere."

Bee turned his face to stare at McTierney but didn't say anything.

"And men. They're in shorts too. People run around, get hot, get excited, things can happen. I'll tell you for nothing that I bet there's an affair or three going on at that club right now."

Nobody challenged McTierney's assertion and the room fell silent for a moment, until Bee picked up the gauntlet, "I think we can file this conversation under riotous speculation," he said, "Bartlett please continue."

"Thank you, sir. The general feeling amongst the club was that Josh, that's the former coach, had been mistreated."

"Okay."

"And there's some surprise, even amazement about the promotion of Ruth."

Both Bartlett and Bee looked at McTierney, who raised his palms in front of his body and said nothing.

"I also picked up two or three other club grumbles, which might not mean much but they do suggest all is not well in paradise."

"Go on."

"There's a feeling that the committee want to cull some of the weaker players and create an elite club."

"Nazism in rural Surrey!" Exclaimed McTierney, before quickly apologising, "come on, you've got to admit, it does sound like a purge."

"Maybe," contended Bee, "but I don't think we'll be seeing the Third Reich marching down Green Lane anytime soon." He nodded back at Bartlett.

"Some of the older or weaker players are being made to prove their tennis ability or they face being barred from the club at certain hours or specific competitions."

"Hmm, and has Dawson been at the forefront of this campaign?"

"No. It seems he was against the move."

"Not likely to be a motive for murder then," concluded Bee.

"Perhaps not. Although as he is the most prominent personality in the club he does tend to be associated with whatever policy or decision the club makes."

"Okay, your point is duly noted," conceded Bee. "What else do we have?"

"There is a general gripe that the membership costs are rising, even though the number of members is growing. In effect this means that people are paying more but getting less access to the club, as the number of courts is limited and there are more people trying to book them. This is exacerbated by the number of court hours that are given over to coaching programmes and private lessons. All of these are associated with Russell Dawson as he runs the coaching academy."

"Hmm, so where we started with the idea that Dawson was loved by everyone, we are now finding some people who aren't fans."

"Yes I'd say that was true, and I have one member in particular who could have a grudge against him."

Both Bee and McTierney lent in on the table to hear the revelation.

"Greg Savage has been club champion for the last two years and some people believe him to be the best player in the club, rather than Dawson. He was in the club open final a few weeks ago and most people expected him to win and complete a hat-trick of wins. Now Dawson doesn't play in the club tournaments."

"Taking the high moral ground," added Bee.

"Too much to lose, more like," said McTierney.

"Whichever. You could argue that he remains independent because he always referees the final, and he does play in the number one position in club matches. Anyway the club take the competition seriously; they have a proper umpire's chair, line judges and ball boys, the full works. It's one of the biggest days in their calendar. This year the match was much closer than expected and in the deciding set Dawson made a dubious call to over-rule a line judge and give a point to Savage's opponent. Most of those watching thought he was wrong, but in his defence he does have the fancy seat and obviously there's no hawk-eye technology at the club. Nevertheless Savage lost it, called him a cheat, and then lost the match to boot. So I think you can safely say he's not

Dawson's number one fan."

"Interesting, not exactly a strong motive for murder, but we ought to interview this Savage chap next week, make sure he has an alibi for the time of death."

"I can handle that," offered McTierney.

"Good, thanks. Anything else Bartlett?"

"No, that's pretty much it, sir."

"Good job. Let's leave it there for the week, I have to go and brief the chief before I leave, but don't let that detain anyone else."

MCTIERNEY DIDN'T NEED to be invited twice to shut down his laptop. As his fingers ran across the keyboard his eyes ran across the room to Bartlett. She caught his eye and read his mind.

"I can't tonight, I have a date with an old friend."

A mixture of disappointment and worry flickered across McTierney's face.

"A girl friend," she emphasised the word girl. "it's Alison, the girl I used to live with, whose cactus I killed."

"I guess I won't have to be gallant and give up the football for you tonight." The happiness had returned to McTierney's face.

"No way would you have done that for me."

"I would," protested McTierney.

"Tell you what, if England make the semis or the final or something important, I'll watch that with you. Otherwise why don't you find us a restaurant for tomorrow night. Now I must be off, I want to get some flowers for Alison on the way home."

RON THREW HIS laptop bag over his shoulder and ambled down to the car park. He looked to the skies; a fresh breeze was chasing the rainclouds away to the east. The sun was making an over-due appearance and he reasoned that it would be a warm pleasant evening. No need to move his car a mile across town, especially through the Friday early evening traffic. Instead he opted to leave his car and wandered back to his hotel. Without Jess, there wasn't anything to hurry for so he choose a residential route rather than one clogged with car fumes.

As he walked he began examining the houses along his route; an eclectic bunch of detached grand properties each standing back from the road waiting to be introduced to their neighbours. Brick, stone and timber facades each raised as uncompromising as the next. None offered a welcome to the casual visitor. Although most were adorned by trees and bushes, the foliage was in place to provide security and distance, Large Volvos, Range Rovers and BMWs stood as guard dogs in the designer driveways. Ron mused how the houses were more socially distanced than most of the inhabitants would be now freedom was re-asserting herself in the mind of the public.

ONE HOUR LATER Ron sat on his hotel bed and weighed up his options for the evening. Should he watch the game in his room with a beer and a meal from room service or slip down to his new local. The smart option would be to stay safe and isolated with nothing more than a bottle of beer for company. He was aware that covid cases were rising, getting somewhere close to 10,000 cases a day so someone had said in the station that morning. But that would be dreadfully dull; – the Friday night equivalent of a glass of sparkling water. Then again, he had a position to uphold, a respectable member of the community and a nasty crime to solve, indeed that was the whole reason he was here in the first place. The game would be the same whichever screen he watched it on. He kicked off his shoes and stepped into the shower.

Thirty minutes later he popped his head into the Red Lion, "Any chance of a table for one? I haven't booked anything."

"No problem Ron, I'm sure we can find a space for our friendly neighbourhood copper." Take a seat over at table 3 and I'll send Julie over to take your order."

Ron's evening started happily with the ubiquitous pint of beer, some flirtatious chatter with Julie complemented by a big-screen football match. Despite the 0-0 score line, the game was exciting and Ron soon found a couple of football fans to share his evening. Together they discussed the chances of an English win, following their positive start despite the disappointing performance of the England Captain. As Ron's beer count rose his arguments became more simplistic yet more forcefully delivered. By the time his two new friends were ready to leave the pub Ron was preparing to write to Her Majesty demanding that manager Gareth Southgate be knighted for his services to the country. He flopped back against his chair and looked around the pub; it was closing time and people were scattering. He waved to Julie for another pint and she slipped into the seat next to him.

TEN

IN KEEPING WITH the longest day, the sunshine was putting on a show and had cleared the early morning mist and was flexing its muscles ready to make home workers curse the lack of domestic air-conditioning across the nation. McTierney squinted at the sun as he strode across the car park and entered the rear of the police building. He stopped and looked at his watch, not quite 8 o'clock – maybe even Bee would be pleased at his arrival.

Despite the performance of the sun, McTierney flicked on four rows of strip lighting as soon as he reached the ops room. Bee scowled and dipped his eyes as the white lights flashed like sabres across the ceiling. Bee had taken the seat at the head of the white composite tables and had control of the on-screen projector; McTierney took a position at the end of the long side of the table, close to the flipchart easel. Along the solid wall behind him were twenty or thirty photographs of the case; starting with a large colour photo of the victim in the centre and spreading out in the style of a mind-map with names and places scribbled in capital letters amongst a host of arrows and question marks.

"Morning sir," said McTierney.

"Good weekend?"

"Very," said McTierney as Bartlett led two new officers

into the room. Then he turned to the newcomers and attempted to start a conversation about the football with the new recruits, but Bee was having none of it.

"We have to focus on this case at the cost of everything else; there is nothing more important than solving this murder. Nothing."

McTierney stopped mid-sentence and fell into line. Then realised that this was the extent of the extra resources; Bartlett, Bee, and himself, plus the supplement of two young officers who he hadn't seen before. Their wide-eyed enthusiasm told him that this was their first taste of a murder case and that they would only be used for the most routine of tasks; paperwork and report writing. I hope you like this room boys because you'll be spending a lot of time here, he thought.

Bee summarised the status of the case, threw in the thoughts of the chief super, laid out their current theories and distributed the primary tasks for the next couple of days. Top priority was to find out everything there's to know about Dawson and then Bee closed by asking if anyone had any questions, no one did. McTierney had been spot on with his forecast for the two newcomers. But there were two interesting additions; firstly Kelly was expected to deliver his DNA analysis tomorrow and secondly Bee was hopeful of securing additional support once he had made his request to the chief.

The meeting broke up and the participants headed for the door and ultimately the station canteen for a refreshing coffee. McTierney hoped to catch up with Bartlett but as he was about to do so, Bee reached across and grabbed McTierney by the shoulder. "Hang on a second, I'd like to get your thoughts on this note in Dawson's diary."

McTierney turned back unable to disguise his disappointment.

He watched Bartlett skip off to the canteen and didn't speak again until she was out of sight. Only then did he look directly at Bee. "What was it, you wanted?"

Bee opted to blow some smoke at him, "You have a creative thought process, different from my own, so I wondered what you thought of this entry in Dawson's diary. The one that appears to be an appointment to meet his killer."

Bee pulled out a photo of the calendar in Dawson' laptop. Thursday June 10th. The screen was divided into 30-minute sections and on the 10pm line, Dawson had added the words, '10pm Meet'.

Bee began, "If you have an appointment to meet someone surely you would write down their name and the place."

"That's normal."

"So why didn't Dawson write down the place and even the other party?"

McTierney shrugged. He didn't want to be here playing this game, but Bee wasn't quitting.

"Maybe it was so obvious from the name of the person that a place was redundant?"

McTierney frowned, but Bee continued.

"If I was meeting the chief super. I'd expect it to be in his office so I wouldn't need to write it down."

"Maybe he didn't know. Didn't know the place, that is."

"What?"

"When he made the appointment the other party said I'll let you know where nearer the time and only told him minutes before they met so he didn't need to write it down." McTierney had joined the game, and in no time he was on a roll. "Or maybe Dawson had something to hide, perhaps he has a woman and was meeting her in their usual place."

"You really do see the best in people."

"You asked me to be creative."

"I'll tell you what I think; I think this tells us that Dawson knew his killer and not only that but that he knew him well."

McTierney's head bobbed in agreement.

"There's a comfort in the absence of detail. I'm willing to bet that when you were invited to come down here, you made a record of all the details, because it was unfamiliar to you. I know I did."

"I'll give you that."

"It's only when you make an appointment that is so recognisable to you that you start to skimp on the details, because you've written them so many times before."

"Sounds like we are back to my theory of another woman."

Bee frowned at his DS and ignored the comment. "I think we need to look closely at Dawson's close associates and favourite haunts. Can I ask you to take the lead on that part and we'll review it in a couple of days?"

"Sure. I think that's got some mileage."

"While I've got you, how did you get on with the ticket tout angle?"

"Looks like a dead end. Your contact at the Met told me that Wheeler never strays far from London and neither of us could see how any scam that Wheeler might be working on could make much money."

"People kill for a variety of different reasons; doesn't have to be a lot of money involved."

"No, but Wheeler doesn't feel like the perpetrator here, and if your theory about Dawson's late-night meeting, being with someone he knew intimately, is correct, that would exclude Wheeler."

"Fair enough," Bee nodded his acceptance of the point.

BY THE TIME McTierney had escaped from the operations room, Bartlett was nowhere to be seen, in fact she was halfway to a coffee meeting with a couple of her tennis partners. Without a colleague to chat to, McTierney was lost and resigned himself to the task in hand and slumped into his chair and began digging though Dawson's business records courtesy of his laptop. Bee strode down to the ground floor to find an old colleague from the drugs squad to pick his brains about the find in Dawson's car.

A clap of thunder woke McTierney from his reverie, he looked down at his doodle on his notepad, an assortment of pound and dollar signs in ever increasing size. He had been examining the finances of Russell Dawson and had only one conclusion. He wanted to share his news, but not with Bee, that path would more than likely bring hassle and aggravation, not favourite playmates of Detective McTierney. He flicked through the local news service on the internet and was about to forward an article when he was interrupted by the arrival of Jess Bartlett. His mood lifted instantaneously.

"Hey, how's things with the county's sexiest detective?"

Bartlett scowled and stepped smartly across to her desk.

"Can we keep our friendship secret, at least at work. I don't want to attract any sly remarks around the canteen."

"Yes sure, sorry." McTierney's happy face was short lived.

Bartlett scanned the office and seeing that no one was paying much attention to them, she reached across and stroked his hand. "Thanks."

Standing back up she returned to DC Bartlett; "I've had an interesting day; shall we go and brief the boss?"

McTierney was only too eager to join a conversation and was by her side within seconds.

Fifteen minutes later Bee, McTierney and Bartlett congregated around the large white table in the operations room. All three had interesting stories to recount; Bee allowed Bartlett to take the lead.

"I caught up with Ruth Jones and I asked her about her promotion to deputy coach at the club. I think I've discovered something to burst McTierney's bubble."

Bee lifted his shoulders and a smile ran across his face.

"It appears that Ruth doesn't like men. She prefers women. So there wouldn't have been any sexual element to Russell's decision to promote her."

McTierney looked disappointed, while Bee beamed across the table.

"She was mildly surprised by the appointment and spoke highly of Dawson."

"I imagine she did if he'd recently promoted her," sneered McTierney.

"Did she have any comment to make on the assertions by your tennis clubmates?" asked Bee.

"She did, but as you might imagine her viewpoint reflected that of the committee more than it did some of the older players. For instance she doesn't see a problem with the level of coaching in the club; instead she sees it as the lifeblood of the club; developing the younger players and all that."

"The usual tensions of any club then."

Bartlett squeezed up her nose. "I think so. I don't think we'll find some smoking gun or even a blood-stained mallet or whatever the murder weapon was, hiding at the back of the tennis club."

"Keep pushing. I don't think everything is as rosy as the club captain made out."

Bee switched his attention to McTierney, "You've been tapping away on your keyboard all day, what have you discovered?"

"Something and nothing. Would you say being a tennis coach is a route to riches?"

"Not especially. What have you found?"

"Looking at Dawson's finances it appears there's a lot of money to be made from a tennis club, or at least Dawson was making a lot of money."

Bee rubbed his chin and stared at the ceiling, "I suppose this area will have a high proportion of wealthy parents itching to spend a small fortune if their little Hannah or Marcus can be the next Sue Barker or Andy Murray."

"Maybe that's exactly what they've been doing. Dawson and his wife have a joint account that appears to run their household expenses; usual stuff, direct debits for the mortgage, gas, and so on, nothing unusual there. But he also has fifty thousand sitting in a separate account in his name only."

"That's some rainy-day fund," said Bartlett.

"It would buy a lot of umbrellas, that's for sure. And it's

one way traffic, he's been paying in odd amounts here and there, mostly in cash. No withdrawals."

"Interesting. I wonder where that money comes from."

"In addition he has a business account, which is new, six months old, but he's already starting to make money here. I think someone estimated his takings at £1,000 a month; it's more than double that, and the business is flying."

"It is tennis season."

"I know, but even so; his profit margins are above 30%. It's all a bit too good to be true."

Bartlett shrugged her shoulders; "Maybe he's a good tennis coach and a good businessman. Everyone at the club comments on how many tennis classes they run and he's universally recognised as a good player."

"I'd agree that he's a good businessman. He has a distribution contract with Wilson; they give him some demonstration equipment; he finds the buyers and Wilson deliver the racquets and the shoes etc. Dawson picks up his commission at the end of the month. No stock to worry about; no cash flow challenges; easy money I'd say."

"Especially if you factor in the tennis club being closed for much of the last ten months due to covid." McTierney smiled and pointed his finger at Bartlett in recognition of a good point.

The atmosphere in the room started to change; where twenty minutes ago it had been jovial and light, now it took on a different texture. Bee pulled himself forward in his seat, placed his elbows on the table and lent into the discussion. "Do you think we are on to something here?"

"Not sure." McTierney shrugged. "I didn't expect to find so much money slushing around and it's not clear if all of this can be attributed to some good tennis coaching. But maybe it can. Although it also fits with the profile of a successful drug dealer." McTierney allowed the point to hang, hoping someone might bite. Nobody did so he continued. "I did discover that Dawson had been nominated as coach of the year in 2019; he didn't win the prize, but it does suggest he's pretty damn good."

"Indeed," said Bee as he scribbled something in his notebook.

"Andy Murray features in his list of contacts."

Bee looked up this time. "The Andy Murray?."

McTierney nodded and pleased to have regained his audience he continued. "But something he did win was distributor of the month for Wilson in May." McTierney waited for Bee to finish writing and to look up. "I spoke to a trade sales manager at Wilson who lauded Dawson's sales performance and explained that they give all their sports distributors monthly sales targets and Dawson had smashed each one."

"Wow!" Added Bartlett.

McTierney smiled across at her. "Quite, so Dawson appears to be a nice bloke, popular with everyone, good at his job, making money hand over fist both for himself and for the club."

"Then someone pops up to kill him and spoil the party," said Bartlett.

"Something else this tells us. It does add some credence to the idea that he might have been approached by another tennis club," said Bee.

"Let's not forget he did have a big bag of drugs sitting in his car."

"Yes, you're right Bartlett, and tomorrow Kelly will be here to share his analysis on that."

ELEVEN

IT WAS 8AM sharp and the operations room was as full as it had been during the last two weeks. There was excitement in the air, not unlike an election night, although most people knew what was going to happen, there was a restlessness around the central table.

"Good morning gentlemen. Thank you for attending this morning's discussion. It seems like we have a full house, not unlike The Kensington Oval, when Sir Viv is walking in to bat. That's The Oval in Barbados, not the joyless place you have in South London."

Bee raised his right hand to stop Dr Kelly. "For those who don't know, this is Dr Kelly the pathologist we are using on the case. He is on loan from Horsham, and a keen cricket enthusiast, as you'll probably gather over the next thirty minutes."

"Thank you inspector. Let's get this party started." Kelly flicked on his power point presentation. "We'll start with our victim. Russell Dawson died sometime between 10pm on Thursday June 10th and 2am on Friday June 11th. Cause of death was blunt force trauma to the back of the head. I can't be precise about the likely murder weapon, perhaps a mallet or a hammer but something with a smallish impact area of 3 cm."

He looked to Bee, dipped his face, and peered over his glasses, "I don't suppose we have found anything new that could be the murder weapon."

Bee shook his head, "No we haven't."

"Pity." Kelly looked down at his notes, nudged the presentation on by a slide and continued. "The body had been left exposed to the elements overnight, principally rain, so we're unable to lift any usable DNA material from the body."

"Pity." Bee echoed Kelly's earlier comment.

Kelly stared at him for a few seconds before resuming his review. "But we did find some DNA on the inside of the victim's tennis sweater."

Bee looked up and blushed, offered a weak smile and returned his focus to his notebook.

"There's no match for the profile on the national database."

"But still interesting," said Bartlett.

"I did examine the body for any evidence of drug use." Kelly turned back to Bee, "I believe you discovered some drugs in the victim's car." Bee ignored the look.

"I'm pleased to say that despite the large quantity of drugs found in the car, which were largely class B stimulants but with some class A pills, there is no evidence to suggest that Dawson was a user. As you might expect the general state of the body was good; it would be fair to say that he looked after his health."

McTierney picked a multigrain energy bar from his pocket and placed it on the table. It looked as though this was the first step to him eating it. Kelly scowled at him. "Please no eating in my debrief."

McTierney replaced it in his pocket and picked up the gauntlet. "That's useful information, thank you doctor." Then he turned his attention to the others around the table. "An open question for the room. With lots of tennis players looking to improve their performance, the use of these stimulants could be common, especially at the lower levels. No one is going to be caught out and if it helps you win a few more games, then so much the better."

"What's the point you're making?"

"I guess what I'm saying is that there could be a ready-made market for light stimulants in the tennis world."

"Light stimulants? These were class B drugs, sergeant."

"I know that. I'm trying to piece together a highly successful coach, a car full of drugs and a bank account awash with spare cash."

"Yes, I guess there is something to investigate there. Can I propose that you catch up with Phil Church, our drugs liaison specialist after this session?"

The group turned back to face Dr Kelly.

"Moving on, the car has offered some interesting secrets. I've identified five different strands of DNA from it. One of which belongs to our victim. Two further strands, both discovered in the rear seats are more than likely those of his children, but I'll leave that for you to prove. That leaves two other profiles, neither of which are on the national database." Kelly allowed the point to sink in as the room made notes.

"Finally I believe the car seat has been moved from its regular position." Kelly moved the slide on to show some photos of the car seat and people sitting in it.

"I believe the last person to sit in the driving seat of Dawson's Nissan was probably 4 to 6 inches taller than him.

That would make the driver 6 feet 2 or perhaps 6 feet 4 tall. Footwear might complicate that assessment but I've no doubt that the last driver was taller than Dawson."

There was a rustle of interest amongst the audience as each of them recognised as compelling clue when it arrived.

"Excellent," commented Bee. "We know that Tina Dawson is shorter than her late husband so it won't be her."

"No, although I suspect she will match one of the outstanding DNA profiles," added McTierney.

"That's easy to check, I'll pop back to the house and get samples from the whole family so we can exclude them from the investigation," offered Bartlett.

"Please do," said Bee.

"That's about it from me," said Kelly, "I'll declare here and you know where to find me if you need me."

"Thanks, doc. Most helpful."

Kelly packed up and left the room, and Bee stood up to address his team. McTierney moved around the table to sit next to Bartlett, leaving the two newbies together and balanced up the room.

"I had been hoping that our pathologist would deliver the first real breakthrough clue, but it doesn't seem so. I'm standing here feeling like Sisyphus." Bee looked around the room at a couple of blank faces. He stopped and stared at McTierney. "For the uninitiated, Sisyphus was a King of Corinth, who tried to cheat death and was condemned to repeatedly roll a heavy rock up a hill in Hades only it have it roll down again once he neared the top."

"I thought he played left back for Olympiacos," said McTierney, earning him a smirk from the two newbies.

Bee scowled back and wrapped his knuckles on the table.

"It's back to the tried and tested routine of pounding the pavement, door to door enquiries and cross-checking statements to validate alibis. Some might say proper police work without the fancy science. Let's work through what we know so far."

Bee walked across to the mind-map he had started on the board.

"Number one, the killer can drive. He may not have his or her own car, or even a licence, but he drove Dawson's car back to the tennis club sometime between 10pm on the Thursday and 8am on the Friday. Possibly his DNA has been found by the doctor, which would be a major bonus."

"Beyond the DNA angle we don't have any leads on this." Added McTierney.

Bee ignored the point. "Secondly, if Dawson was driving to meet his killer; it suggests that the killer is local, and so for this reason we'll drop the focus on Wheeler." Bee's eyes searched for McTierney who nodded his support.

"Additionally Dawson obviously knew his assailant and quite probably through the tennis club, so the killer could be a club member."

This point was met with a general murmur of approval around the room. Bee pointed to one of the new constables, "Chivers, can you ascertain a full list of all the club members."

"Thirdly the killer is strong enough to comfortably carry Dawson onto the tennis court and dump his body. Based on Kelly's analysis he is also over six feet tall. So I suspect we are talking about a male killer."

Again McTierney sought to challenge the idea. "It could mean we have two killers."

"I think it's unlikely, Kelly only found relatable DNA in the back of the car, so where would the other killer sit? Perhaps we shouldn't exclude it, but it doesn't feel right to me."

McTierney nodded and Bee continued.

"Finally number four; the killer lives in Reigate or close to it. We know this because traffic cameras show Dawson driving around the one-way system at 9:45pm on Thursday night suggesting the meeting he was heading to, can't be more than 3 miles from the centre of the town."

This time there was general agreement.

"When you get that list of tennis club members, get them to include the home address and if possible, a list of the taller members of the club," McTierney added to Chivers' work.

"Right that's it, not an impressive list, as the chief likes to remind me, so I want some progress this week. McTierney, as you seemed fixated with the drugs angle can you meet up with our man Church and dig into that. I'll investigate the money side of the tennis club. Any questions? No. Good. Let's move."

Bartlett and McTierney and the two newbies each exchanged a few words as they pushed back their chairs and made ready to leave the room. Bee moved across to interrupt Bartlett.

"I'll take McTierney along to meet Phil Church."

But as they arrived at the office door, Chief Superintendent Beck greeted them curtly.

"Ah Bee, that's where you're hiding, I need a few minutes with you."

"Don't worry sir," said McTierney, "I'm sure Bartlett can walk me down to Church's desk," and the pair slipped past the chief.

Superintendent Beck didn't have time to waste, he sat on the edge of the table and dropped a copy of the local paper down in front of Bee. The front page bore a colour photo of Russell Dawson from his Wimbledon hey-day and some intrepid reporter had dug up the story of his match against Federer.

"Have you seen this?" Said Beck pointing at the photo.

"No sir."

"It's very disappointing Bee. Murder all over the front page. The public will get worried and once the press link Dawson with Wimbledon this case could take on a new dimension and run for weeks."

"The pathologist has finished his briefing; he's suggested a few new avenues for us. I'm hopeful we'll see some progress soon."

Beck nodded his approval and pushed the paper across the table to Bee, then raised his head and looked directly at his inspector.

"Bee, I'll come straight to the point. Two topics. Not for debate. Firstly, there is concern in the community over this murder in the heart of the town. People are feeling threatened, worried, so the chief wants us to put some more police out on the beat. He's going to be announcing it tomorrow in a press statement, hoping to grab the moral high ground before the press go overboard."

"Good idea, sir," "it's important to maintain the trust of the public."

"Thanks I thought you'd agree. By the way I'll be taking one of the men from your group, who do you want to lose, Collins or Chivers?"

"What? No we need both to help us crack the case. We're under resourced as it is."

Beck stared at his detective inspector. He didn't need words. Bee opened his mouth to protest further but said nothing. He sighed, then muttered, "take Collins."

"Thank you, if and when we get some people back from isolation, I'll return him. Now, point two. We need to reduce our running expenses. This new kid down from Norfolk, McTierney, how's he doing?"

"Not bad sir, but you can't take him away, we'll have nobody. This is a complicated case; the pathologist has given us nothing, we're going to need to rely on rock steady standard police work. We need him out there talking to people, tracking down this killer."

"I thought you'd say that. Here's my proposal. You can keep him, but he's out of the hotel from the weekend. No more expenses for DS McTierney."

"We can't expect him to commute back and forth from Norfolk and he can't work from home. He's got to be in the vicinity so he can be out on the streets 10 hours a day."

"I agree, so what's your solution?"

"Can we charge Norfolk? Tell them we'll develop his skills, give him new expertise."

"I've tried that, they won't wear that, and I can't say I blame them."

"Can't we keep him at the hotel for another couple of weeks, I feel we are on the verge of a major breakthrough, the case could be cracked in that time."

Beck offered his stone-faced mute reply.

Bee looked flustered, "Give me a day to think of something."

"Can't do that, I need you focused on the case. Here's my solution. I know you live alone, got some space up in your farmhouse?"

"No, that's my sanctuary."

Beck remained impassive.

"It will contravene the covid regulations."

Beck raised his left hand. "I'm not asking you to share a bed with him, and you've got so much space up there, you'll barely see him. Besides they're only guidelines and you see so much of him during the day if you were going to catch anything from him it would have happened by now."

"But it's where I think, where I escape from this mayhem."

"Don't worry, it'll only be for a couple of weeks, I heard that you're on the verge of a major breakthrough."

Beck pushed himself off the desk and headed for the door, he stopped turned back to Bee. "Keep up the good work, inspector."

Bee waited for the chief to move and then kicked the nearest chair over. "Bollocks! No way is McTierney living with me!"

TWELVE

PHIL CHURCH WAS a young man, McTierney guessed he would still be in his late twenties, he wore black jeans and an Ed Sheeran white maths symbols t-shirt. He didn't look anything like a policeman. He sat in the canteen stroking his goatee as he listening to McTierney describe the drugs they had found in Dawson's car. He nodded a couple of times, grunted, and shrugged his shoulders as McTierney repeated his earlier assertion that up-and-coming tennis players might be tempted to take short term stimulants to improve their tennis game.

Church took a swig from his coffee cup, wiped his hand across his mouth and lent into the conversation. He liked to make his points forcibly and jabbed his index finger onto the table as he spoke.

"What you've found is fairly innocuous. Two hundred white ecstasy pills, and a quarter of a kilo of amphetamine powder." He looked for McTierney to nod his agreement.

"I don't know how much you know of the Surrey drug scene, so I'll give you a quick overview. As a street drug, amphetamines usually come as a white, pink, grey or occasionally a yellowish powder. Sometimes, as you have here, they can also be pills. Pills are a favourite form for dealers cos they're ready to use. Street purity here is usually less than 15% with most deals having only 10% amphetamine. Powders are snorted up the nose, mixed in a drink or prepared for injection in the case of a heavy user. You don't get many of those in this town."

He looked up to see if McTierney was following.

"Not in Norfolk either, but it's growing. Easy access into the ports from Eastern Europe."

"Yeah, I can imagine, it's no longer the West Indians that we have to worry about; it's the Beast from the East, and I'm not talking Russian ice storms."

McTierney nodded and Church continued. "Sounds like you'll know this bit, but I'll say it anyway, amphetamines are synthetic stimulants; drugs that speed up the body's processes including heart and breathing rate. Basically they increase energy levels and alertness. Users may feel more confident, happy, or creative."

"Hence some of the slang terms such as whizz and ecstasy."

"Yeah, exactly."

Church twisted in his chair, "The Home Office tells us that 9% of adults from 16 to 59 have used amphetamines at some point in their life. It would come in at number 4 on the chart of favourite illegal drugs."

He stopped, looked over his shoulder before turning back and tutted heavily. "Some say it's like drinking 10 cups of coffee in an hour, but without the need to go to the toilet." He shook his head. "Until you crash and need a shit. Taking a lot, can induce panic or paranoia once the effect wears off and the user comes down. Not pleasant."

"I guess not," said McTierney. "Is there a major problem in the town?"

"No, not especially, but it's growing. I mean we're not Oslo, but there's a lot of spare money floating around this town and invariably that attracts dealers and dealers create users and users create problems, both for themselves and for others and of course, for us."

"How bad is it?"

"Fairly stable at the moment, we're running at roughly 100 deaths a year in the county. All the covid stuff and the lockdown in particular has unsettled things. The nightclubs are shut for a start. Fewer people are travelling. All the supply chains are being disrupted. But there's no doubt we're on a slow decay to madness."

"100 deaths doesn't sound outrageous in a wealthy area; I was expecting more."

"We're doing some good things across the county to combat it and we're much better off than Kent; they have twice the problem we have."

"How come?"

"Various reasons; some of it structure, they have twice as many airports as we have and all of theirs are little fart-arse ones that don't operate 24 hours a day and have next to no security. Of course we have Redhill, which has been known to have the odd unscheduled landing late at night, but nothing like the same problem."

"What are you guys doing to combat the drug trade? Maybe I could take some ideas back to Norwich."

"Although I say so myself, we're pretty good at separating victims from criminals and then looking after those who are suffering. Reigate has the highest number of individuals in treatment in the county."

"Yeah?"

"442. I think the local support groups around here are doing a grand job. They've set up a few safe havens and are getting people off the street, away from temptation. We still need to tackle the stigma attached to drug misuse. But a couple of women in the team; Kimberly and Romy are doing a grand job."

"One person with the right approach can make a huge difference."

"Agree, and we've got two! Your friend Bartlett knows Romy; she could tell you about her."

McTierney jotted something down in his notebook and Church smiled at his new convert, before stepping up the pace.

"But the problem is the justice system or at least the sentences. We grabbed a dealer in Redhill a couple of years ago; caught him red-handed with 7 bags of cocaine, ready to push out onto the streets. Had him banged to rights. What happened? He gets 20 months and a £150 fine. Christ he's probably out by now." Church shook his head and waved towards the door.

"That kind of sentence is no deterrent; not when he can make a grand a night pushing coke. We're pushing water upstream."

"Yeah. It doesn't help when you get politicians telling us how cool they were when they took drugs in the younger days."

"Oh you mean that idiot Gove. Christ I'd like to meet him on a dark night in Priory Park! I'd soon knock some sense into him."

The two men laughed and took a swig of coffee.

"We could sit here all day putting the world to rights.

How do I help you my friend?"

"Two things I guess, Phil. Firstly I wanted your thoughts on my theory about whether a tennis coach be a dealer."

"Oh God yes. Easily. Anyone could be. In his position with access to lots of rich kids he'd be a prime target for a distributor to find. The covid lockdown has helped us in a way, in that it has reduced the number of people on the streets and made it harder for the dealers to find their targets. Nightclubs being closed must have driven some of them out of their minds."

"And out of business?"

"Yeah, quite probably. Not that there's a lot of direct dealing in the clubs around here. John Watson runs the Mishiko club here in town, he's got a virtually monopoly of late drinks in town, and he's far too smart to ruin that little goldmine by allowing any drug trading on his premises but we're not far from Croydon and that's a hotspot."

"I guess it's easy to get into London too."

"Thirty minutes on the train. But you don't need to go that far to see some action."

"No?"

"No, although I've never caught anyone red-handed, the talk is that the well-known burger joint in Redhill sells more than fries and milkshake. A couple of years back, it got so bad that they had to employ a security officer to regularly clean out the toilets, and we're not talking toilet brushes."

McTierney's eyes widened.

"Add to that a couple of coffee shops here in Reigate, plus the huge expanse that is Priory Park and you've got a steady supply."

"Who buys it all?"

"The town is full of rich, bored kids. There are more fee-paying schools in this neck of the woods than anywhere else in the south-east. All those spoilt brats have rich daddies falling over themselves to give their little Johnny and Mary anything they want. If I wanted to get into the drugs trade, this is exactly the place I'd target."

"So my theory of a drug trade built around the tennis club is a possibility."

"I don't know the place, or the victim, but it has a lot of the characteristics that you'd look for if you were a dealer."

"Okay, thanks, not what I wanted to hear, but it's what I expected. How do I start digging into it?"

"As a new face here, something you could do, would be to hang around some of the coffee shops and see who comes to talk to you. Unfortunately by now all the dealers know my face. You're bound to get offered some weed; I'd bet my pension on that. Before lockdown I reckon every other dinner party in town finished with a casual smoke in the garden."

McTierney smiled his recognition.

"Now during covid, we've got a rise of lifestyle users."

McTierney frowned and Church explained, "Regular working people who enjoy a taste of drugs at the weekend, perhaps an illicit dinner party with a bit of white powder to snort – it beats Black Forest gateau or tiramisu."

"Right, I'll give the cafe a shot." McTierney pushed his chair back ready to move.

"Late afternoons are supposedly the best time. Oh and one other aspect to keep in mind I get the feeling from my niece that the schools see their share of weed."

McTierney shook his head. "Sitting talking to you for ten minutes can make a man depressed. How are we ever going to win the drugs war?"

"We could do worse than copy the US."

McTierney screwed his face up.

"No listen. We set up a national force like the FBI, which is used to tackle national crime gangs."

"Okay."

Church was on a roll, "County lines are a problem whereby a supply line is developed from a major metropolis such as London and a call centre develops where a local dealer can call into a drug call centre and order a delivery of crack cocaine or heroin. The delivery is then dispatched by motor bike down to the user. It's like the Sainsbury's food delivery but with drugs."

McTierney's eyes widened.

"It means a few big dealers can control a large area without having to travel. The impact of covid and the restrictions on movement have forced drug barons to be more creative. Happens all over the country, probably all over Europe."

"And the US tackle these supply lines?"

"All the FBI do these days is tax and drugs."

"Tax and drugs and rock 'n' roll!" McTierney added a flourish where he smashed an imaginary high-hat drum.

"You should be on the stage. A gallows stage."

The two men exchanged smiles and a friendship was born, McTierney pushed back his chair and made to move away.

"Before you go, how are you getting on with Sting?"

McTierney frowned.

"Detective Inspector Bee, aka the grumpy bastard, who can't keep a partner beyond 6 weeks."

McTierney grinned, "Yes of course. We've had a few

rocky moments, but he's been okay the last few days. How long have you known him?"

"Long enough to know that you'll be back in Norfolk by Christmas."

McTierney stiffened.

"He's a perfectionist; wants everything done by the book and done yesterday. He's no life apart from the force. You need to watch yourself, or you'll get stung!"

McTierney smiled. "Great, thanks for the tip."

"But I'll say this for him, he always gets his man."

THIRTEEN

IT HAD BEEN a difficult day for Bee, despite starting positively with Dr Kelly's scientific briefing and the suggestion that they were looking for a tall, muscular individual it had toppled off a cliff once he'd met the chief. The idea that he invite McTierney to come and live with him was still bugging him. He found himself muttering about it as he made his way down the back stairs and out to his car. Where he would normally be the most courteous driver on the Queen's highway he found himself shouting at a BMW driver who cut through on an amber / red light at the traffic lights. 'I need to go for a run, clear my head and ruminate on this challenge,' he said to himself.

For a few years Bee had contemplated running the Pilgrims Way from Winchester to Canterbury, or at least part of it, but he never felt in shape to tackle the taxing 153 miles. For now it resided on his bucket list, while he built up his stamina running across the Surrey Hills. This day he stayed local; he jogged down to the end of the farmhouse trail, looked across the fields and opted for the village run, that would take him downhill initially and torture himself on the return; he resolved to keep on running until he had a solution. The first couple of miles didn't produce anything beyond angst and regret. 'Why had he pushed so hard to bring in an extra detective?' He stepped up the pace to punish himself for that moment of weakness. 'And McTierney didn't show any potential'. He pushed the pace for another quarter of a mile. 'And he had no respect for Bee, or anyone for that matter.' Faster still. 'Except Jess Bartlett!' He sprinted the next 200 yards in fury and collapsed against a post box.

"Bloody McTierney!"

He shouted across the landscape in between a bout of heavy panting. Then remembering where he was he threw a glance in every direction, while he brought his breathing back under control. There was nobody about to admonish his outburst. He puffed out his cheeks and checked his phone to gauge his pace; he nodded his approval, but it was time to get going again. He ran to the corner of the lane and turned away from the few houses he had passed and set off towards the emptiness of the countryside. After a hundred yards he reached a stile and as he clambered over it he spotted a puppy on the other side.

"Hello fella, what are you doing here? I bet someone is out looking for you."

The puppy scampered over to Bee and he bent down to inspect the collar.

"You're not so far from home are you, Frankie?" Bee picked up the terrier puppy and turned back the way he had come. Beyond the post box where he had set his seasonal best for the 200 yards he found Hart Cottage and knocked on the front door. A flustered woman came to the door and called out to someone behind her as she opened it.

"Good evening madam, I think I've found your missing puppy."

"Ah, thank you so much. Lucy, look some kind gentleman has found your puppy."

This time it was human scampering as a young girl with blonde pigtails ran to the door. The puppy and the young girl were excited to see each other and Frankie scrabbled to escape Bee's hold. He handed the puppy over to a mixture of human and doggy squeals.

Lucy's mum patted the dog and turned to Bee. "Thank you so much for bringing him home; we thought the garden was dog proof but he must have found a way to escape. My husband has gone out searching for him, while we waited here in case he came back on his own."

"Not a problem. It's the most useful piece of policing that I've accomplished all day."

"Oh, you're a policeman, how appropriate that you should find him."

The mother turned to her daughter and repeated the point, "Lucy, this man's a policeman, fancy that, you're missing dog being found by a friendly detective. Now come and say thank you."

Bee squatted down on his haunches to match up to Lucy. She put Frankie down on the floor and followed her mother's lead. She reached out to Bee and gave him a big hug. "Thank you officer."

Bee was unprepared for the embrace and left his arms outstretched behind her back before gently tapping her on her shoulders before he pulled her close. He was so touched by the display of affection that he was lost for words for a few seconds.

"That's okay, this is a nice part of my job."

Lucy hadn't finished, "I bet you can do anything because you're so clever. You must be the best detective in the whole world. Will you come to tea on Sunday? You can see if Frankie's behaving himself."

Bee struggled to find a word to reply and allowed his jaw to drop. Lucy's mother wasn't faring much better. "I suspect this policeman has got lots of important things to do, catching criminals and the like."

"Exactly," added Bee, thankful for the intervention.

"Pleeease." Said Lucy. "Frankie would like it."

"You're most welcome, if you can spare the time," Lucy's mother qualified.

"How about a cup of coffee and a quick check on Frankie."

"Okay," said Lucy, "if you promise. Because I know a policeman can never break his promise."

Bee smiled, "I promise, Sunday at three, but only for half an hour, and it will have to be in the garden to keep everyone safe."

"That's Frankie's favourite place," said Lucy and she turned and dragged her puppy off inside.

Back on the trail Bee couldn't fix his mind on a route; he zig-zagged across footpaths not building any speed and not granting his mind a rhythm from which to solve his current problem. His thoughts were shattered by a squadron of emerald, green parakeets squawking and squabbling as they darted across the sky. He reached a corner where the path crossed a road and stopped for a car to drive by. His mind was still confused, "Damn, damn, damn!"

He checked his phone; he'd been out for 90 minutes and made no progress at all. Clouds were building on the horizon; rain was coming but hopefully not until the morning. "Come on Bee, you're supposed to be best detective in the world, surely you can sort this little problem."

He turned for home, put Springsteen to play on his phone and within three hundred yards The Boss had suggested a solution as Bee ran home along his own 'Thunder Road'.

FOURTEEN

McTIERNEY LOOKED DOWN at the piece of paper Bartlett had given him. Holmthorpe Industrial Estate was a hotch-potch of buildings of all shapes, sizes, and ages; some painted some not, some brand new, most rundown. This wasn't the salubrious leafy avenues that he was used to seeing. There wouldn't be an Ocado delivery van anywhere to be seen here unless it was being repaired in one of the dozen or so garages that he was trundling past. It was no use, he stopped at the burger van and asked for directions. Back in his car he made the three turns that were necessary and found himself outside a dilapidated grey industrial unit. The front comprised one large dirty roller door, pulled down to the floor. Next to this there was a painted wooden door that wouldn't look out of place on someone's kitchen, but didn't belong here, above the only chance for sunlight to penetrate was provided by a white painted double-framed window that probably came from the same house as the door. McTierney pulled his Jaguar on to the concrete forecourt in front of the building and stepped slowly towards the building making sure to lock his car. There was no number on the building but this was unmistakeably the building next to Halfords Auto Centre so it had to be the place. He knocked on the door and pushed at it at the same time, to his surprise the door swung open and he heard music playing inside. He was faced with a set of stairs or a second door that opened out in the main warehouse space. He called out to announce his arrival and stepped slowly through the internal door.

The unit was spartan apart from half a dozen pinball machines gathered together in the centre of the area. On the end machine the gaming table was open and a man was bent over it fiddling with something inside.

"I'm looking for Greg Savage, I wonder if you might know where he is?"

The man took his time to lift his head out of the table and turned back to face McTierney, looking him up and down as he did. "I might. Depends, who's asking?"

"Detective Sergeant McTierney, Reigate CID." Ron enjoyed it when a suspect tried to play hard and fed him some more rope. "I'd like to ask him a few questions if he's about."

"What sort of questions?"

"Questions connected to a murder enquiry."

"Oh."

"So do you know where he is or do I need to keep on looking?"

"Yeah. I'm Savage. But I need to get this machine back in operation today, I don't have much time, so make it quick."

McTierney bowed his head and stepped purposefully across the concrete floor until he stood directly in front of the other man. He lifted his face and drilled his eyes into Savage's face. "I'll make this simple for you. This is a murder enquiry and people get upset about murders. So either you answer every question I ask you, fully and politely, here and now, or I'll take you down to the station, keep you there all day, while we collect the correct paperwork for the interview and then I'll get a search warrant based on your reluctance to talk and I'll come back here with a team and rip this place apart. It's your choice, personally I prefer the later, because I'm a nosey bastard and I'll go through this place like a dose of salts, but I know my inspector will want me to do it by the book, so you have a choice."

Savage stepped back from McTierney, ran his fingers around the spanner in his hands, took a second to weigh up his options and folded. "Okay, what do you want?"

"As you put it so nicely, why don't you make me a cup of tea, while I get my notebook out."

Savage snorted but pushed past Tierney towards a kettle in the corner of the unit. He didn't bother to clean the mugs but dropped a tea-bag in each and flicked the switch on the kettle.

"In case you're worried about covid I can tell you I'm double vaccinated and tested negative two days ago, so you're not at risk."

"Don't bother me, my granddad's Chinese, so I'm alright."

"How do you work that out?"

"The way I look at it, this is a Chinese invention."

"Oh yeah?" McTierney turned his face into Savage and stopped to listen.

"Stands to reason. All of them, the Americans, the Russians and the Chinese are competing to be top dog, right?"

McTierney nodded in agreement.

"This is the Chinese trying to do it with genetics. They're working on something in Wuhan, then there's a slip up; it gets out, but they're able to control it, because they're used to it."

Savage waved his rag at McTierney to emphasis his point. "There's few cases in China, but there's millions elsewhere. Western Europe grinds to a halt, but life pretty much goes on in China. How come?"

Savage waited for McTierney to reply, but no answer was forthcoming.

"Because it's genetically profiled. This virus won't attack Chinese people as much as it will white westerners. It's their way to get ahead in technology, finance and what have you. It's brilliant. Nasty but brilliant. Yellow peril on the march."

"Sounds a bit fanciful if you ask me. And there are people of Chinese origin dying in Europe and America."

"Not many."

A lull developed between the two men as Savage relished his moment and McTierney debated with himself whether it was worth arguing.

"There's no milk unless you want to walk around the corner to Tesco's."

"Black's fine by me." McTierney decided to move on. "I understand you know Russell Dawson."

"Huh, that shit. Yeah I know him. Is he your stiff?"

"He's the victim, yes."

"I've never liked the guy, but it's not good that he's gone."

"You weren't best friends then?"

"You're quick aren't you Sherlock. No we weren't friends at all. He robbed me of the tennis championship. Always had a thing against me."

"Why was that?"

"Dunno, didn't like the competition if you ask me. He

liked to be top dog at the club and felt threatened by someone able to take him down."

The kettle boiled and Savage splashed some water into each cup.

"Could you beat him?"

"Could I? Could I ever? Whipped him 2 and 3 last time we played. He didn't like that."

"Did you play each other often?"

"Not since that time. He couldn't handle another beating. Blamed the last one on him carrying a knock. Bullshit. I'd worked him out and he knew it."

As Savage's confidence grew he turned his body to face McTierney and puffed out his chest.

"When was the last game?"

"About a month ago, maybe longer."

"When did you see him last?"

"The day of the club final; that Sunday, what was it? June 6th I think."

Savage looked up at calendar hanging on the wall and checked the date. There was a red ring around the date. "Yeah, there you go, all marked on the calendar. I haven't been back to the club since."

"Can you account for your whereabouts on the night of Thursday June 10th?"

"Not easily. I was either here, or possibly in the Sailor; that's a pub around the corner, and then at home."

"Anyone verify that?"

"Maybe, you could try the barman, Jeff."

McTierney scribbled down a few notes and allowed a stillness to develop to see if Savage would bite, but the silence hung.

"Do you know anyone who would want to see Dawson dead?"

"You mean apart from me? Can I give you another suspect?"

McTierney smiled at the question; he was starting to like this bloke.

"No I don't think I can." Savage stopped to squeeze the tea-bags out of the cups and handed a cup to McTierney. "But I didn't kill him, I'm glad he's out of the way, but it wasn't me."

Savage dropped the tea-bags into a half-empty cardboard box on the floor that was doubling as a bin. McTierney's eyes followed the tea-bag and noticed a couple of boxes of disposable overalls on the floor. He kicked one; "is pinball a dirty business?"

"Can be. There's a ton of fancy electronics under each playfield keeping all the lights on, so you can't let any moisture or grease get inside or you'll screw it up big time."

McTierney nodded his thanks and took a sip of the tea, he turned his head away to hide his disgust at the taste and his eyes fell onto the pinball machines.

"What got you started with pinball?"

"My dad loved them, so they remind me of him. Then I discovered you can make good money with them."

"Yeah? What kind of money?"

Savage walked across to the set of machines in the unit and McTierney followed him.

"Any one of these would set you back best part of ten grand. Twelve for you."

McTierney laughed. "Seriously, that much?"

"Easily. A good condition table with a rare backglass,

maybe something from a movie, and you could be looking at twenty grand. Especially if it's a Lawlor or a Krynski."

"Who?"

"Pat Lawlor and Ed Krynski are the two most famous designers associated with pinball tables. Rumour has it that Stan Lee paid Krynski a small fortune for a bespoke Spiderman table."

McTierney nodded his appreciation and hurriedly swallowed a mouthful of tea. "So are you any good at the game?"

"Yeah, not bad. Are you angling for a free game constable?"

"Sergeant, actually, and since you offered so nicely and in the interests of community relations, I wouldn't say no."

Savage shook his head and then swept his long black hair up and over his forehead, but it flopped back. As he did McTierney thought he saw a long scar running down from his left ear. "Go on then, try The Star Wars table, second to last on the left; it's got the easiest set up."

"Thanks," said McTierney and he yanked back the plunger to set the silver ball running. "What makes this one easy?"

"The key to the game, sergeant, is the incline built into the playfield; normally about 6 or 7 degrees between front and back, but the higher you go the harder and faster the game becomes, so punters get through their cash a bit quicker. This one is set at 4 degrees so if you're half decent you could be here until lunchtime."

McTierney was occupied by his game and slammed his right hand on to the flipper button for that side. "Don't think I'll be here that long."

"Is it worth me telling you that the primary skill of a ball player involves proper timing and technique in the operation of the flippers nudging the silver sphere infield without tilting and choosing targets for scores or features?"

Savage lent over the table to study McTierney's performance before continuing, "A skilled player can quickly learn the angles and gain a high level of control of the ball." He turned his head to face McTierney as the ball disappeared down the centre of the playfield. "That should stop the ball draining down to the bottom." He paused, "but you don't seem able to do that. What a pity."

"I had it mastered, but I can't stay here all day."

"Right you are."

McTierney rocked back from the table, looked down at the tea mug that he had placed on the floor and decided against picking it up.

"Thanks for the tea. From now on I'm going to think of you as Tommy."

"Goodbye sergeant."

McTierney walked to the door, halfway across the floor Savage called out to him.

"Hey, I have an answer to your question."

McTierney turned his head.

"Josh. Josh Hammond. He was Dawson's number two coach, damn good player too. Dawson kicked him out for no good reason. He's someone who'd have a grudge against Dawson. Least he should."

FIFTEEN

BEE WOKE EARLY and lay in bed watching the sunlight creep silently across his bedroom floor as he pondered the case. He knew he should be making more progress, but something about the case didn't add up. They hadn't unearthed any significant clues at all in the first two weeks. That was disappointing and unacceptable to Bee. Yes the covid pandemic was making things more difficult, people were less active, no one was out or about to spot anything untoward and even worse no one wanted to stop and talk about it. Witness statements had become virtually extinct. But none of this should stop good police work. He needed to re-double his efforts, after all it was barely 12 hours since he's been acclaimed as the cleverest detective in the world. He smiled at the memory; it had been a strange but happy moment. He would go back and have tea with Lucy and her family. But for now he needed coffee, breakfast, and a chat with Josh Hammond.

Bee found Hammond at the Redhill Tennis Club in the midst of a group lesson where he was instructing a group of middle-aged ladies. Ladies who lunch thought Bee as he signalled to Hammond to come over to the side of the court. A tall sporty-looking guy, straight from the pages of a modelling catalogue. Sallow skinned with black hair, artificially enhanced with a few strategic highlights and a stud earring. He was wide shouldered, well-built but with a childlike cherry blossom pink across his cheeks. The youth scowled across at Bee and then with the kind of swagger that looked cool, rather than arrogant, he sauntered over to the gate and sent a self-confident nod in Bee's direction.

"Your colleague in the clubhouse told me you're Josh Hammond."

"What of it?"

"I'd like to ask you a few questions."

"I'm coaching at the moment."

"This won't take long. I'm Inspector Bee from Reigate CID, investigating the death of Russell Dawson. I believe you knew him."

"Yeah, I did. So what." Hammond turned back to the group of ladies and called out to them encouraging them to play on for a few minutes.

"I'd like to hear your version of the story of your departure from the Reigate Club."

Hammond drilled his eyes into Bee as he spoke to him. Bee felt grateful that the interview was taking place through the wire fencing that surrounded the court.

"Not much to say. I'd outgrown the place. I could see I wasn't going to make head coach there anytime soon so I decided to move on."

"So you're saying you resigned and left of you own free will."

"Yeah. That's what happened."

"Interesting. The committee members I spoke to at Reigate are under the impression that Dawson sacked you."

"No. I told him I wanted out."

"How would you account for the difference in opinion?"

"I don't know. Maybe Dawson didn't want to lose face and told the committee he'd got rid of me. You'll have to ask them."

Bee pondered the answer and squeezed his chin. "Maybe. Do you have a copy of your resignation letter?"

"Ha! You're joking aren't you? Do you have a copy of the sacking letter or whatever you want to call it?"

Bee smiled. "No. No I don't actually."

"Hm, No surprise. There's not a lot of paperwork in this profession. You don't get pension plans and stuff. It's all zero contract hours work. If it rains I go hungry. I'm sure it's different for you."

"It can be." Bee nodded.

"That's one of the reasons I moved here. I get a retainer salary. Not much but it's a step in the right direction."

Bee turned over a page in his notebook and changed tact. "I see. How would you describe your relationship with Dawson?"

"It was good. He was okay. Not bad as a boss. No major complaints."

Hammond looked back over his shoulder at his group who had given up playing and were now grouped around the net, chatting. "Look is this gonna take long? I'd like to get back to my class."

"Not much longer. Can you tell me where you were on the night of June 10th, – it was a Thursday."

"At a guess, I'd either have been here playing tennis, or at home."

"Where's home?"

"I live with my parents in Reigate."

"And they can vouch for the fact that you were home that night?"

"Yes."

"Good. Be aware that we'll check it."

"Knock yourself out."

Bee looked up from his notepad and saw the dark eyes still grilling him. He coughed, "Last one, can you think of anyone who would want Dawson dead?"

"Not really. He was a decent bloke. Perhaps Greg Savage. They never got on. Savage was always a bit big for his boots. Thought he was a much better player than he really was."

Bee tilted his head to encourage Hammond to say more.

"You know the old story, good on paper, crap on grass. That's Savage all right."

"That'll be all for now. Enjoy your lesson."

SIXTEEN

BARTLETT ADDED HER sixth plastic cup onto the small tower she had been slowly building in front of her. She had been reading an article over the weekend about the health benefits of coffee; evidently it carried a high level of antioxidants and other beneficial nutrients that lowered the risk of contracting several nasty diseases to those who drank it. She recalled that type 2 diabetes was on the list. But she wondered if six cups in four hours would start to reverse the benefits. It was supposed to improve your energy levels and reaction times, but if it did then today it must be outweighed by the tedium generated from working through a set of bank statements. She didn't feel the least bit energetic. Perhaps one more coffee would kick start her verve. She decided it was worth the effort, pushed back her chair and headed down to the canteen.

Back at her desk nothing much had changed; the Reigate Priory Tennis Club accounts were a mess as far as she could see. They hadn't been audited in three years; there had been two changes of treasurer and the accounts tin that the latest treasurer had given her was stuffed with little bits of paper that wouldn't have been out of place on a school papier-mache board. Worse still there seemed to be no correlation between the transactions in the bank account and the paper notes she had spread across her desk. Various strips of paper had been gathered together and broadly represented business for a given period, but no attempt had been made to prepare a profit and loss for the club.

It was clear that the club account was busy; membership income generated over £70,000 annually and in addition there was a separate account where donations had been collected from a large number of members and a couple of local business sponsors with the intention to fund a major upgrade to the grass courts.

But it was in the labyrinthine payments side of the account where Bartlett had her greatest concerns. Money flowed out of the club like water through a cullender. She found a series of payments to two accounts held by committee members using the description 'furniture'; a regular standing order to another committee member and a myriad of cash withdrawals on one of the four cards issued against the account. But she considered the icing on the cake to be a couple of payments to companies based overseas – what was a rural English tennis club doing shipping money out of the country? She was aware of the plans to redevelop the clubhouse, but she wondered if this was a smokescreen hiding a bizarre group of payments.

She threw her pen down on the desk, pushed her chair back and rubbed her eyes. She needed a break and preferably some fresh air. She looked at her watch it was pushing 1 o'clock, a walk in the park was calling to her. She reached down to collect her bag but looked up when she heard the main door to the floor swing open. It was McTierney. Perfect.

"What are you working on?" He called out.

She briefed him on her morning's investigation and he listened intently for a couple of minutes but then started to open his mouth to speak. Bartlett knew he loved to chip in and kept her story flowing as McTierney twice lent in to start speaking and then backed off. Finally she let him interrupt her.

"That's great work. But give it to the specialist accounts team, they're meticulous with this sort of thing. You've got the gist. The club's awash with money and open to some dodgy practices and possibly fraud."

"Looks that way."

"So get Sting to bring in the specialists and move on to the next thing. We've got plenty of leads to follow up on."

"You're right, I need to get back to Tina Dawson and clarify the rogue DNA profiles that Kelly identified."

"Quite. That would be useful. More so than crossing the t's on the tennis bank account."

"Sold. Your prize is to buy me lunch while I listen to your morning's adventure."

They laughed as they walked back up the stairs but their mood changed the moment they pushed back through the double doors of the first floor. Bee was standing in the middle of the floor looking dismayed but a grin sneaked across his face as he heard them approach.

"Damn, two minutes too soon," muttered McTierney in Bartlett's ear, and she giggled.

Bee raised an eyebrow, "Good lunch, team?"

"Marvellous sir, now what can we do for you?"

"I want a quick debrief with you both ahead of tomorrow's regular catch up. Can we have 15 minutes in the ops room?"

Bee didn't wait for a reply and walked across to the room with McTierney and Bartlett close behind. They flopped into seats on separate sides of the main table and each recounted their most recent discoveries. They concluded with Bee's assessment of Josh Hammond.

"I don't think he told me one word that was true, and I'm not saying this because he had an earring, he's hiding something, I know it. I'd like you go back and rattle his cage a bit McTierney and see what you think."

McTierney smirked and nodded his acceptance.

Bee relaxed back into his chair and ran his hand through his hair. "Now let's focus on the question of why the killer would go to the trouble of moving the body. This element continues to bug me and I think it holds the key to solving this murder."

"I think you're right. It's rare to find a killer move the body. I can't recall another murder case where this has happened," agreed McTierney.

Bartlett joined the debate. "I have two thoughts; the murderer either moves the body because he wants to make a point about the place; maybe the tennis court is symbolic in some way."

"Yes, that could fit with either Savage or Hammond being the murderer because both of them had disputes with Dawson that centred on the tennis court," added McTierney.

"I like the thinking," Bee concurred.

"Or it's because the original place would give us a major clue as to the identity of the murderer."

"If it was in their front lounge," offered McTierney.

"Yes, but I can't imagine anyone kills someone in their lounge," challenged Bartlett.

"You'd be surprised," said Bee. "The trouble is we've no leads at all." The others shook their heads and an uncomfortable silence developed.

McTierney picked up the gauntlet. "I'm going out on a limb here, which I admit I like to do, but something needs to happen." Bee and Bartlett exchanged glances and focused on their colleague.

"I have no evidence for this, but I don't buy the idea that the tennis court is a significant feature. I prefer the idea that the original location would be a major clue."

"Go on," said Bee.

"If the tennis court was significant it would suggest a well-planned and methodical killing. But the twin wounds; of the head injury and then the stabbing suggest this wasn't methodical. I'd go so far as to say that it wouldn't surprise me if the death was unplanned and gave rise to an elaborate cover up."

"It's an interesting theory. But we've absolutely no evidence to support it."

"Not yet."

"Does that imply you have a lead?"

"No. But I will say that it's not easy to move an 80kg body, you need some upper body strength for that. Again both Savage and, I guess Hammond, would fit the bill for that."

"Yes I'd agree that Hammond could be in the frame."

All three nodded and tutted their agreement.

"Two suspects but nothing to connect them to the crime," summarised Bee.

"Where are we on basic motive?" asked Bartlett.

Bee tilted his head and said "I'd go money I think. There

seems to be a lot of money around the club and thus far neither Savage nor Hammond seem to have much of it."

"It's sex or lust for me," countered McTierney.

Bee shot him a glare, "Another theory devoid of evidence?"

"For now," McTierney admitted.

Bee tutted and folded up his notebook and lent towards Jess Bartlett.

"Now Bartlett, can you go and speak to the chief about enlisting the support of the financial team from County, I have something I need to share with McTierney. Nothing you need to worry about."

Bartlett got up slowly from the table and shared mystified looks with McTierney.

"Go on, I'm sure he'll tell you later."

Once Bartlett had left, McTierney lent across the table and rubbed his hands together.

"Don't get too excited, I doubt you'll see any of these as good news."

"Oh," McTierney slumped back in his chair.

"Three things, firstly I had a call from Stuart Page, our mutual friend at Lavender Hill."

McTierney looked up. "Oh yes."

"He said he's been trying to call you, but you hadn't returned any of his calls."

"It's on my list for next week."

"You might want to bring that forward. It seems he's had a call from Woking tennis club alerting him to a Wimbledon ticket scam."

"Interesting," said McTierney sitting up.

"Even more so when I tell you the name of the fraudster."

"Mark Wheeler?"

"The very same."

"Now it becomes very interesting."

Bee smiled, "I'll leave it with you to follow up. But make sure you do!"

McTierney nodded.

"The rest is not as entertaining. Notwithstanding what Bartlett might extract from the chief this afternoon, we're not getting any extra resource."

"No?"

Bee shook his head. "There's too much clamour for extra police on the streets to keep the public safe. Apparently we have 18% off sick with covid related illnesses, plus the Met are demanding an extra 50 officers to help them police these football matches and there's a damn anti-covid demonstration in Central London this weekend."

"What?" McTierney threw his arms up in the air.

"I know, ridiculous. But the chief's hands are tied on that one. Now he's trying to find 10 extra officers to show a presence on the street. So we'll be losing Collins from next week."

"With all due respect to the chief; he's too busy shooting the alligators, when he should be draining the swamps."

Bee frowned at the remark but didn't rebuke McTierney. "It's not an easy time for him. Overtime is going through the roof."

"At least we've got plenty of money."

"Funny you should say that, because we haven't and here's the good bit." Bee paused and took a breath. "Your time at the hotel is coming to an end."

"What? Is he sending me back to Norwich? I've only been here a couple of weeks."

"No, he's not doing that. He's stopping your accommodation expenses."

"Does he expect me to pay for myself? That's taking the piss."

"No, nothing so barbaric. He wants you to move in with me and take a room in my farmhouse."

McTierney's eyes popped out. "What?"

"I wasn't jumping for joy either."

The two men laughed.

"You're serious aren't you?"

"Afraid so. I was shocked when he first suggested it, but as the chief said, it should help us crack the case sooner and that's a win for everyone."

"Do I have a say in this? A choice."

"Of course, but it's harsh. Take it or return to Norfolk."

"That's not a choice. That's an ultimatum."

"Your last night in the hotel will be Friday."

"Tomorrow."

Bee nodded slowly and passed his card across the table. "I'll be around on Saturday to help you move your stuff in and show you the ropes."

McTierney sat speechless.

"I'll leave you to contemplate. I have an alibi to check."

SEVENTEEN

THERE WAS ONE story that dominated the news the next day and it had nothing to do with the murder of Russell Dawson, although you could argue it did feature a death. The death of a political career. The front page of The Sun proclaimed a world exclusive and that plus several more pages inside were dedicated to the professional destruction of the then Health Secretary Matt Hancock. He had been caught on camera in an intimate embrace with his aide, Gina Coladangelo. Although a long-standing friend and supporter of Hancock she was neither his wife, nor mother to any of his three children. As the leading proponent of the covid safety programme he had spearheaded the government's campaign to promote cautious and responsible behaviour across the country and his position appeared untenable.

The police station canteen was buzzing with the news, every officer had a view of the subject; and none were sympathetic towards the beleaguered politician. The spectrum of views ranged from 'sack him now, Boris,' to 'hypocritical bastard,' to 'what does she see in him?' Each was laced with a dose of hilarity and rage.

Even Bee allowed himself to vent his disgust at the appalling double standards on display. He shared his opinion with the chief. "As I understand it, there is a ministerial code of conduct under which ministers are expected to maintain high standards of behaviour and to behave in a way that upholds the highest standards of propriety.

"Quite so," agreed Beck. "Lord forbid that any of our own officers should behave in such a way."

"If it was anyone on my team; they'd be out the door immediately."

"I think I should send a communique to the team, re-enforcing what we do. It's important that we retain the public's trust. I understand that there's a lot of angst for the public over the continued precautions and delaying the so-called 'Freedom Day' hasn't helped, but we need to demonstrate that we are all on the same team."

"Absolutely chief."

With that Superintendent Beck turned on his heels and made his way out of the canteen, stopping briefly to allow McTierney to pass him at the door.

McTierney walked slowly into the canteen and nodded to a couple of colleagues rather than join them in his usual banter. Bee caught his eye.

"What's on the agenda today?"

"I need to write up a couple of reports and then Church asked me to stake out a couple of the coffee shops in town, see if I could attract any drug interest."

"Fair enough; I'll send you my address later in readiness for tomorrow. I live in the village of Outwood to the east of the town. If you can find the Bell public house then I'm across the road from there and up a farm track. I'll expect you around noon."

McTierney nodded his agreement. He looked around the room and saw Bartlett sitting on her own over by the window; her young face was etched in anxiety. He sent her a quick wink and wandered up to the counter and inspected the chocolate bars as he waited for the canteen to empty out. As the last three guys from traffic departed he scuttled over to where Bartlett was sitting.

"How are you doing?"

"Terrible. I'm in pieces. All this uproar about Matt Hancock, as soon as Inspector Bee finds out what we've been doing, he's going to sack us. I don't want to lose my job. Jesus I can't afford to lose my job."

McTierney reached out to take her hand but thought better of it. "Don't worry. They won't find out."

Bartlett looked at him with despairing eyes.

McTierney continued "Don't worry, nobody knows anything. We've been very careful. Nobody saw you come into the hotel and nobody saw you leave."

"So we believe. I'm worried, really worried. Inspector Bee would go nuts if he knew. I feel I've let him down after he gave me this chance on his team."

"Let's not let that happen."

There were tears welling up in Bartlett's eyes but she took a deep breath and held them in. "You should've heard him and the chief banging on about it this morning. You'd think it was high treason."

McTierney looked for her eyes, but Bartlett had her head down. "Come on Jess, look at me."

Reluctantly she raised her head. McTierney held her gaze. "Look there's lots of differences between us and Hancock. We're not married for a start. Neither of us has any other partner sitting at home waiting for us to return." He waited for her to acknowledge the validity of what he had said, but she didn't.

"We're both single people using each other as our support bubble. There's only two of us; we're okay. We're both double jabbed. We both take the bi-weekly police covid test and we're both clean, so we're doing the right things."

"Are we? I don't know I'm scared." Bartlett dropped her head again.

"Yes we are. We are not a threat to anyone. Not even each other." McTierney let the point rest but Bartlett didn't respond.

"I looked at the guidelines this morning. Firstly social distancing in the workplace is not a legal requirement, it's only a recommendation. The Health and Safety Executive, essentially that's the government, says where possible people should keep 2 metres apart. If this isn't viable, keeping 1 metre apart with risk mitigation is acceptable. So we're not breaking the law."

"What about in the hotel? That wasn't 2 metres apart."

McTierney smiled, "No, most definitely not. But that's not work. It was pleasure, pure unadulterated wonderful pleasure."

"Stop it." Bartlett reached out and slapped his arm.

"When we're off duty, we can argue that we are a regular couple sharing our bubble together."

"Bee doesn't think we're ever off duty."

At that moment the canteen door swung open and Phil Church walked in. He spotted McTierney and Bartlett and strode across the canteen a broad grin spreading across his face with every stride. "You two are not doing a Hancock are you? Woo, old Sting won't like that."

"Don't be ridiculous of course we're not," replied

McTierney.

"You're looking very guilty."

"Everyone looks guilty to you, you're an undercover cop."

"Yeah suppose you're right. I'm gonna grab a coffee, do either of you want a refill?"

Both McTierney and Bartlett shook their heads and Church left them for a couple of minutes. They exchanged nervous glances and their conversation dried up. Then just as she heard Church pick up his coffee, Bartlett whispered, "I think I should go."

"No, not now it'll look suspicious," comforted McTierney.

Church pulled up a chair and joined them "So what do you make of old Hancock? He's a boy. Got his hands all over his personal aide. Dirty bastard."

Bartlett gave a weak smile and McTierney offered a half-laugh. Church didn't respond to either and launched into one of his tirades.

"I don't like Hancock, but I can understand him. People need to understand that public figures have a life."

"What about his wife?" asked Bartlett.

"Ah yes, I'm not defending him per se. I think he's an arse. But mark my words there'll be a back lash against authority; somewhere in the country in the next two weeks a couple of coppers will take a kicking and it will all be because of him."

Bartlett recognised that Church was about to launch into a speech and lent back in her chair.

"Let me make it about us instead. The police are under constant scrutiny for anything and everything we do. The public have to accept that police officers are human too."

He looked to his audience for acceptance and both nodded in agreement.

"None of us get paid what bloody Hancock gets paid; none of us gets the privileges he gets. But we are every bit as much in the front line as he is. Any kind of problem; we get the call."

Two more nods of approval.

"All I'm saying is that we are due a bit of slack sometimes. This isn't an easy job. Never has been and now with covid kicking around it's twice as difficult. The public should show some appreciation for the work we do and the circumstances in which we do it. They should be grateful that we keep them safe – ungrateful bastards."

McTierney snorted some of his coffee back into his cup.

"You all right there my friend?"

"Yes, yes," replied McTierney nodding and coughing at the same time.

Church continued, "Look around the world today – is there a better police force anywhere in the world? No. No one even comes close to the good old British bobby. You know the standard joke about the police force in heaven. Saint Peter is organising things for God and is determined to have the best of everything, after all this is heaven."

McTierney bobbed his head, "Okay."

"So he gets to choose the best of everything from all the nations on the earth. So it's Sweden for the women," Church cast a quick look at Bartlett, "no offence, my darling."

"None taken."

"It's France for the chefs and it's dependable old Britain for the police."

McTierney laughed. “Okay then tell me what the situation in hell would be?”

Church tilted his head and thought for a moment, as a smile spread across his face.

“For a start Sting would take the place of St Peter.”

“Fair enough.”

“Then it’s Bulgarian women, probably wrestlers every one of them,”

“Without question.”

“German chefs and Turkish police; you get beaten up first and then questioned.”

“Yes I’ve seen Midnight Express.”

“Wouldn’t catch me over there.”

“No it’s not high on my list.”

“Anyway, I must go and do some work. It’s only CID who get to sit around and drink coffee all day.” He stood up, walked to the bin dropped his cup in it and headed for the door. As he approached it he turned back and called out, “Don’t forget you’re working the coffee shops this afternoon.”

As the doors swung shut, Bartlett lent in towards McTierney and whispered “What do you think of him?

“Don’t really know him, but he seems okay.”

“I don’t like him. There’s something devious about him”

“You have to be a bit weird to work with the drug teams.”

“I don’t mind weird, but there’s something untrustworthy about him. I wouldn’t want him covering my back.”

“You don’t need to worry about that. That’s my job.”

Bartlett smiled, but it was short-lived.

“Look I have some news,” said McTierney.

Bartlett's face perked up.

"Given what's happened this morning I don't know if it's good news, but here it is. The chief wants me out of the hotel, and Bee has offered me a room at his place."

"What? Beck wants you out. Maybe the hotel told him that I'd visited you. This is terrible." Alarm spread all over Bartlett's pallid face once more.

"Calm down. No they didn't. If the hotel had said anything I'd be in his office right now getting my arse kicked but I'm not so he doesn't know and nor does Bee."

Bartlett picked up her purse from the table and squeezed it.

"It'll be okay. I'm not sure today is the right time to tell Bee that you'll be coming over to stay at his house; – we'll have to work on that. But we'll be all right."

Bartlett took a deep breath and bit her lip. "I don't know if I would feel comfortable being with you in the inspector's house. That's too weird to contemplate right now."

"So let's make tonight a night to remember in the Cranleigh."

Bartlett nodded weakly.

"And stop over analysing everything. We'll be fine."

EIGHTEEN

"COME ON, WE need to get back to work, or someone, you know who, will be asking questions."

"Do you think you could do the follow up chat with Tina Dawson and get the DNA samples, I don't feel like facing the world at the moment."

"Yes sure. I'll go now and slip it in before I go to Woking tennis club."

"Thanks."

Bartlett and McTierney went their separate ways; he out to the car park and on to Richmond, she up to the first floor where she popped in her airpods, buried herself in some paperwork and didn't speak to anyone until lunchtime.

The minutes were trickling by like hours for Bartlett and she'd added only three lines to the report she was trying to write. Eventually she admitted defeat and logged off the system. She decided to change her surroundings and swap the police station for the tennis courts. Stepping out into the Surrey sunshine she took a couple of deep breaths and immediately felt better. She looked down at her shoulder bag, checked her notebook and pen and walked down to the main road. For once the weather was living up to the expectations of a June day; she decided to walk through the town to the tennis club. When she reached the main road, she changed her mind. She was struggling to focus today, and went back for her car, which would save her having to return to the station later in the day. She opened the door of her Fiat 500 and dumped her bag on the passenger seat, as she did she caught sight of her tennis racquet sitting on the rear seat. Another change of plan, but this would be inspired.

Jess wasn't the greatest tennis player but she could hold her own against most players and played for fun. As a teenager her mother had insisted that she adopt a sport so her daughter would gain and even maintain some degree of physical fitness. Jess had rebelled against every sport that had been pushed at her. She found hockey way too aggressive, running without a purpose was boring, and the netball girls were too cliquey. She had tried hard to enjoy swimming but found that the ratio of changing and faffing around compared to the time she spent swimming was too great, plus the pool in Redhill seemed to take its water from the Arctic. So she arrived at fifteen without any sporting pedigree and an increasingly anxious mother. Then one day her best friend at school, Helen, announced she was going to try out for the school tennis team. It was a sunny day and without anything else on her agenda Jess had followed her down to the tennis courts. Fate played her part and ensured that only seven girls turned up that afternoon and so Jess was cajoled into playing. Although she wasn't a natural player, she enjoyed it, went back the following week, started to improve, and before long she was a regular in the school team playing girls doubles with Helen.

She arrived at the tennis club and spotted the coach Ruth Jones bustling about around the stores shed. Away from the police station and the potential ramifications of her indiscretion, Jess felt her confidence flooding back and she strode up the gravel path to Ruth. As Jess had thought, Friday afternoon was a prime coaching session for the club with many of the young players coming along for an hour or two, once they had turned out of school. Ruth explained that they started with the younger players and moved through the teens and finished with an hour-long practice for the junior team.

"Would you be happy to introduce me as a trainee coach? I want to chat to some of the junior team and get their take on Russell's role at the club and that of Josh and Greg Savage."

"In principle yes. But it depends on our numbers. The Lawn Tennis Association restrict us to a maximum of 8 players. But with the spread of covid, enthusiasm for tennis coaching has waned so I doubt we'll break that limit."

"Thanks, I find that some kids can be intimidated by the idea of talking to a policewoman but if they think I'm a coach they might open up a bit more."

"Let's give it a try. Are you getting any closer to finding who did it?"

"Afraid not."

"Shame, he was such a positive influence." Ruth pulled out a basket of balls and stacked up a few cones for the upcoming session.

"Only the good die young."

"No one will be here for another twenty minutes so why don't you get changed and we can have a quick knock and I'll run through with you what we do in the sessions."

"Sounds good."

The ladies made their way into the clubhouse and on to the changing room.

"Plus if she turns up you can meet our star prodigy, Sophie."

"I think I've heard her name."

"Probably, she was a qualifier for Wimbledon this year. Russell spent hours preparing her, but sadly she crashed out."

"Maybe next year." Jess started to change while Ruth stood by the door to keep the conversation going.

"Yes maybe, although she seems to have taken the loss of Russell badly. Of all the youngsters here I would say she is the most affected. Her game has dropped off a cliff."

The students in the first two groups didn't have much to say about Dawson beyond that they liked him and they were sorry he was no longer teaching them. None of this surprised Jess and it allowed her to focus on her backhand which needed some coaching of its own.

At 6 o'clock six teenage girls came giggling onto the two courts that were allocated to the lesson. They chatted easily amongst themselves as they stood on either side of the net tapping balls back and forth. Two minutes later Sophie joined them and teamed up with Jess as Ruth stepped out to stand between the courts and organise the session. Sophie greeted Jess politely but didn't say anything more and looked over her shoulder every time a new car pulled into the car park. She had shoulder length hair, smooth skin and her eyes glinted like precious stones from beneath long dark lashes as she watched each ball onto the centre of her racquet. Jess tried to engage her on conversation.

"Hi Sophie. How was your day?"

"All right."

"Are you playing tennis at school?"

"Sometimes."

"Are you enjoying it?"

"It's okay."

Jess pinched herself for asking another closed question and in doing so missed a ball on her backhand. She pulled a spare from her pocket and plucked a new question from the back of her mind, but Ruth called the group to order.

"Good evening girls. Tonight we are going to work on volleys, but before we do that let me introduce Jess. She is helping out tonight to see if she likes the idea of being a coach. So welcome her to out group and engage her in a bit of chat to help her feel at home."

The girls on the other court looked her up and down, grunted and silently dismissed the idea of Jess being a coach. Ruth set up several tennis drills and moved the girls around to ensure Jess had time with each of them. Each of them offered her a polite smile but little more, nobody wanted to talk about Russell in any detail, although they did appear to be more positive about him than any other coach and nobody had any comment to make about Greg Savage.

Jess concluded that most of them were just being teenage girls and obsessed with their own world of music, make-up, and social media and oblivious to everything else. But there was something different about Sophie; she seemed to be an outsider to the group even though she was the star attraction. Jess wanted to dismiss it as petty teenage jealousy, but Sophie also seemed obsessed with something, but something different. All the other girls laughed joked and messed around, but Sophie didn't laugh once. Was she simply a tortured genius? Jess was captivated and wanted to know. Ruth brought the session to a close and the girls skipped off the court; the six friends all rubbing shoulders together totally ignoring the covid restrictions while Sophie stopped to use the hand sanitiser by the side of the court and walked three paces behind them. Jess sensed an opportunity and nodded to Ruth.

"Sophie," No response.

"Hey Sophie." This time much louder.

Sophie turned back but looked aghast at the attention.

"Sophie, I'd love to hear about your experiences at Wimbledon, could I sit and chat with you for a few minutes?"

Terror flooded across Sophie's face and she babbled a reply, "No sorry, I have to go," and with that she scampered on ahead of the others.

Jess turned back defeated and walked in with Ruth Jones.

"That's disappointing, I've got a feeling she has something bothering her and I'd like to help."

"Maybe," Ruth shrugged her shoulders, "I think they're all struggling with the combination of exam pressures and worries about university. There again perhaps she's just your regular teenage girl worried about her social media likes."

NINETEEN

WHILE BARTLETT WAS trying and failing to talk to young people at the tennis court, McTierney was being equally unproductive in each of the two Reigate coffee shops, that Church had recommended. As he sat stirring the fourth flat latte of his afternoon he contemplated the futility of the task. A single conspicuous male sitting in the corner of a coffee shop with a much-thumbed copy of that day's newspaper. Had he been a drug dealer himself, he wouldn't have come over to talk to the stooge in the corner. He tried again to make a double tiered pyramid from the biscottis he'd received free with his coffee, again they tumbled to the floor. This time he couldn't be bothered to pick them up. Ten more minutes and he'd quit; there was only so much coffee he could drink. He had grander plans for the evening. He stared around the shop, the place was empty and had been for the last ten minutes. Sod it, I'm off he decided. He picked up his cup, dropped the fancy biscuits back on the saucer and took it back to the counter. The young barista stopped his restocking of the chocolate counter and looked up. "A refill?"

"No way, I've drunk enough of this stuff all day, I need something stronger."

"You want to see the school-teacher about that. But I haven't seen him today."

"The school-teacher? Who's the school-teacher?"

Suddenly the youth realised they were having different conversations. "Sorry what did you ask for? Another latte?"

"No, I'd like to know who the school-teacher is and what he sells here."

"Beats me mate. Never heard of him."

"Does he supply drugs in here?"

"No way, this is a coffee house. Best coffee in town."

"Don't give me that shit. Tell me who the school-teacher is or I'll bring every police officer in town down here, park a big fucking police van outside and make sure everyone knows it was you who tipped us off."

A look of fear raced across the face of the youth who stepped back from the perspex screen that separated customers from staff.

"Think about it sonny." McTierney stabbed his finger against the partition. "You'd be the one. Do you want that?"

The youth froze for a moment and McTierney pressed on. "All a want is a name or a contact point. Nothing else. No one will ever know we've spoken."

The youth weighed his options and then turned and bolted through a staff only door at the back of the shop.

"Shit!" yelled McTierney as he looked for a way around to the back. He darted left, found a gap, and sprinted around to the door, shoved it open and pushed through. Ahead of him was a corridor, at the end a door to the outside swung open.

McTierney started calling out for a manager. No one replied. "Looks like I'm locking the place up tonight. Terrific."

★ ★ ★

JESS HAD BOOKED a table for the pair of them in The Giggling Squid, as the clock passed 9pm, they had both unloaded their stress for the day into the evening conversation and were starting to relax. Ron experimented with their Rising Star Red Duck Curry, while Jess stuck to her favoured Thai Melting Beef dish, both swapped forkfuls as their occupational angst gave way to their private laughter.

"I bet old Bee will have a strict set of rules for you at his house. It'll be bed as soon as the news has finished."

"I don't mind that, if you're there to keep me company."

"I've told you I don't know how I feel about visiting you at the inspector's house; it's beyond creepy."

"How about me coming over to your place. Isn't that just as problematic?"

"I haven't told my aunt about you yet. I'm not sure how she will react when she realises you're older than her."

"I'm not that old!"

"I know, but I'm so young by comparison," Jess laughed.

Ron took a sip of beer, looked directly at her and asked, "Does it bother you?"

"No," she shook her head.

"Seriously?"

"Yes seriously, It doesn't bother me. I'm as happy as I've ever been."

"Good. So am I." He lent in to kiss her.

"But Aunt Claire won't be." Jess folded her arms in mock school mistress pose. "What do you think you're doing young lady, bringing home a man for sexual pleasure in my house? A man who will be drawing his pension within a matter of months."

"I won't," protested Ron as he reached across and tickled Jess' ribs.

She giggled loudly and then remembered where she was. "Shall we get the bill?"

"YOU SLIP UP the back stairs and I'll meet you in my room." Ron handed over his room key. "I need to tell the manager I'm moving out tomorrow."

Ron bounced up the stairs and burst into the room. Jess was sitting on the end of the bed.

"You haven't even packed yet, what have you been doing all day?"

"Don't forget I spent half the day running around covering for you."

"Oh yes, thanks for doing that." She reached out and kissed him gently but he pulled her closer.

"You can repay me tomorrow by dropping over to the coffee shop and getting the details on their Friday night staff."

"No more talk about work, we're off duty now."

"You're right."

"I know you like games, so here's a game for you. I like things to be organised, I don't know why, it must be in my blood. I want you to get your packing done, so here's the deal. I see that you've got four cases to pack; so for every bag that you pack I'll take off one item of clothing."

The smile on Ron's face broadened.

"But."

The smile froze.

"There's a small but. You have to finish all the packing in ten minutes or nothing else comes off."

Ron lent across and kissed her. "Deal. You have to find a clock and I'm starting now."

"I have a timer on my watch and your time has started."

Ron began like a whirlwind he opened his two large suitcases and threw clothes in there with abandon.

"Wait, wait, wait!"

Ron looked up.

"Don't trash your clothes, especially not the yellow Hilfiger shirt or the grey green sweatshirt, that's my favourite. I'll give you two extra minutes if you fold your clothes."

"Deal." Ron was back on his mission.

"And I get to wear the sweatshirt."

"Deal."

"And keep it," whispered Jess.

"I heard that, but I know you'll look good in it, so yes. And that's one case done."

"Already? Crumbs that was quicker than I thought, I might have to re-negotiate this deal."

"No you don't. Can I choose?"

"No you can't. Carry on, the watch is ticking."

Ron took a sports bag over to his table and with one broad sweep of his arm he brushed all the items on the table into his bag. "That's two."

"That's cheating Mr McTierney. If you keep doing that, you won't get everything in your bags."

"So I'll claim new ones on expenses!"

"Right, if you're going to cheat so am I. I'm taking off my favourite purple top. I hope you appreciated that I had my favourite top on for you tonight."

"I did. But I'm appreciating it more now I'm saying goodbye to it!"

Jess smiled back at him. "But I'm replacing it with this New York sweatshirt of yours, that you've so kindly agreed to give to me." She pulled it over her head. "There."

"I can't argue. It looks much better on you than it ever did on me."

"I like this because it makes me feel like you are here with me, even if you're not and that makes me feel safe."

Ron stopped his packing and walked over to the bed and pulled Jess close. "You'll always be safe with me."

"I know."

He kissed her gently and whispered, "I love you."

"Say that again."

"I love you Jess Bartlett."

Jess's eyes sparkled at the words.

This time Ron shouted it "I love you Jess Bartlett."

★ ★ ★

ALTHOUGH HE DIDN'T have much to pack Ron made the job last for 40 minutes; Jess sat on a chair reading her Vogue magazine while he floundered.

"You were packing much quicker last night when you thought I might take my clothes off. What's with the delay?"

"I'm not convinced that living with the inspector is such a great move. I don't think he and I have anything in common except work and I don't want to talk shop every evening."

"I don't know, you both like your sport. That should give

you something to talk about." Jess sat up and looked out of the window to think, "Then there's booze; I've been told he likes a drink a two and that Scotch whisky is his favourite."

"Yeah?"

"Perhaps you should pop into Morrisons and pick up a bottle as a thank you gift."

"Me! Thank him! He should be thanking me; I'm the one doing him the favour!"

Jess lowered her gaze; "Maybe but think how big it will make you look if you act like he's doing you the favour. You'll knock him off his stride from the word go."

"Hmm I like that."

"Good, now can you get a move on, I'm starving."

TWENTY

WHILE RON AND Jess were enjoying a 'last-breakfast' in Café Rouge in the middle of Reigate, Scott Bee was steeling himself for Ron's arrival by taking on the Reigate park run. It had only been re-instated for a couple of weeks since the lockdown measures began to be lifted and as yet the numbers were still relatively low. With a shortage of runners and a feeling that he had plenty to do that morning Bee finished in the top ten and posted his best time at the Reigate course. He strode away from Priory Park with his chest puffed out and dropped into the local DIY shop to buy a flat padlock for his study. If he was quick he could get if fitted before McTierney arrived.

RON PERSUADED JESS to have a second post prandial coffee and it was approaching noon before he finally said goodbye to her and headed off to Scott's home. Bee lived in a remote four-bedroom converted farmhouse at the end of a long drive four miles to the east of Reigate in the village of Outwood. Apart from the current farmhouse he couldn't see another property; a slice of rural solitude – exactly as he liked it. But this morning the peace was shattered by Scott charging around his house; he had fitted the padlock across his study door and then had second thoughts about the image it would create and removed it leaving four small holes in the door. He changed his tactics and walked around his house collecting valuables and shifted them upstairs to his study. That would be a much subtler approach. He returned to his kitchen made himself a coffee and sat at his island to read the paper; then noticed the cafetiere and his favourite Buzz Lightyear mug; should he move these as well? No that would be madness. He had finished returning all his valuables to their original positions when McTierney knocked at the door.

"Morning boss, hope I'm not too early."

"No, not at all, come on in I'll show you to your room."

"Here, I brought you a moving in present, a little bird told me you're partial to a drop of the Speyside spirit. This one's been hanging around for 12 years, – should be ready to drink about now."

Scott took the bottle of Macallan. "That's remarkably kind of you and totally unnecessary but thank you."

The two men fetched Ron's few bags and dropped them into the hallway. Original parts of the house dated back to nineteenth century but over its life it had received several upgrades and makeovers. The most recent was a two-room extension on the ground floor to the right of the hallway which had added an extra bedroom and a downstairs bathroom, Scott had decided to give these to Ron; it would keep the two men as far apart as logistically possible within the property. Scott opened the door and showed the room to Ron and walked back to the kitchen to continue with his newspaper. Thirty seconds later Ron appeared back in the kitchen; "how about a tour of the shop?"

"This is the kitchen, what else do you need?"

"The beer fridge, the tele, the sofa; it would be good to see the whole place, help me start to feel at home."

Scott hesitated for a couple of seconds and accepted his fate. "Sure let's go."

The main part of the house offered a simple square design; four rooms on each floor. Downstairs were four reception rooms; a lounge, a dining room, a kitchen and a utility come domestic room which Scott used for washing, ironing and a giant American fridge. Upstairs the four rooms were two bedrooms, a main bathroom and Scott's study. Ron was happy with a cursory glance at each room until they arrived at the spare room, where he pushed into the room and started to inspect the contents. He ran his fingers across the strings of the Fender guitar and whistled, "cool, can you play?"

"A bit, but please don't touch the guitar it has special memories for me."

Ron moved on to the study where his eye caught the Star Wars chess set standing on a separate table in the corner. He picked up Darth Vadar and turned to Scott who was scowling.

"Fancy a game? I used to play chess at school."

"Maybe later," said Scott as he gently prised the black king from Ron's fingers and replaced him on the board.

In the centre of the room was a black leather swivel chair, Ron spun it around and flopped down into it. "This must be where you come to think"

"Sometimes. It's my study."

Ron glanced up to the shelf above and to the right of the large wooden desk which sat against the far wall. His eyes followed the series of detective novels which sat on the shelf. "Sherlock, Sherlock, Sherlock, Agatha, Agatha, and…" he tilted his head to read along the spine, "Raymond Chandler."

"Chandler created the detective Philip Marlowe, he's my favourite. Perhaps you've heard of him?"

"Can't say I have."

"I guess Cagney and Lacey is more your style, especially the blonde."

"Now, now inspector."

"Sorry."

"I'm guessing this is him," said Ron holding up a photo frame.

"Yes, although to be precise it's Humphrey Bogart playing the role of Marlowe from the film, 'The Big Sleep'. Probably his most famous, you may even have heard of it."

Ron shook his head.

"To be honest, I prefer The Long Goodbye which starred Elliot Gould in the Marlowe role. You'd probably like the nymphomaniac wife." Ron looked hurt and didn't reply.

"Here's a bit of trivia for you; Arnold Schwarzenegger made an uncredited appearance in the film."

"Getaway."

"No honestly; I wouldn't lie to you."

"You learn something every day. To demonstrate my delight at that piece of trivia I'm going to give you my best joke."

"There's no need."

"The IKEA football team are playing tonight; their manager Alan Key," Ron paused and waited for a response, which didn't come, "is expected to start with a flat pack four!"

Scott grimaced, "Not as bad as it could've been I suppose. Come on I picked up a couple of pasties for lunch."

Scott started back down the stairs but before he got to the bottom he realised that Ron hadn't followed. He scampered back up the stairs to find Ron on the threshold of his own bedroom.

"I don't think you need a tour of my room."

"Just checking it out, you never know when it might come in handy."

Scott pushed around him and attempted to block Ron from stepping further in the room.

"Nice lamp," said Ron pointing to a brass chain with a waxing crescent moon adjacent to a white spherical lamp. He lent back and switched on the lights and a pale glow filled the room.

"Impressive. I bet the girls love that."

Scott ignored the comment. But Ron was on a roll and had noticed a bowl of lemons by the bed.

"Less cool are the lemons, what are they for?"

Scott pursed his lips. "Lemons provide us with a true vitamin boost; they are full of super healthy phytonutrients. These phytonutrients go on a hunt in your body for so called free radicals that cause damage."

"Getaway."

"You should start your morning by drinking a glass of lemon water; it's important to drink it on an empty stomach. That way it's most effective when it comes to cleansing toxins from your body. Plus it stimulates weight loss." Scott looked at Ron's midriff but said nothing. "That's because your liver produces more bile if you drink the lemon water on an empty stomach. In turn that leads to you being less hungry and digesting food quicker."

"Stone me Scott what the fuck have you been reading?"

"It can also help you against depression. I think it's important to look after yourself both mentally and physically."

"Whatever you say. Did you mention food a couple of minutes ago?"

"I did," said Scott as he started down the stairs, eager to bring this investigation to a halt.

Lunch refuelled Ron's enthusiasm for exploring his new surroundings and he left Scott to clear the table and wandered off to the lounge. Scott had a tea towel in his hand as Ron returned with a silver photo frame in his hand.

"Who's the girl in the photo?," he asked pointing to a baby standing in front of a church with a tall copper green spire.

"It's my um god-daughter,"

Ron frowned, "You don't seem sure."

"Of course, I'm sure," snapped Scott, taking the frame from Ron. "Would you mind not playing with all my possessions. It feels like my whole life is on display here and you've come to critique it."

"Sorry, trying to make conversation."

"I know, I don't mean to snap, but this is hard for me." Scott looked down at the photo of the young girl and grimaced. "I want you to know that I'm doing this as a favour to the chief. I don't like it but I know things are difficult at the station with covid and the impact on resources."

Ron stared at him.

"And I know it's not easy for you to be away from home, missing out on all the home comforts, but please don't abuse it. I don't like change; I find it difficult."

Ron nodded, "How about I give you some time this

afternoon and tonight I'll buy dinner and a few beers in that pub I saw at the end of your drive."

"Yes that would be great on both counts. Thanks."

AS THE TWO men walked down the long drive from Scott's house towards the Bell pub, Scott reached out to repair their burgeoning friendship. He slipped his hand into his pocket and stole a glance at the list of conversational topics he had scribbled on a post-it note.

"It's obvious you enjoy football; which team do you support?"

"The glorious Manchester United."

"I'll file that under predictable and boring."

"What about you?"

"I used to support Chelsea but all the money pouring into the game is ruining it as a sporting spectacle, so now I prefer the non-league teams. Occasionally I'll get over to Dorking and watch the Wanderers, with a bit luck they'll make the top tier next season. But if you want a team you'll recognise to poke fun at; then it'll be my home-town of Northampton."

"I can't abuse them it'll be like kicking a kitten."

"I'm sure the moment will arise; anyway do you play at all? The police run a team and due to the shift patterns we're always looking for players."

"I do a bit," replied Ron. "I'm a Colesque left back."

"Really? Ashley Cole? That would be excellent, we are a bit light on the left side of the team." "Not Ashley, the lesser-known Ted Cole." Ron burst into laughter.

Scott stopped and sighed heavily. "Do you ever take anything seriously?"

Ron turned to face him. "Of course. But I think it's important to laugh and to enjoy life. Laughter is good for you; it stimulates the release of endorphins and reduces stress. So it's every bit as good for your health as your bowl of lemons." Ron punched Scott on the shoulder and Scott smiled.

Ron continued; "especially in these covid times when people have been left feeling anxious and isolated and uneasy about going out and socialising. Humans are social creatures we should meet up, mix, share, trade, and have sex. An anthropologist will tell you that the function of laughter is social cohesion."

Scott looked open-mouthed at him, "what was your phrase? Stone me Ron, what the fuck have you been reading?"

The two men stood and laughed together.

Several hours later and with stomachs full of steak and beer the two colleagues staggered back to the house. Ron led the way into the lounge.

"I fancy listening to some music, what have you got?"

Ron bent down on his haunches and began flicking through Scott's CD collection which was housed in a series of wooden units. He ran his finger down the line of CDs and started tutting as he went.

"Something bothering you sergeant?"

"No, no. Well yes. I'll overlook the decision to house them in alphabetical order."

"That's good of you."

"But there's no AC/DC or Aerosmith in the A's."

"Nor anywhere else."

"All the space that should have been given over to Status Quo or The Scorpions appears to have been usurped by Bruce Springsteen."

"An upgrade, I think you'll find."

Unable to hold his pose on his haunches Ron rolled over onto his backside and sat on the floor. "Twelve Springsteen albums, surely by any measure that's too many."

"You can't count; there should be fourteen."

Ron turned back to the unit and counted out loud. "Oh yeah, fourteen. But my point still stands."

"I could argue with you but instead I'll refer you to the noted music journalist David Hepworth who described Bruce's 'Born to Run' as 'lightning in a bottle'.

Ron sat silently on the carpet for a couple of seconds, recharging his batteries before replying.

"Must have been a bloody small bottle."

"You heathen."

"Talking of bottles," Ron looked up with puppy dog eyes, "Did someone present you with a bottle of whisky today? Why don't you open it, it might convert me to a Springsteen fan?"

By the time Bruce had reached track 9 and was singing about 'My hometown', Ron and Scott were on their second tumbler of whisky and the mood had turned melancholic.

"You manage to see sunshine in every event; I don't know how you can do it. What's your secret?"

Ron paused, took a long sip of his whisky as if weighing up his response and when he spoke he looked directly out of the window.

"When I was 13 my elder brother took me for a drive in

our father's car. It was a Ford Cortina Mark 2; my father had been working on it and had tuned the engine. It was a bit quicker than it should have been and a lot quicker than my brother expected. It was three days since he'd passed his test and he wanted to show off his good driving to his little brother. And he was a good driver but not as good as he thought. He wanted to show me how fast he could drive and well you can guess what happened." Ron stopped and took a huge gulp.

"He lost control of the car. We raced along an old Roman road that ends in a sharp bend, we skidded, a 73 yards skid as it happened and ended up in the ditch. He died at the scene; I saw his dead body slumped over the steering wheel as I climbed out of the back window."

A silence enveloped the men for a couple of minutes.

"I'm sorry. I didn't know. I would never have asked."

Ron turned back to face him.

"It's okay. I don't talk about it often, but I don't mind you knowing."

Scott nodded.

Ron finished his whisky and picked up the bottle to refill his glass.

"So now I make the most of every day I'm on this planet because you never know when your time is up. My brother had everything to live for; a fabulous footballer – he could really play, excelling at school and planning to go to university, plenty of friends and a drop-dead gorgeous girlfriend."

"Sometimes there's no rhyme or reason to these events."

"I know. But every morning I thank the heavens that I have one more day to enjoy."

"What prompted you to join the force?"

Again Ron stopped to consider his reply.

"You don't need to say if it makes you uncomfortable."

"No it's not a problem. Sometimes the memory of that afternoon can knock me off my stride. It's straight-forward; that day I was too weak, too scared to help my brother so at his grave I vowed to help other people any time I can. Maybe somewhere in my brain it helps me compensate for not being able to save Derek. So the police seems like the best place to be."

Again the conversation lulled allowing Bruce's lament about the 'Streets of Philadelphia' to fill the void. Scott swirled the ice-cubes around his tumbler and then from nowhere Ron launched into a speech.

"When I was a young man, I hated all kinds of things. I was full of hate for what had happened. For people I felt had wronged me, people who had actually wronged me, people I'd never met, Ford cars, Sunday best, manufactured boy and girl bands, Arsenal FC, musicals, Harry Potter, golf, steak and kidney pudding, quizzes, MTV, grapefruit and Noel Edmonds, the list is long and eclectic. I have gradually learnt that it takes all sorts of clothing, musicians, and foods to make a world. And all sorts of vehicles are suitable to get around town, although I've never driven a Ford. More importantly I've learnt that hate is a hugely pointless emotion. It's far better to laugh at the world. You carry a lot more people with you. That said I haven't gone completely soft. I do try to let things flow, but I still hate bullying, cruelty to animals, Noel Edmonds and not getting a real live human being when you call the bank. All the usual suspects. I also take an unfashionably dim view of dickheads in supped up tractors racing through towns and villages, and I will get that red Range Rover."

Scott applauded. "Good to see Noel Edmonds remains as a constant throughout your life. It's important to have an anchor."

"He's certainly one of those!"

Scott spat out some of his whisky as he cavorted at Ron's joke.

"I feel I should match your revelation and tell you something about me, although I don't think I have the repertoire. My story is much simpler. My father died when I was young, a year younger than you when you lost your brother. My mother was lost without him and although she tried to keep going for my sake; she never came to terms with her loss and died of a broken heart. So I joined the police to make sense of things, to bring some order to life when there was no order and no sense in my own. I think I hoped that by solving the puzzles of other people's lives I would eventually solve the puzzle of my own. It hasn't worked out like that, but now the police is my family."

Springsteen reached the end of the CD and the room was engulfed in silence.

"So we're both fucked then!"

TWENTY-ONE

THE TEAM ASSEMBLED in the operations room and Bee began running through their priorities for the week. There was only one item on the flipchart when Chief Superintendent Beck opened the door.

"A word." He glanced around the room but said nothing to anyone else and stepped back out of the room.

Bee shrugged his shoulders at the team and followed his boss out of the room, being careful to pull the door closed behind him. Beck put his left hand on Bee's right elbow and escorted him quickly along the corridor talking as they walked.

"Have you heard the news? There's a councillor on the local radio station ranting about police inefficiency. Saying we don't know what we are doing; that we've no idea who killed Dawson and that the streets of Reigate aren't safe."

"That's disappointing but, I'm sure they are making outlandish headlines sir, trying to gain some popularity for themselves."

"Are they? It's not good you know. We need to make some progress on this case and quickly. It's a bloody murder enquiry and we need a sense of urgency here."

"We are making progress sir. We had an interesting development on Friday, which might prove fruitful."

Beck stopped walking and turned to face his inspector "Why don't I know about it?"

"It's early days yet. It's something McTierney stumbled on. I want to check it out myself before we get too excited."

"Hmm, very good. Carry on. I want an update by the end of the week." Beck turned and left Bee alone in the corridor.

Bee walked back into the operations room and gave no signal of the tirade he had suffered. Instead he appointed a couple of tasks and then rallied his troops. "We're going to find the man that destroyed the Dawson family, who took away their father and we're going to send him to jail for the rest of his life. Now let's get to it."

Bee stood in the operations room and allowed his team to file out. He contemplated the words of the chief super, perhaps it was fair to say that up to now the operation has been running on optimism, and even then the fuel for this could be said to be running low. He wondered if any doubt was percolating through to his team. McTierney always seemed to be confident, but then that was his nature; he'd be confident if asked to race against Usain Bolt. Elsewhere maybe doubt was starting to take over; he was never good at reading people and certainly couldn't read Bartlett. There was no point in asking her, she'd simply tell him what she thought he wanted to hear. He would have to up his game and lead from the front. He considered the coffee shop incident represented the best opportunity of a break-through, so he'd best get involved. He turned and stepped out of the room and called after McTierney.

Trade was brisk in Zero's coffee shop and Bee's request to speak to the manager was met with a gruff response, "You could at least buy something, this is prime time."

"We'll take two coffees and a quick chat over there by the window."

The two detectives took their seats and were duly joined by the woman from the counter.

"Can we make this quick, young Tracy up there is not the brightest. If I don't keep my eye on her she'll cost us a fortune in freebies for the boys."

"We're investigating a murder, so this'll take as long as it needs," announced Bee.

"Yeah, yeah, go on then," said the woman rolling her eyes.

"My colleague was in here on Friday afternoon trying to question your manager."

McTierney smiled at the woman, who scowled back.

McTierney picked up the story, "He mentioned a drug dealer called 'the school-teacher' and then when I attempted to question him further he turned and ran out the back door and into the distance." McTierney pointed towards the door. "We'd like to talk to him further so can you give us his home address please?"

"Hmm that'll be Darren; he's a bit of a hothead, but great with the customers and he's whizz on all the hot drinks."

"Great, but where does he live?"

"Somewhere in Redhill I think. I'm only the duty manager for today, you'll need the big cheese to give you his details."

"Where might we find him?"

"Her. Judy C, she doesn't work Mondays; likes to have two days off. She'll be back in tomorrow."

McTierney scribbled the name in his notebook.

Bee took the conversation on. "While we're chatting and enjoying our coffee what can you tell us about any drug trades that go on in or around here."

"Not me, I don't know nothing," her arms shot up in defence.

"Have you ever heard of the 'school-teacher'?"

"Last school-teacher I knew was Mr Wilkins in year 11 at the big school down by Woodhatch and that was ten years back."

"That's cute, but do you have any knowledge of someone calling himself, or herself, the school-teacher and looking to sell drugs in the vicinity of this coffee-house?"

"No."

Bee held her gaze tempting her to say more, but she remained silent.

"Good. Here's my card. Ask Judy C to call me tomorrow with an address for Darren, we'll let you get back to your customers."

As the two detectives walked away from the coffee shop they crossed the road and headed towards the central car park of the town. At the top of the alley way stood an Asian lady selling copies of 'The Big Issue'.

Bee stopped and handed a five-pound note to the woman.

"Wow, that's a bit much for one of them," said McTierney.

"Perhaps," Bee shrugged his shoulders, "I look at it as an investment."

McTierney screwed up his face.

"The easier society makes life for those who are struggling, or in this case not working; then the less crime there will be and the easier life will be for us policemen."

"Do you think your five quid will make any difference?"

"In the big scheme of things? No probably not. But it makes me feel better, knowing I've done my bit to help."

They walked on to big supermarket in the centre of the town, collected a couple of meal-deals and walked on into the big green expanse of Priory Park, where they found a bench to sit and eat. Bee and McTierney sat side by side staring directly out into the park, announcing their news like a pair of newsreaders on morning television.

"Do you think we're getting closer to finding the killer?" asked Bee.

"Yeah I do."

"Is this the half-full glass talking?"

"I know you like your evidence, and I don't have much to put on the table, but my gut tells me we're close. He's definitely out there somewhere."

"One of the joggers going round the park?"

McTierney laughed and turned to face Bee, who had a smile on his face. "Inspector have you started telling jokes?"

"Maybe living with you is starting to rub off on me. But no. I think we can file that under 'unusual behaviour for now'."

McTierney grinned and the two men reverted to their forward focus. "I think he's out there, keeping a low profile, but he has a connection to the tennis club and a foot in the drugs trade."

"I can't see Dawson, who we know to be a decent tennis player, doubling as a drug dealer."

"Maybe he was using, hoping to delay his slide into

obscurity."

Bee turned to face the suggestion with a look of disgust.

"We all get old, and no one gets better with age. If he peaked twenty years ago at Wimbledon, maybe he's trying to slow down the inevitable decline. Savage reckons he's got the beating of him."

"Yes, but I'm guessing this Savage guy might not be the most credible witness to have in court."

McTierney nodded and digested the point as he digested a mouthful of tuna baguette.

"Do you think we've met him yet or would you rule out all of those we've interviewed so far?"

"Savage wouldn't think twice about breaking the law if he had something to gain." McTierney paused, "but I can't see him as a murderer, maybe it's worth you taking a look at him."

"Will do." Bee was following a couple pushing a pram along one of the many stone paths that criss-crossed the park.

"This Wheeler bloke, the bent ticket agent has clearly been trying his luck to secure Wimbledon tickets to flog on the black market, but I don't get the sense that he's capable of a theatrical murder."

"What did you discover?"

"I spoke to the leading coach at Woking Tennis Club, a Laura Crow. She said Wheeler had approached her, Dawson and two others at a Wimbledon qualifier event held at Woking a month or so ago. They sent him packing with a flea in his ear. Apart from a few idle threats and a dozen swear words, she said he disappeared and she hasn't heard from him since."

"You think he's a bit of a chancer?"

"Definitely." McTierney took another gulp of his drink. "Beyond that, it's not him, it's no one at the tennis club and certainly not Janice at the sports shop; she's more likely to shag him than kill him."

Bee let the comment hang in the breeze.

"You ought to rattle Hammond's cage. Cocky little sod, but probably not a killer."

"Do you get many murders here?" McTierney bowed his head to take a bite from his baguette.

"Not really."

"The chief seems worked up about this one. I'm guessing he didn't barge in this morning to give you a pat on the back."

"No, you're not wrong there. I think this case has caught everyone on the back foot. We're lucky, our crime rate is low. I'm convinced it helps having a presence on the street to keep crime down…"

"Sitting here, Reigate looks like some Disney created quaint little town where crime doesn't exist. I'm expecting the pigeons to break into song any minute."

"Ha! It certainly does, but a different sort of crime; husbands lying to their wives and slipping off to meet their girlfriends."

"That's not crime. That's life."

"Cheating is the tip of the iceberg. Here it's silent crime; tax evasion, greed, corporate fraud, cyber-crime and of course a sprinkling of drug related crime to underpin everything else."

"Sounds like white-collar stuff."

"Take a look around you." Bee swung his arm forward in a big arc. "White-collar people, committing white-collar crime."

"All nice and clean."

"Yes, and with covid closing Gatwick airport, there's no air pollution either. But you don't have to travel far to see the picture change. White crime gets a bit darker by the time you get to Redhill, I believe you've been over there once."

McTierney nodded.

"Two stops down the line and you'll reach Croydon and beyond that it's London and everything it has to offer."

McTierney swung his face back towards Bee. "Here's a radical thought. Maybe the killing of Dawson took place outside of Reigate and the body was dumped back here to send a message to the people of Reigate."

Bee pursed his lips. "Certainly wound up the chief."

McTierney looked across at Bee as he sat mulling over the idea. Bee ruminated as if he was physically chewing on the idea. "No, I don't think so," he declared. Then he turned to point at McTierney, "But I'll tell you what. I think we should spend some time considering this case from a different angle."

"What?"

"Who benefits from the demise of Russell Dawson?"

"No one in particular."

"As far as we are aware. But that may not be the case. Can you find out if he left a will and who is the main beneficiary?"

"Sure."

"Now let's get back to the station and see what Bartlett has been up to; she should be chasing up Dr Kelly to process the DNA swabs you collected from Tina Dawson. This has been a useful chat we should come here more often."

"The magazine girl would appreciate that."

THEY ARRIVED BACK in the station to find Bartlett in an agitated state.

"There you are. I have news."

"Let's drop into the ops room and you can share it."

"It won't take much to beat our findings for the morning, the coffee shop manager is off on a Monday," said McTierney.

Bartlett dropped into her usual seat and lent across the desk eager to unload her news.

"Firstly I've completed the background checks on Savage." She looked around at her audience waiting for one of them to guess her news. Neither party was playing the game, so she continued. "He's a nasty piece of work. Savage has done time on two occasions, once for GBH and again for handling stolen goods. Plus he has a caution for fighting outside a football stadium."

McTierney looked up, "which one?"

Bartlett checked her notes. "Arsenal."

"Yeah figures."

"And he's been banned from the England supporters club for repeated disturbances both here and on the continent."

"A bit quick to use his fists," added Bee.

"That would fit with the idea that he lost it with Dawson in that match at the tennis club."

"Good work, Bartlett. Pop back to the club and ascertain if they would describe him as violent."

She nodded and turned over the page in her notebook.

"And while you're there can you talk to the membership secretary and ask him if he knows of any member who's also a school-teacher. It's a bit of a long-shot but we should check it."

"Yes, got it." Bartlett scribbled herself a note and then composed herself for her second item.

"The next bit's not so interesting. The lab has reviewed the DNA profiles from the car. Unsurprisingly three of the unknown four match the other members of the Dawson family."

"I guess we knew that would happen," said McTierney.

"But the fourth?" asked Bee lifting his chin.

"As yet unexplained but Tina remembered that they had the car serviced only a couple of weeks ago, which the handbook verifies and it's expected to be the prints of the mechanic from the local garage. I'll get a swab tomorrow and get it confirmed."

Bee nodded. "Yes we should cross that T, but it doesn't seem likely to yield much."

TWENTY-TWO

THE EARLY MORNING discussion centred around following up on the name that McTierney had gathered from the coffee shop. There wasn't a lot of enthusiasm for the idea that a school-teacher might be behind the drugs trade in Reigate, but it was a lead that couldn't be ignored. Bee had completed some preliminary work and determined that there were 47 schools in the immediate Reigate area, as defined by the government website. This comprised 38 primary schools, 14 secondary schools and 10 performance schools.

"That adds up to more than 47," said McTierney.

"I know, but that's how the government categorises them, some schools fall into two categories and are double counted."

McTierney threw his hands up in horror.

"I know, I know. And this is data from 2019 and I know of at least one new school that has opened since these numbers were collated."

McTierney shook his head in disbelief and started muttering about government inadequacies as Bee issued three sheets of paper. "I took the liberty of allocating these schools between the three of us. Let's see if we can get round all of them within the week."

Bartlett and McTierney picked up their sheets and nodded their acceptance.

"What exactly are we going to say when we turn up?" asked McTierney, "We can't ask to meet the teacher who dishes out the drugs."

"Clearly not," Bee glowered over his glasses.

"I suggest we each have an unofficial chat with the head and ask them if they have any knowledge of drug dealing in or around the school."

McTierney raised his hand, "Surely no one is going to say yes to that. They'll tell us to clear off, – especially the 38 primary schools."

Bee looked peeved, but McTierney continued. "We should prioritise the 14 secondary schools and colleges, they are far more likely to have had some experience with drugs, even if they are reluctant to admit it."

Bartlett looked left and right at her two colleagues as if crossing the road between them and then spoke. "I know this would take a bit longer, but could we go to the schools with a drugs awareness programme. Maybe drag in a couple of the drugs team."

"That alone will slow us down," said McTierney, "although I like the angle."

"I could get the chief to make this a priority for the drugs team, and that would give us some more resource," Bee chipped in.

"Good," said Bartlett, retaking control. "What I had in mind was two or three of us visiting each school, ostensibly to set up the awareness discussion and use the opportunity to ask a few open questions to teachers and pupils and see what drifts to the top."

"Yes, I like it."

McTierney turned to Bee; "Can we map these secondary schools against the CCTV you were looking at and rule out the schools that Dawson couldn't have been driving to."

"Good thought. We have only one camera offering us anything but it should rule out a few schools. I'll tackle that and get the chief on board; McTierney can you develop a plan with the drugs team and Bartlett can you follow upon some of Dawson's sales contacts, see if that generates any interest."

The team scattered in pursuit of their assigned missions.

MCTIERNEY AND BARTLETT were discussing their lunchtime options when Bee left his office and found them in the main open plan area. "Before you make any plans, I've had a phone call from the manager of that coffee shop and she's provided an address for your runaway barista. Shall we pay him a visit?"

McTierney looked up at the office clock. "He's probably crawling out of bed right now; let's ruin his breakfast. Is it far?"

"No, Redhill. Five minutes from here, especially the way you drive."

"It's a requirement of the job."

The two men skipped down the stairs and out to the back car park. McTierney took the opportunity to demonstrate that he could drive sedately and gently eased his Jaguar along the A25 that joined Reigate to Redhill.

"You'll see a different side of our community with this house call," said Bee.

McTierney turned his head, "How do you mean?"

"Last time I saw any statistics this was the second most dangerous town in the county; 20 crimes a week last year."

"Charming; violence and sex?"

"Naturally. And to keep us on our toes; possession of a dangerous weapon is unusually high."

McTierney tutted and rolled his eyes. "So where's the most dangerous place?"

"Care to guess?"

McTierney sucked on his lip. "I don't know the area. Maybe Croydon. That name seems to come up a lot."

"Yes but that counts as a city in these stats."

"Don't know," McTierney shrugged his shoulders.

"Epsom."

"As in the race-course?"

"The very place, and we're not talking about the bookies."

Bee directed him to the North-East side of the town; an area that looked a million miles from the houses that McTierney had often walked past in Reigate. They pulled up in a dull grey street full of dull grey houses; McTierney made a point of locking his car and looked up and down the street as he did. It seemed the architect had been working in monochrome the day he drew these houses although no self-respecting architect would put his name to these properties. A large puddle stood in testimony to the vagaries of the British summer and reflected the houses to underline the greyness.

Concrete was the material of choice here, although it probably wasn't much of a choice. At the end of the row of houses stood a set of concrete garages where the weeds were pushing up through cracks in the ground. Two youths were kicking a football back and forth, they looked up briefly to sneer and carry on. The 5-minute journey had taken them back 20 years.

They walked towards a green door where the paint was flaking off. Bee looked for a bell, but a scribbled note declared it not to be working. As Bee made ready to knock on the door, he stopped and turned to McTierney; "you might want to cover the rear, I'll give you a couple of minutes to get around that alleyway." He motioned to the end of the terrace. McTierney nodded and jogged to the corner of the houses and disappeared.

Bee knocked on the frosted glass pane in the door, the glass rattled in the frame but no one answered. He knocked again, still no reply, then lifted the letterbox and shouted 'police'. He couldn't see the source but heard a scrape of a chair and a back door open. He stepped back and followed the path McTierney had taken. As he turned the corner he met McTierney holding a youth by the scruff of his shirt.

"Darren Fisher I presume. How nice of you to talk to us."

"Ain't saying nuffin to you pigs."

"And such a pleasant tone."

"Fff."

"Now Darren I'll make this easy for you. You have a choice. Either you stand here in this alleyway out of sight of all your mates and tell us what we want to know." Bee stooped to stare at Darren to make sure the message was getting through. "Or we'll drag you out there into the street and take you down to the station. We'll keep you there all day and bring you back in a marked police car so everyone gets to see you with us. Your choice."

"Bastard."

McTierney decided to join the party. "And you'll be in a cell tonight and miss the football, so all your friends will ask you where you've been."

"Get off," Fisher wriggled to break free from McTierney's grasp although the two policemen blocked both escape routes along the alley. "I don't know what you want, I don't know nuffin."

"Don't be so modest, Darren, I'm sure you know a lot. Now let's start with why you ran from the coffee shop the other day?"

"I was scared. I didn't know who this guy was, I thought he was gonna do me. He'd been hanging around the shop all afternoon, I thought he was waiting 'til we closed and then he'd knife me and empty the till."

Bee looked down over his glasses and surveyed Fisher, weighing up his reply. "How many times have you seen a police officer pull a knife on a member of the public?"

"More often than you'd believe."

"Now tell us what you know about the school-teacher."

"I don't know nuffin."

"Yes you said, but we don't believe that. You mentioned his name first, remember? So you'll have to do better than that."

Darren wriggled again and this time McTierney released his collar. "It's true I don't know nuffin." Darren lowered his head, "it's a name I've heard. Nuffin more."

Bee sighed. At that moment Fisher sprang to his left but McTierney was ready for him and shoved him back against the wall. "Not leaving us yet are you Darren?"

Fisher scowled at McTierney. "The inspector is a patient

man, but I'm not, so you've got one last chance to say something meaningful or I'll drag your sorry arse across the street making so much noise that everyone will stick their head out of their windows. Now get talking."

Fisher fidgeted against the wall then dipped his head and whispered. "I don't know him but they say the school-teacher is the bloke to go to for drugs in the town."

"Yes, we'd worked that bit out for ourselves. You'll have to do better than that."

"I don't know, I don't do drugs, I wanna be an athlete. I've never spoken to him."

"But you must know what he looks like."

"Look all I know is that he's a big bloke, a bully, he takes no shit from anyone. I don't even know if he's really a school-teacher. He wasn't at any school I went to."

"If you don't know what he looks like, how do know he wasn't a teacher at your school?"

Fisher fell silent.

"Come on you've obviously seen him, so tell us what he looks like?"

"All I know is that he's a big bloke; he's English or white anyway. Dark hair and built like a brick shithouse."

"How poetic. And what drugs is he dealing?"

"The usual; coke, pills, hash. I think he can get anything you want. But I don't do drugs."

McTierney grabbed his shirt sleeve and rolled it up, there was no obvious needle mark. Fisher yanked his arm back. "I told you, I don't do drugs."

"Fine. On your way." Bee nodded at McTierney and turned back towards the street.

BACK IN THE station Bee pulled his team together to update them on the plan to approach some of the senior schools in the area.

"The chief is fully on board hence we have Church and Carol Bishop on secondment for the rest of the week. The CCTV analysis allowed us to rule out a few schools on the western side of the town but there's still a long list.

"How many?"

"I've cut the original 14 down to 11. We need to get through these by Friday."

The plan was met with a series of nods.

"There are three with lowish pupil numbers, less than 200; Cornfield, Merstham Park, and Woodfield. We'll put those at the bottom of the list."

"Fair enough."

"We'll start with one of the big ones first thing tomorrow, Reigate College."

"You know it's close to the end of term for these schools, we might get some push back, with a request to leave it until next year."

"We can't allow that." Bee looked from McTierney to Bartlett to check his message was getting through. "We'll take all five of us en masse, start by addressing the head and then split up and see what we can find. Some of these places have over a thousand students, there's a lot of ground to cover."

Silence around the room suggested there was general agreement to the plan.

"Any questions?" Asked Bee.

"Just one," said McTierney, "Are we going to finish at half four today so we can get home for the England game?"

"I don't know why you're so obsessed with the game; there's no way England will beat the Germans. The best we can hope for is to lose on penalties."

"Come on, you've got to start believing there's a chance. This German team is a shadow of some of their great ones; we've never had a better chance of winning."

"That's the sort of banal claptrap that I imagine you say every time we play them."

"But it's true!"

"Hardly. We haven't beaten them for over fifty years."

"Why not? We have a team on form, a stellar manager, home advantage and their form has been sketchy at best." His eyes widening with each word.

"The only footballer who has done anything to warrant this praise is Rashford and his school meals program. His campaign to support food bank charities and to extend the availability of free school meals is extraordinary."

"Yeah, but can he score one against the Germans?"

"Doubtful, the German team always come good in the big tournaments. They've been pacing themselves for these last few games."

"Course we'll win, you've got to have a bit of belief. Southgate is our messiah he's going to lead us to the final and Kane will come good tonight."

Bee held up his hand to stop the avalanche of positivity steamrollering towards him. "You only need to look at their past history and anyway the key factor will be their mental strength; they know they can beat England whereas England are hoping to beat Germany."

"Hmm." McTierney shock his head but Bee hadn't finished. "Even if you only look…"

"If you two don't stop arguing, the game will be over." Bartlett chipped in.

The two men fell silent and stood like admonished school-boys for a few seconds before McTierney returned to the topic. "So do you fancy coming over to watch it? After the game we can grab a bite in the local pub."

"No you're okay. I'll see you boys in the morning."

"YOU GET THE tele on and I'll get the beers, I put a few in the fridge this morning."

Ron returned to the lounge and flopped on the sofa and passed a cold can to Scott. Although they sat on the same sofa the two men watched the game in different worlds; Scott rested his back against the sofa calm and relaxed, whilst Ron was on the edge of the seat offering advice to every player and cursing each decision which went against the England team. Fifteen minutes in and Ron needed a second can. Scott waved away the option.

By halftime with the game still scoreless Scott had abandoned his calm exterior and was on the edge of the seat, but Ron had moved way beyond that. He sat with his leg under his bum, then he pulled it out, then he switched to the other leg, then he stood and walked around the back of the sofa, slipping off to the kitchen for another can. A sheen of sweat appeared on his forehead; he rubbed the back of his neck and chewed his nails. "Lord, let us win this game and I won't swear, speed or break the law for a week."

"Break the law?" Scott turned to examine his colleague.

"It doesn't happen often, and it's always minor."

"Best I…"

But the rest of Scott's statement was lost in a scream as England scored. Ron jumped from the sofa and hugged Scott spraying him with lager at the same time. In a matter of seconds the tension of the previous 75 minutes evaporated and joy engulfed the pair.

But as quickly as the euphoria had arrived, it disappeared as Germany broke through the English defence and the German striker advanced on the goal. He shot and the household held its breath, the ball sped passed the goalkeeper but missed the post by an inch. The household breathed again.

"Oh no. Life has given us hope, only to snatch it away at the last minute. We're going to lose this."

"No we won't, Germany always take that type of opportunity against us but tonight they've fluffed it. We're gonna win this and we're going win the final. The Queen will be knighting the England manager in a few weeks' time!"

Scott shock his head in disbelief but nothing could shake Ron's confidence. Two minutes later, the England captain Kane stooped to head in a second goal and Ron was up on his feet dancing and singing. "And now you're gonna believe us, and now you're gonna believe us and now you're gonna believe us, we're gonna win the cup."

"Thank heavens I don't have neighbours."

The whistle blew to end the game and start Ron's celebrations.

"Is it worth talking to you?"

"Nah, let's go to the pub."

They wandered down the road from Scott's house and fell into The Bell where the landlord greeted Ron with a hearty smile. "Good evening Ron, enjoy the game?"

"Oh yes. We'll have two pints please Tom."

"Sure grab a seat over there and I'll bring them over."

Scott looked dismayed; "Do you know I've been coming to this pub for two and a half years and he still doesn't know my name. You've been here for ten minutes and you're his best mate."

Ron put his arm around Scott's shoulder and pulled him close before he shouted in his ear, "Don't worry about the past, it's the future that's important. When he comes over I'll introduce you."

"I don't want to be introduced in my own local."

"Whatever. Weren't the lads brilliant? And now Kane has started scoring we'll go all the way."

"Yes. Happy days indeed. I will admit that it was an exciting game and good to finally beat the Germans, shame it was played in a half empty stadium."

"Don't be grumpy, Saint Gareth and the boys have brought happiness to millions tonight."

"Will you stop calling him Saint Gareth. He's just a football manager."

"All across the country people will be out celebrating."

"I hope there's no trouble on our patch, I wouldn't want to get called out tonight."

"So turn your phone off."

"I can't do that, where's your commitment?"

Ron shrugged his shoulders and picked up the pint that had been placed on his table. "These moments don't come around often; we should enjoy it while we can."

Their enjoyment ran late into the night. They left the pub after 11pm and staggered across the country lane and back to Scott's house. Although he hadn't kept pace with Ron, Scott had drunk more than he could take and was starting to sway and slur his words. At the front door Scott fumbled with his key and dropped it twice before lining it up with the lock. Once inside he headed for the sofa and flopped across it as Ron tottered on into the kitchen. "One more before we call it a night?" He called out from the fridge. Scott didn't answer.

"There was something I wanted to ask you. I want Jess to come over and stay. Maybe Friday and Saturday, that'll be okay won't it?" He plucked the last two cans from the top shelf and headed back into the lounge. Scott was laying passed out on the sofa. Ron stood one of the tins on the floor next to him. "Have it when you wake up." Ron turned and headed up the stairs leaving Scott to sleep it off.

TWENTY-THREE

BEE WALKED GINGERLY across the office hoping to slip unnoticed into his office, he was within ten feet when McTierney called out from across the open plan office.

"Hey inspector, how are you this morning?"

The words bounced aggressively around his skull like exuberant children demanding to be heard. He turned back slowly, grimaced and waved.

"When you're ready come join us in the ops room. I have some news, that I think you'll like."

Bee plonked his case on his desk and sighed. He had no choice. He had to go and listen to this awful man. How could he drink like a fish and not suffer any form of hangover? He dragged his feet as much as possible but perhaps this could be the breakthrough that he desired. When he sat down in the ops room the painted smile on his face used every ounce of enthusiasm he had left. "So McTierney what can you tell us to brighten our day?"

"I've won the Euro millions lottery. Last night my numbers came up."

McTierney beamed as he moved around the table to open a paper bag and hand out a selection of pastries that he had brought up to the office along with a coffee for everyone.

Bee sat dazed for a moment and then his consciousness

kicked in. He stood up walked around the table and thrust out his hand. "Congratulations. We'll miss you."

"Hang on, I'm undecided about what to do. I thought both of you could tell me how you'd spend a lottery win, give me a few ideas, before I decide what to do."

He turned to Bartlett; "What would you do Jess?"

Bartlett tilted her head left and right and hummed. "I think I'd want to secure my future, so I'd probably buy a house and put some money away for a rainy day."

"Very commendable," said Bee.

"But I'd still have a major blow out and get myself a new wardrobe with one of these fashion advisers to help me."

"There's nothing wrong with your wardrobe, you've got some beautiful things," said McTierney.

"I know, but it'd be nice to have an expert recommend something chic and daring, that no one else in Reigate is wearing," she paused, "afterwards she could help you."

McTierney offered a weak smile. "What about you inspector?"

"Hmm, I think I'd like to make a difference to the world. Nothing wrong in securing your future," he smiled at Bartlett, "but I have a house I'm happy with, so I'd use my windfall to do some good, maybe fund a cancer research project. Doubtless our laughing policeman here would blow his fortune on having a good time with wine, women, and song."

McTierney faked a look of hurt. "You're both been a touch snippy with me when I'm the one with the lotto win. But as it happens I would share my winnings with my friends."

"Of course you would," sneered Bee, "but we're getting

carried away; how much did you win?"

"Twenty pounds, the majority of which I spent on these coffees and pastries for my friends – you two!"

"Twenty pounds. That's it. You drag us through this charade and all you've won is twenty quid. Christ I thought you'd won a jackpot."

"All I said was that I'd had a win. It's your assumption."

"Hmm. Now assume this. Get out there and catch this killer or you'll be buying your next lottery ticket in Norfolk."

LATER THAT MORNING the team swelled by the presence of Church and Bishop from the drugs squad marched up into the reception of Reigate College. Bee went to the desk to address the receptionist while the others loitered.

"This takes me back to my college days," said Carol Bishop, "I did my A-levels here twelve years ago. Biology and applied science. Wonderful days. A bit scary at first, there were so many students, but when I found my feet I loved it."

Bartlett joined the conversation, "Yes I had a great time here."

"Did either of you see any drug abuse?" asked McTierney.

Neither woman spoke and Church filled the vacuum. "I doubt it's any different to any sixth form college, if you want to find illicit entertainment, the opportunities are endless. Especially here, there's over two thousand students all starting to break away from their parents apron strings. This is where they find their independence."

"Any drug dealers in the college?"

"Doubtful, but if you're a student here, either in the college or in the town and you want to try something, it won't be too difficult to get started. The problem comes when you want to stop."

Bee returned to the group, "We have an appointment with the Principal Nick Chapman. I phoned him earlier to set the scene; I've positioned this as a reconnaissance visit leading to a drugs awareness programme for the start of next term."

"I guess we'll be picking up the pieces come September," said Church.

"Possibly, but I would have thought that an awareness programme would be high on your agenda."

"We can cope with it."

Two minutes later and they were all squeezed into the principal's office.

"Good morning to you, when the inspector spoke to me, I hadn't quite understood the scale of the mission. I'm not sure we can accommodate all of you."

"Don't worry Mr Chapman, we'll be discreet and quick. We want to talk to a few teachers and get a sense for their perception of drug knowledge, use and abuse around the college. Apologies for being a little heavy-handed but we're aware that we need to hold these conversations quickly before the schools and colleges break for the summer."

"Certainly let me introduce you to my deputy and a few of the teachers who are in the staff room today. I'm afraid while you're walking about the college you'll all need to wear face masks. We are a likely breeding ground for the virus, lots of students in close proximity and no vaccinations."

There were 15 lecturers spread around the staff room and

Bee elected to divide and conquer by dispatching his troops on solo missions. He elected to talk to the principal and deputy himself as they took a short tour of the college.

"Let me come clean with you right from the start. This investigation is linked to the recent murder at the tennis club."

The principal stepped back in surprise. "So all this drug's talk was a smokescreen?"

"No not exactly. We are pursuing a lead that suggests the killing has a drug connection and that the killer may be a dealer known as 'the school-teacher'. We have a general description of the man as a large stocky individual."

The two college men waited for Bee to continue.

"That's it. Not much to go on I'm afraid."

"Not much? I'd say that was nothing inspector," said the deputy. "The name could easily be a nickname. It seems unlikely that any drug dealer would want to advertise his whereabouts to the police."

"Yes, we have considered that element, but we have a duty to investigate every lead that comes our way, so indulge me. Do you have any members of staff here that would fit the general description and who you think or know might be familiar with drugs?"

The principal stopped and turned to the inspector. "Mr Bee. Let me make this clear. None of my staff are as you put it, 'familiar with drugs'. If I thought that to be the case, it would be incumbent on me to relieve them of their duties. The college has a zero-tolerance policy for drugs, as I'm sure you can imagine."

Bee pursed his lips, let the principal finish, and then delivered his reply.

"Yes I quite accept that, and I didn't mean to imply drug usage was high, open or accepted in the college. But put yourself in my shoes for a moment; we all know that there are drugs available in this town; we all know that some students will try them. I'm not interested in any casual drug taking that may or may not take place on your premises, but I am interested in finding a murderer who is casting a shadow over this town. If that means I have to offend your honour by asking uncomfortable questions, then so be it. If I need to drag every one of your staff down to the station, then I will. Don't doubt it for a second."

Chapman stood quietly looking at his feet, and Bee continued in a calmer tone.

"If it makes you feel better, I can tell you that we are holding this type of conversation with every secondary school around the town. You are not being singled out; we started here due to the proximity of the college to the police station. So perhaps you could re-consider my question."

Chapman looked up and down the corridor; "there are three lecturers who I might consider as large and stocky men; Lane, Steel and Waltham. I've no reason to suppose any has any connection to drugs. If I had to nominate someone as most likely to know a thing or two about drugs it would be Isobel Hernandez in the Arts department, but I must stress I have no evidence for that, and clearly she doesn't fit your profile."

"Thank you Mr Chapman, that wasn't so difficult now was it?"

Chapman raised his hand to make a point and the conversation was developing into a stand-off. But at that moment Church and another of the lecturers came around the corner.

They stopped in mid-conversation to watch the spectacle.

Fifteen minutes later Bee gathered together his troops in the reception area and they left en masse to discuss findings back at the station. Church stood away from the group and was shaking his head, while Bartlett made her apologies and slipped out down to the tennis club where she had arranged to meet the membership secretary over lunch.

IVAN WRIGHT WAS an enthusiastic club member who readily gave his time to the sport he loved. He greeted Bartlett with a warm smile and insisted on giving her a tour of the clubhouse, despite her being a member. He stopped by the two wooden boards of honour and quickly found a reason to point to his own name as men's champion of 1989.

"A memorable year; the fall of the Berlin Wall and I won the club championship." He laughed.

"I believe so, but long before I was born, Mr Wright. Now can I ask you a couple of questions."

"Certainly my dear," said the old champion with a twinkle in his eye. He led Bartlett over to the sofa and sat down next to her.

"Greg Savage, I understand he played here until recently. Did you know him?"

"I did, yes that's correct, he's a fine player."

"Would you describe him as a violent man?"

Wright sat and thought for a moment, "It's not the first word I would use but I wouldn't say it was wrong."

"Perhaps you could explain."

"He was and is an emotional player, he plays with his

heart as much as he plays with his racquet. On his day he's a master, but if you can get under his skin and rattle him, then he's a different player. He starts to swear and curse and many's the time I've seen him throw his racquet down and even smash it."

"Interesting. But let me try a different angle. I know you don't ask members for their profession but do you happen to know if there are any school-teachers amongst the club?"

"Now there's a question." Wright lent back against the sofa and rubbed his chin. "I can't say for certain but I think Spencer Lewis is a teacher at the King's School here in town and I believe, though I'm not quite as sure, that Debbie Unsworth is a teacher at Micklefield."

"Excellent," said Bartlett as she scribbled the names into her yellow notepad.

"Of course, we have 617 members so there's a lot here I don't know, but I make it my mission to get to know everyone either by face or by name."

"Super, while we are chatting, let me ask you another. Do you know if Russell Dawson ever offered coaching sessions to any of the schools in the neighbourhood?"

"I do. We have two teaching contracts; one is for The Parish School and the other is at Reigate Priory School. The Parish is Tuesday afternoons and the other is on Wednesdays."

"Fabulous; you've been a great help."

BARTLETT ARRIVED BACK at the station as the canteen was closing and found McTierney and Phil Church deep in conversation in the operations room.

"What did I miss?"

McTierney turned to welcome her. "Not a lot really."

"I don't know, I think Sting was close to getting thumped by the principal at Reigate College."

Bartlett raised her eyes.

"I was telling McTierney here, that if I'd been a few seconds later coming round the corner I think old Chappers would have swung for the boss."

"I didn't realise you knew the principal."

Church looked down at McTierney, "of course, it's my job to know all the players in the drug trade."

"Are you saying Chapman is a dealer."

"No, but he's in a great position to know what's going on. So I have to know him."

McTierney nodded, "Makes sense. So what do you think to this school-teacher theory?"

"I'm not convinced there is some big drugs lord running the trade in Reigate. I don't think the town has the scale to warrant it. Yes there's a few pills and tablets available if you want them, and perhaps something stronger, but we're not Soho. I think Bee's got his knickers in a twist over this school-teacher idea. I tried to tell him, but he won't hear it."

"I think the chief is getting twitchy about the lack of progress and upping the pressure on him."

"Could be, I saw the chief heading for Bee's office earlier."

Phil Church stood up, nodded to Bartlett, and made for the door. McTierney pulled out a chair for her to sit down. "I've been going through the list of sales that Dawson had made. There's nothing there." He waved his hand at a list of names and scribbles on the desk. "He's just a bloke selling tennis racquets and the odd pair of trainers. Nothing to warrant a murder."

TWENTY-FOUR

BEE CALLED A sudden ops meeting for 2pm in the afternoon and used it to distribute a sharp demarcation of tasks. McTierney was allocated a desk role to investigate Dawson's will; Church, Bishop and Bartlett would continue visiting schools and colleges around the area in the hope of identifying the school-teacher and Bee himself was going to visit the two primary schools where Dawson used to provide after-school tennis training. He didn't bother to open the floor to questions and dismissed his troops without his regular encouragement, merely demanding they return for a 5pm meeting with Dr Kelly.

As Bee left the room there was a quick exchange of confused glances across the team as they pushed back their chairs and made ready to pursue their respective errands.

"What's up with the boss today?" asked Bartlett to the room.

"He's your boss," replied Carol Bishop, "but if he's always like this, I'm glad I don't have to see him too often."

"It's my fault," confessed McTierney, "but you're all getting off lightly."

"How so?"

"Because I had it all last night. How I'd persuaded him to drop the focus on primary schools and as soon as we do, up pop two leads which feature primary schools."

The group stared back at him not understanding.

"The tennis club told us that Dawson has contacts with two primary schools, so he's convinced that one of those could lead to the elusive school-teacher, who he sees as central to the case."

Church shook his head. "He needs to open his eyes and keep his options open. Who's going to tell him?"

All eyes focused on McTierney.

"Me? Whoa, steady on. I'm still the new boy. He won't take any advice from me."

McTierney finished by passing the stare to Bartlett.

"No way, forget it, I'm the junior."

"Bee needs to embrace change and somebody needs to make him, or we'll be going around in circles for days," said Church as he headed out the door.

McTierney hated the desk admin side of this job and sauntered downstairs to get a hot drink before he opened up his laptop and picked up the phone to make a couple of calls. His coffee had gone cold and his elaborate eagle doodle had spread across two pages before he typed up the summary of his findings on to the case folder. Dawson hadn't written a will and therefore there was no obvious beneficiary to his death. Popular legal opinion suggested that his wife would inherit after a lengthy process. He concluded by typing 'No further investigation required' hoping that would be sufficient for Bee.

BARTLETT, BISHOP, AND Church spent the early afternoon

visiting two senior schools. First choice was the Royal Albert and Alexandra School which catered for a thousand pupils half of which were boarders. Church believed that the high number of live-in students increased the possibility of misdemeanours and especially drugs. A theory which they struggled to ratify during their sixty-minute tour of the establishment. As they walked back to the visitors car park and admired the view of rolling Surrey hills, they shared brief snippets from their individual chats but none of them offered any reason to return.

Next on their list was St Bede's School set in the northern part of the town and accommodating 1,700 pupils, although the year-numbers started to decline in the sixth form. The scale of the school stretched their visit towards a second hour but offered nothing more exciting than the RA&A school had done. Their enthusiasm was waning as they headed back to the station for the afternoon rendezvous with Kelly.

BEE SPENT HIS afternoon following up on the two primary schools where Russell Dawson had held coaching contracts. There was a familiar pattern to his visits; each school stank of disinfectant which even permeated the offices of the headmasters and overpowered the taste of the tea and biscuits he had been offered by each. Both schools were shocked at the demise of the tennis coach and concerned at the lack of communication that had followed from the tennis club. Every classroom he entered he was met by rows of facemasks and open windows as the schools did their best to contain the growing number of covid cases that was starting to stalk the community. Testimony to the efforts of the schools to tackle the virus he encountered a battalion of three cleaning trolleys at The Parish School, more heavily armed than some Challenger tanks. But nowhere did he discover anything remotely useful in tackling the case. The only aspect of his afternoon that offered anything untoward was as he walked the corridors of Reigate Priory primary school and turned a corner to face a group of school-girls laughing raucously; they fell silent at the sight of the headmaster walking towards them and bowed their heads as he and Bee passed by. At that point Bee realised he was wasting his time and decided to head back to the station.

THE TEAM ASSEMBLED in piecemeal in the operations room; first to arrive was McTierney who had been counting the minutes until 5pm arrived. Shortly after him Bartlett popped her head around the door, decided she had time to visit the washroom and disappeared again. When she returned she was reading a text on her phone.

"Hey, if you ever get bored watching that football stuff that you're so keen on, you might want to try a bit of tennis. Wimbledon started this week and Ruth has sent me a text about the future of British tennis."

"Oh yeah?" McTierney didn't sound that interested, but Bartlett continued regardless.

"She's calling out some 18-year-old girl called Emma Raducanu who's won the first set of her first-round match."

"She doesn't sound British. Are you sure you've got the name right?"

"So Ruth tells me. She's describing her as an extraordinary talent and cool under pressure."

"A bit like me then!"

"Yes that's right, just like you, but without the ego." Bartlett threw her pen at him across the table.

McTierney picked it up and was about to retaliate when Inspector Bee entered the room and brought an end to the frivolity. He was followed by Dr Kelly, who looked dishevelled and harassed.

"Dr Kelly has some news for us," announced Bee tersely as he took a seat close to the door and turned to stare at the pathologist who dropped a couple of books on the table and began to fiddle with his papers as he searched for his notebook. He began to talk as he looked.

"Good afternoon all. Yes as the inspector says, I do have some news for you." Kelly looked down as his pad as he spoke.

"I'm sorry to say that I have made an error on the DNA analysis. Simple silly mistake but should never have happened. I can't apologise enough, but what with cases here and cases in Horsham, I'm struggling to keep on top of everything. But that's no excuse. I wanted to explain to you how it came about."

"We understand doctor. Could you give us the news?" Bee interrupted Kelly's ramblings.

"Certainly." Kelly raised his head for the first time since he had entered the room.

"Something of a yin and a yan."

"The news?" said Bee.

Kelly nodded. "The fourth DNA sample in the car relates to Jack Bates the mechanic at the Kwik-Fit garage in Redhill.

So we can close off that line of enquiry."

There was a murmur of contentment around the room, nobody was surprised by the revelation.

"But I've found a new sample."

Everyone in the room woke up.

"I thought it wise to re-trace my steps and search the body for any missed samples and picked up a new sample on the inside of Dawson's tennis top."

"The inside?" said McTierney.

"Yes, the inside. Quite unusual and before you ask I don't think it could have transferred from the outside."

There was an exchange of glances around the room.

"Could this be evidence of a struggle or a fight of some sort?"

"That I can't say, you'll have to do the detective work. All I can say is that the profile is not contained on the police database. So he's a newbie. Or even she's a newbie."

"This puts us right back at square one," moaned McTierney.

"No, I don't think so," said Bee. "We've ruled out a number of options."

"Maybe but now the good doctor has opened a new can of worms."

"As you feel so passionately about it, perhaps you could take the lead on this item."

McTierney nodded and dropped out of the conversation in a sulk. Phil Church smirked at him from across the room.

The inspector thanked Kelly for his input, made a quick summary of the status of the investigation and allocated a series of new tasks for the forthcoming day.

McTierney bounced back into the meeting, "If I'm making enquires around town tomorrow, I'll drop in and talk to this Hammond guy. You didn't like him much did you boss?" Bee looked over the top of his glasses at McTierney and allowed the heat to drift away from the comment. "Not especially. He wore an ear-ring and try as I might, I can't see that as a good look for a man."

"Doesn't make him a criminal." Church joined the debate.

"No of course not. But his demeanour wasn't welcoming either. It was all a bit disappointing."

"Maybe he didn't like the look of you either!" Church laughed at his own joke.

Bee glared across the room at him.

McTierney came to the rescue. "I know you don't like raw speculation, but all this talk about car mechanics has got me thinking." All heads turned to face McTierney. He shuffled in his seat and then a smile broke out across his face.

"Perhaps one reason we haven't found much DNA is because the killer wore a coverall or a clean suit or whatever they're called... The type of overall you see a mechanic wear or come to think of it someone cleaning a pinball machine."

"Savage?" said Bartlett.

McTierney nodded. "Worth checking out. Using one of those suits would help the killer avoid leaving any DNA in the car or on the body."

TWENTY-FIVE

"WHERE'S CHURCH?"

"I don't think he's joining us this morning sir."

Bartlett presented her information as pleasantly as she could.

"Humpf. No loss I suppose. What about Carol Bishop? I think she always brings something to the party."

"I believe Church pulled her off the case to accompany him."

Bee bowed his head and looked over his glasses at Bartlett with dismayed eyes. "What did he actually say?"

"Not much. Something about having to deal with a situation at Gatwick Airport that required real police work and he couldn't…" Bartlett hesitated.

"You're being nice to spare my feelings." Bee smiled.

"A little sir."

Bee raised his hand. "Fine. We don't need his type." He reached out and squeezed her shoulder. "I've got the A-team with me this morning. I can feel that we are on to something today. We'll start at the grand old school of this town. I'll get my best brown jacket."

"POOR TIMING INSPECTOR. You should've been here Tuesday or better still last week. Our school year closed at lunch-time yesterday," said Mr Neil Pinkerton the headmaster of the Reigate King's School.

Inspector Bee was sitting in a fashionable office which mixed classic educational memorabilia with eclectic furniture. Pride of place was given to a Hogwarts' style 'sorting hat' which sat on a walnut table in the window of Pinkerton's study. Jess Bartlett couldn't take her eyes from it.

"That's most unfortunate," replied Bee his hands clenched. "in these circumstances I think I'd better come clean and explain the real reason for our visit today."

Pinkerton's eyes grew wider and his face twitched as Bee re-counted the full story of the murder of Russell Dawson and the potential lead of a 'school-teacher'. Pinkerton held up his hand. "Inspector I understand your consternation about a lack of progress with your enquiry, but I absolutely must refute the suggestion that we would employ a school teacher here who was doubling as a drug-dealer, not to mention a murderer."

"Yes, I appreciate your position, but nonetheless a murderer is at large in our society and it's incumbent on myself and my team to fully investigate every avenue. As such I must insist that we are allowed to talk to whichever staff you have available."

Pinkerton's bowed his head, pushed his glasses up onto his forehead with his left hand and sighed. "Very well inspector if you must. Let's make this as painless as possible. I'm not sure which members of staff will be in school today, it's not uncommon for them to stay home on the first day of release and this year we have a covid related deep clean scheduled for next Monday and Tuesday so I don't expect many will re-appear before the middle of next week."

Pinkerton rose from his expansive desk and set off at the pace of a gazelle in flight leaving the two detectives in his wake. His party reached the maths block which was shrouded in darkness despite the proximity of the summer solstice.

"I think we can assume that mathematics has finished," he announced with a wave of his hand and sped on. It was a similar situation in the Arts department, the library, and the canteen. He was about to shortcut the science building when Bee grabbed his arm and cupped his hand to his ear. "I think I hear a distant hum coming from the upper floor; let's investigate."

Pinkerton didn't bother to hide his irritation. "Yes, right, fine. Up we go." He leapt up the stairs two at a time. Bee and Bartlett trailed behind. When they arrived at the top, Pinkerton stood tapping his foot.

"I can't think why anyone would be in their classrooms today, but let's whizz you around. I doubt you'll be satisfied until you've seen it for yourself."

Bee bowed his head to avoid Pinkerton's eyes and turned to grin at Bartlett before he fell-in behind the head to march along the top corridor. As they approached the end of the passageway the noise grew louder. Bee couldn't decipher it. A cacophony of whirring and crashing interspersed with a dash of Tchaikovsky's Nutcracker ballet. They reached the final classroom and the mystery revealed itself as Pinkerton opened the door.

The food science teacher was conducting her own deep clean of her kitchen-classroom accompanied by the music of her favourite Russian composer. She stood in a full-length blue apron protecting a rainbow patterned t-shirt with her long blonde hair rolled up on top of her head and a pair of yellow rubber gloves on the end of her arms. She looked like anything but a school teacher.

Pinkerton swayed backwards to take in the sight.

"Mrs Garnett, good to see you. Have you fully recovered from your dose of covid?"

"Yes thank-you headmaster. Much better now."

"May I ask what you're doing? I hope you received the memo about the intensive cleaning programme we have scheduled for next week."

"I did, but I can't let anyone else clean my kitchen. I must clean it before they come. I can't let them find a dirty kitchen." She plunged her hands into a bowl of soapy water to emphasis her point.

Pinkerton grimaced as if confused by the logic. He opened his mouth to speak but closed it again, before choosing to introduce his guests. "As you wish Mrs G. I'm escorting our local police around the building. We wondered what the noise was?"

"Tchaikovsky isn't noise headmaster. It's musical poetry."

"Indeed so, one of my favourites," said Bee stepping around Pinkerton and anxious to join the conversation. Pinkerton frowned at the intrusion.

Garnett lifted her right hand out of the sink, brushed it quickly on her apron and offered it to Bee. He hesitated, but unable to think of a better response, he gingerly lent forward and shook hands with the wet yellow glove.

"Since we have the inspector here in the room where it happened, maybe we could test his expertise."

"No, no, I'm sure the inspector has far more important

things to do," said Pinkerton hastily.

"No, not at all. I enjoy a challenge."

Garnett didn't wait for further encouragement.

"It's the strangest thing. I only noticed it a couple of days ago and I think it must have happened when I was off school with that dreadful covid bug."

Bartlett stepped away from the conversation and over to a gleaming red food mixer which stood on the workbench nearest the window. Across the room a red sentry stood on every desk. She ran her hand gently across the top of the machine as if inspecting the quality.

"Oh please, don't touch anything, you'll contaminate it. Now I'll have to sanitise that again once you've gone." The fussy cleaning lady had been transformed back into the strict school teacher and Bartlett jumped back in embarrassment. "Sorry," she mumbled.

Garnett huffed and turned back to the inspector.

"Now where was I? Oh yes."

Pinkerton drilled his eyes into his food tech teacher and she quickened her story.

"One of my best kitchen knives has been replaced. It looks the same but it's a newer version. Who on earth would do such a thing?"

Bee's ears twitched and he lifted his nose a few degrees. "Tell me more."

"It's that block on the main bench, the one I use." She walked across to the desk and carried the block back to the middle of the classroom. "The middle knife of these three is subtly different to the other two. It has the same colour and design but it's newer. All the others are kitchen worn from hundreds of visits to the dishwasher. But this one has hardly been used at all."

"May I?" Bee reached out took the block.

Garnett nodded and he lifted the suspect knife between his thumb and fore-finger.

He turned back to Bartlett with a contented smile. "I think we've found our murder weapon."

"How can that knife be the murder weapon?" asked Pinkerton.

"Allow me to clarify, headmaster. I think this was purchased in the last two weeks to replace the knife that was used to kill our victim, although he was already dead at the time."

Pinkerton's frown grew deeper.

"The murderer was trying to disguise the original cause of death and stabbed our victim with the knife that I believe used to sit in this block."

Pinkerton and Garnett exchanged open-mouthed stares.

"I'm afraid headmaster, that this means I'm going to need a lot more co-operation and information from you and I'm going to need it now."

Pinkerton hesitated and then quickly caught up with the conversation, "Yes, yes sure, whatever you need. I'm struggling to comprehend what I'm hearing."

"No problem, headmaster. The general public are not trained to deal with murder. Now I will need the following as quickly as possible. A list of all your teachers and their contact details, with a priority on those who regularly teach in this corridor."

Pinkerton nodded. "Yes certainly, right away I'll get Louise to print it for you."

Bee turned to back to Mrs Garnett. "Tell me, what were the dates when you were away from the school and this knife could have been replaced?"

Garnett let her eyeballs rise to the top of her eyes as she stood recollecting her dates.

"I got the first symptoms on the Friday, so I took a test on the Saturday and it came back positive on the Sunday so I stayed at home from the Monday. That would've been June 7th. I only returned to work on Wednesday of this week."

Bee turned to Bartlett with excited eyes, "We need to have a look around here and see what we can uncover."

He turned back to Pinkerton, "Do you have CCTV in operation at the school?"

"We do."

"Excellent. I need to see the tapes for the evening of Thursday June 10th."

"Right."

Both men paused.

"I need to see them today, now, this minute. If you could make a call."

"Yes, yes certainly, I'll get hold of my secretary."

"Good, I'll follow you back to your office in a couple of minutes."

Pinkerton scuttled away from the room like one of the many pupils he had dismissed from a classroom.

Bee switched his attention back to Garnett. "What goes on in the neighbouring classrooms?"

Garnett flushed and began to stammer. "Next door is Mr Howes' chemistry lab, opposite is the physics department, that's the domain of Mrs Jarvis and at the end before the fire exit is Mr Buckley's office."

"What does Buckley do?"

"He's head of the sixth form, teaches physics but does

lots of admin for Mr Pinkerton."

Bee squeezed his bottom lip with his thumb and forefinger and walked towards the door, he poked his head outside and look towards the fire exit and walked back still pinching his lip.

"Interesting."

He turned back to Bartlett. "Let's go and take a quick look around these three rooms and see if anything looks amiss."

"What am I looking for?"

"I'm not sure yet. Something to connect this place with the tennis club would be useful. Otherwise, nose about around the desks and drawers and see if anything strikes you as out of place."

After twenty minutes of opening drawers and cupboards, rustling paper and flicking though books Bee decided to stop the search. "We're not getting anywhere here, but if our murderer was here, he's had plenty of time to clean his tracks. You stay here until our SOCO team arrives, then put them to work. Start in Buckley's office, I have a feeling about it. I'm going to catch up with the head and see if the CCTV tells us anything."

Bee found Pinkerton in his office. The headmaster had lost his normal composure and was looking rattled.

"What have you found Mr Pinkerton?"

"It's more what I haven't found. Two tapes are missing."

"I'm not surprised. Who in your staff, besides yourself, has a working knowledge of the security camera network?"

Pinkerton rarely had to pause before he answered a question, such was his command of the school, but this query caused him to stop and contemplate his answer. He counted the reply out on his hand. "My two deputies, the bursar," he paused on his index finger, "Mr Childs who is our head porter, and perhaps a couple of his deputies. Maybe six people in total."

"I'll need the contact details of all of them before I leave today."

"I'll get on it without delay."

"Good, I'll brief my colleague and be back in five minutes for those lists."

Bee turned to leave but stopped at the door, "One final thought; do any of the people who you know to have knowledge of the security cameras play tennis?"

Again Pinkerton had to think before he could speak. The bursar does, that's a fact, and he's a useful player to boot. Not too sure about my deputies and I wouldn't know about Mr Childs or his team."

Bee nodded. "and what about the others on the top floor; who did you say Howes, Jarvis and Buckley?"

"Never seen them play, Buckley plays a lot of rugby I believe."

"Right."

"And I guess I should declare my own hand here. I play a bit. Don't get a lot of time these days but I try to play on the grass when it's fresh."

Bee found Bartlett sitting in Buckley's chair behind a grand desk. "What have you found?"

"Nothing I was trying to put myself in the mind of a killer and imagine what he would do."

"That's always a revealing exercise. Where are your thoughts taking you?"

"I'm thinking that this is a convenient out of the way

office. As head of the sixth form this Buckley person wouldn't get much casual traffic to his door. If he needed some privacy this place is near perfect."

Bee looked around the room, walked over to the solitary window and looked down towards the playground and the edge of the drive into the school. "It also has a lofty view of what's happening down in the school."

Bartlett joined him at the window and nodded her appreciation.

Bee continued "Some of the CCTV footage from the night of the 10th is missing so it suggests our teacher can manipulate the evidence of the school cameras."

Bartlett looked shocked.

"But he won't be able to tamper with the cameras on the Queen's highway. Put a call into the station to have someone secure all the TV cameras for this road for that night."

"Will do sir."

"It's not often the lack of evidence is compelling Bartlett, but in this case I'd say that the loss of video footage from two cameras at precisely the day and time we are investigating is damning."

"It would have been much smarter of our suspect to have wiped all of the tapes clean for that day and made it look like some technical malfunction."

"Maybe he, or she didn't have the time."

"Or the expertise, maybe our suspect isn't on the list of people with knowledge and access to the system."

"That would be unfortunate but we can't dismiss the idea. Good thinking Bartlett."

Bee strode back to his car a happy man he pulled his car around and stopped at the end of the school drive waiting for a gap in the traffic. He was eager to get back to the station but his police training kicked in as a couple of pedestrians sauntered along the pavement. He waited, smiled politely, and waved them across in front of his car. The girl acknowledged his gesture with a friendly smile. Bee jumped – it was Tina Dawson out walking with Greg Savage.

TWENTY-SIX

MEANWHILE MCTIERNEY HAD compiled a list of the tennis players who had played with Dawson in their last match on the night of his murder. He had 5 names, fortunately all the addresses were within 5 miles of Reigate. He knocked on the door of Michael Honeycutt, who took a few minutes to come to the door and didn't disguise his displeasure about being dragged away from a zoom meeting.

"Haven't you completed your enquiries yet officer?"

"No sir. Murder investigations aren't time limited. New evidence has come to light which I'd like to discuss with you. We could do that inside or down at the station." McTierney smiled broadly.

Honeycutt opened his mouth but didn't speak, then stepped back from the door and invited McTierney into his house.

McTierney took a seat in the kitchen and stared at the kettle. It took Honeycutt twenty seconds to catch on but shortly after he did, a second smile adorned McTierney's face. He looked around the kitchen again but Honeycutt intercepted his thoughts – "There's no biscuit barrel sergeant."

"Shame, back to work." He pulled out his notebook. "I understand that you played tennis with Russell Dawson on the evening of June 10th. Is that correct?"

"Yes it is." McTierney scribbled something in his notebook.

"What more can you tell me about that night?"

"Not much. It was a standard game, us against Dorking. I got to the club about 6pm, Russell was already there, so were Findlater and Spencer Lewis. There was a bit of chat, Spencer was pleased to be back in the team, but nothing memorable – just the normal. Then Graham and Barber arrived."

"How would you describe Dawson's mood that evening?"

"Fine, normal. He was always quite positive."

"Can you recall what he was wearing?"

"His tennis clothes."

McTierney blew out his cheeks. "Was he wearing a burgundy tennis jacket?"

Honeycutt frowned and McTierney pulled out a photo of the sweater.

"Yes, I think he did." Honeycutt nodded. "in truth we're all supposed to wear them for the matches, but I rarely do. It's supposed to make us feel more like a team, make us feel more professional." Honeycutt screwed up his nose. "But I think that's a load of old bollocks. Dawson saying that so he can sell a few more sweaters."

Honeycutt looked up to the heavens and mumbled 'sorry Russell.' Then turned back to McTierney, "either you can play or you can't."

"So all 6 of you have identical tops?"

"Yes we do, in fact both the A and B teams have them and a couple of the reserves, so I'd guess there's 15 or more knocking around the club."

"Interesting."

"That's very helpful Mr Honeycutt, that'll be all for now."

THE HONEYCUTT INTERVIEW set the pattern for the next two hours until McTierney arrived at a flat in Earlswood adjacent to the East Surrey hospital where James Barber lived. Where Honeycutt had been abrupt and gruff Barber was polite and genteel. There was no need for McTierney's subterfuge to squeeze a hot drink from the unsuspecting member of the public; Barber plied him with Earl Grey tea and bourbon biscuits. It wasn't often that McTierney's ears worked harder than his tongue, but Barber seldom had visitors to his flat and wasn't about to let this opportunity pass to showcase his grand, if petite luxury flat. McTierney received a full tour of the property with no room overlooked. They were about to visit the communal swimming pool when McTierney broke the conversation and took a seat in the lounge. Barber looked crest-fallen but answered all of McTierney's questions fully. He had a habit to over-elaborate but one such answer compensated for all the earlier meanderings.

"Oh yes, I had my club sweater there. They're a gorgeous burnt mulberry colour. Have you seen one? Russell had such divine taste. Anyway, that night he and I got our jumpers mixed up; he had mine on and deary me, I was wearing his. How we laughed when we realised."

McTierney left with a DNA sample tucked inside his case and his sanity intact. It was approaching noon and despite the avalanche of biscuits that had come his way, McTierney's stomach told him it needed further attention. He was driving close to the town centre and pulled into the Bell Street car park from where he would be able to pick up a freshly made baguette. As he drove around the car park looking for a space he spotted the big red Range Rover parked in a disabled space, the same car that had jumped the lights on the Croydon Road in front of him and Bee. But this morning McTierney had a few spare minutes and he put a call into the station.

The car wasn't listed as a disabled permit holder and the registered owner lived in Reigate – a Mr Gary Buckley. McTierney decided on a working lunch and selected a tuna baguette from the delicatessen opposite the car park. He plucked his mobile from his pocket and typed the address into google maps; the owner lived three streets away and didn't need to use the car park. He took a bite and walked up Cockshot Hill in search of the elusive Mr Buckley.

Buckley lived in a two-storey townhouse presenting an imposing gothic exterior with stone gargoyles. The house offered a large brass knocker which boomed into an empty hallway. McTierney squinted through the glass pane in the front door, the floor had black and white chequered tiles but all the connecting doors were closed. He took a couple of steps back and looked up at the upper stories; 4 large double pane windows stood like soulless eyes in the dull and lifeless front. McTierney was glad that Bee didn't live here. He was about to walk away, when a small middle-aged woman opened the door. Her brown hair was pulled back into a bun and she wore a neat floral dress and greeted McTierney with a timid smile. "Can I help you?"

"I'm looking for Mr Gary Buckley. Is he at home?"

"He's my husband, but no sorry he's not available. He's at work."

"Shame. I'm the police." McTierney presented his warrant card and she inspected it with sharp eyes.

"Could you tell your husband that I'd like to see his vehicle documents; that's his driving licence and insurance for his red Range Rover down at the station in town at some point in the next six days. Tell him to ask for Detective Sergeant McTierney." McTierney handed her a business card.

Mrs Buckley took the card nervously and placed it neatly on a cabinet that stood in their hallway.

"Right, I'll tell him, but I should warn you he's busy of late. He does a lot of work."

"What does he do?"

"He's a school-teacher."

McTierney bounced back down the hill towards the car park with a huge smile growing across his face until it morphed into a full-blown laugh. He skipped around the corner and into the car park, but crashed back down to earth, when he discovered that the Range Rover had gone.

'No matter your time will come,' mumbled McTierney as he unlocked his own car. He sat inside and searched for the address of Hammond's tennis club. He was about to punch the address into his sat nav when he changed his mind and replaced it with his home address. According to the on-line crime report folder, no one had checked Hammond's alibi for June 10th. He shook his head at the thought of Bee ranting about people doing the job properly. McTierney's run of good luck continued as Mrs Hammond opened the door; she was home alone.

"It's routine Mrs Hammond, nothing to worry about but I need to check a few details with you. Could you tell me where you were on the night of June 10th? It was a Thursday if that helps you."

Mrs Hammond thought for a moment and then burst into conversation.

"Oh yes, of course, the 10th, that's Sandra's birthday. We had a small get together at her house. Only a few of us officer, nothing for you to worry about, we weren't breaking the law, a few girls, a cake, and a bottle or two of pink prosecco. You know what it's like when it's a special occasion."

McTierney smiled. "I can imagine. I bet she loved it."

"Oh she did. She lives alone and hasn't been out much what with this covid and all that."

"Sounds delightful. She's lucky to have a friend like you."

Mrs Hammond blushed, "Oh go on. She's such a lovely lady, do anything for anyone."

"What was your son, Josh doing that night?"

"Heaven knows with that boy. He's rarely at home always down at the tennis club. But he did come to pick up his mum that evening, sometime around 10pm I think."

"Sure?"

"Yes, because when we got home, Steve, my husband, was watching the weather and that always follows on from the news doesn't it?"

"I believe it does. Thanks very much Mrs Hammond. Enjoy the rest of your day."

MCTIERNEY FOUND JOSH Hammond sitting in the

clubhouse at Redhill Tennis Club.

"Got a few minutes for a few questions. It's the police."

"Let me go and clear my mind first and I'll be back to talk in a mo."

McTierney watched Hammond walk to the washrooms with an urbane swagger. It was rare for him to agree with Inspector Bee, but here he fell into line.

"Ready now?"

"Uh huh."

"Washed your hands properly?"

A hatred burned in Hammond's eyes but he ignored the jib. The two men walked to a corner table in the club house and took positions on opposite sides.

"I'd like to re-visit the interview you gave to Inspector Bee on Thursday June 24th."

"I've already said all I've got to say."

"Not to me."

Hammond shrugged his shoulders.

"You told Inspector Bee that on the night of June 10th, you were at home with mummy, but when I spoke to her today she told me that she was out at a birthday celebration and didn't see you until 10 o'clock. So where were you?"

"I don't recall."

"Try harder."

"Honestly I don't remember. I don't keep a diary."

"A tennis coach with plenty of appointments and you don't use a diary. Maybe a phone diary?"

Hammond stared back.

"Perhaps a visit to the station will jog your memory. Come on let's go."

"I can't go now I've got a lesson in 15 minutes."

"Your choice. Either you give me a credible explanation for that night, or your next lesson will be in the station. How's that going to help you build up a new clientele?"

Hammond rubbed his hands together as he contemplated the options. The scales tipped in favour of talking. He took a long breath. "I slipped back to the Priory clubhouse. I waited until everyone had gone and let myself in, I'd kept my key. I sat down at the computer terminal and went through the list of club members and their contact details."

McTierney raised his eyes. "Go on."

"I was only after the people I used to coach; I get a bonus for any new member I can bring in."

McTierney tilted his head in judgement.

"Come on, they were my clients in the first place. I'd done all the work developing them; it's me they have a relationship with, not the club."

"Whatever I'm not interested in that."

"You wouldn't say a word if it was some stockbroker switching companies and taking his clients."

"I'm not saying anything now."

Hammond grunted.

"But what I am interested in is your presence at the Priory clubhouse, potentially at the same time as the body of a murder victim turns up. So give me the timings of your visit."

Hammond lent back in his chair and considered his answer. "I'd say I entered the clubhouse about 9:30pm – it wasn't quite dark, but I couldn't wait much longer. I knew I had to pick up mum."

McTierney began scribbling. "And when did you leave?"

"About 15 minutes later."

McTierney looked directly at him for confirmation.

"All I had to do was copy a file. It didn't take long. I knew the password from when I worked at the club."

"Did you see anyone else?"

"Not a soul, and I was looking."

McTierney nodded. "Was Russell Dawson's red car in the car park?"

"No the car park was empty."

"Good. Thank you. That's useful."

McTierney stood up and turned towards the door, stopped, and slowly turned around. "One final question. Do you know Gary Buckley?"

Hammond furrowed his brow, like a contestant on 'Mastermind' trying to drag the correct answer from the back of his mind. "No I can't say I do."

McTierney's shoulders slumped. "No problem."

"But I do teach a Lily Buckley, or at least I used to. She has lessons at the Priory club on Saturday mornings. Good kid too. I must steal her away to Redhill."

McTierney's eyes popped.

As he searched through his rucksack to make another note in his workbook, an eager tennis player walked over to Hammond. "Afternoon teacher, are you ready? I've come to school."

McTierney stopped to make another note.

MCTIERNEY WAS LURKING around the office hoping to accidentally bump into Bartlett; he had watched three-quarters of the day staff leave and was close to admitting defeat when she appeared out of nowhere. "Where have you been today?"

"Checking the phone records of our friend Savage and waiting around for our SOCO primadonnas to turn up and dust an office at the school."

"Good lead?"

"Bee seems to think so. It's a school teacher and a potential match for the murder weapon."

"Cool." McTierney paused for a moment then reverted to his original script.

"Can I see you tonight? How about you come over for dinner. I'll cook. The old goat is going to be out."

Bartlett allowed her head to jiggle left and right as she weighed up the offer. "Ruth has encouraged me to watch the Radacanu game, so yes you can feed me but only if I can watch the tennis."

"Of course. I presume she won last night."

"She did, she beat somebody called Diatchenko in the first round 7-6, 6-0."

"Are you sure she's English? Dodgy name and winning at Wimbledon."

Bartlett glared at him, "I'm serious. You have to let me watch it. No asking dumb questions or making smart remarks through it, hoping I'll get bored and turn it off."

"You won't know I'm there. I'll sit silently by your side throughout the match." McTierney pulled an imaginary zip across his mouth.

Bartlett crossed her arms in the style of a school mistress and stared at him. "You'd better."

"Promise. And I never break a promise."

"Okay. The game should be on around 8pm, it depends

a bit on how quickly the early game finishes, so let's have dinner early. What are you cooking?"

"My speciality; toad in the hole." A huge grin spread across McTierney's face. It didn't reach Bartlett's.

"I'm sure your toad is majestic, but can you make pasta instead? Perhaps a carbonara?"

"Sure," said McTierney, the smile disappearing fast.

"Cool, I'll see you sharp at 7pm." She glanced up and down the corridor and pecked him on the cheek. "That should give you enough time to google the recipe and pop into Sainsbury's on your way home."

JESS ARRIVED AT the house and tapped lightly on the door. Ron rushed to it, pulled it open and shouted, 'come in', before dashing back to the kitchen where he was maniacally stirring a bowl trying to revive a sauce. Jess stepped delicately into the kitchen like a cat tiptoeing past a sleeping dog. "Are you on your own?"

"Yes, me and my new best friend Nigella."

"Nigella?"

Ron nodded towards an open cookbook lying next to the hob already splattered with cream. Jess laughed, skipped over to his side, and kissed him gently on the cheek. Ron turned his head to make it a full-blown smacker. Jess pulled away after a few seconds; "easy Tiger, you'll make Nigella jealous." Ron frowned.

"More to the point you might burn my dinner. Keep stirring. That way I'll know where your hands are!"

Ron smiled. "I hope you appreciate the effort I'm going

through to make dinner for you."

"I do, and now that you've invested in a whole book of recipes, I recognise that it's incumbent on me to ensure you get good value for your money. I expect you to cook a meal for me every week."

Ron hesitated, caught between the delight of more time with Jess and the dilemma of that time being in the kitchen.

"Not only that, but a new recipe each week."

Ron opened his mouth to protest, but instead smiled back at her.

"Would I be correct in thinking this is the first cookbook you've ever owned?"

"You would."

"Excellent, if nothing else I'm making you more eligible by the minute. When you finally trick some naïve country girl into marrying you, she'll be grateful for all my hard work."

"What if that person is you?"

"Then I'll pat myself on the back as I walk down the aisle."

Ron grinned back at her.

"But don't think you get me this easily. No way! It'll take more than a few dozen Italian meals."

"I'm on the case."

"While you're cooking, can I do anything?"

"You could lay the table."

Jess wandered off for a minute but returned holding the photo of the little baby in front of the church in the silver frame.

"Do you know who's in this photo?"

"No, not a clue. Probably Sherlock Holmes as a toddler.

Hey, did I tell you that he has a bat cave?"

"No." Jess gawped at Ron and popped the frame down on the island.

"Yes, he's got a study all kitted out with detective memorabilia. It's where he does his thinking. It's got all sorts of fancy stuff and a top of the range executive chair. I'm convinced he sits in there and pretends he's bloody Batman!"

Jess collapsed in laughter and Ron's sauce burnt in the pan.

ONCE DINNER HAD been resuscitated and consumed they settled down to watch the tennis on Bee's comfy deep blue cotton sofa. Emma Raducanu was pitched against the Czech player Marketa Vondrousova.

"So does your friend think this Raducanu girl will win?"

"Maybe, probably not this year, because she was a wild card entry, but perhaps soon."

"It'll make a change to have a decent British woman player."

"Haven't you heard of Konta? Jeez you're so ignorant if it's not football!"

Ron sat quietly for a moment and contented himself with breathing in the scent of Jess's hair, but as the match started he was eager to speak again. Jess gave him a stern look which delayed the inevitable for a few minutes as Raducanu took an early lead.

"This Vondrousova isn't up to much, but then what do you expect from the Czechs?"

Jess stared at him. "Seriously? Is that your comment on the match?"

Ron offered a weak smile as his defence.

"I think Vondrousova is seeded in the top ten here, and then of course there's Pliskova who I'm sure was a world number 1 ranked player, plus Kvitova who I'm convinced has won Wimbledon at least once."

Ron offered a wan smile.

"And then of course there's Martina Navratilova, multiple winner at Wimbledon and from your generation."

Ron squirmed in his seat and then said, "I thought you wanted to sit quietly and watch the match."

Jess swung out her left arm and walloped his shoulder, before falling back into his arms and cuddling up for the rest of the match. Raducanu secured a comfortable two sets victory and harmony was restored to the lounge.

The clock was ticking round towards 10pm when Scott opened the back door and stomped into his kitchen. He picked up the silver photo frame from the island and placed in carefully back into position on the side. His arrival had kicked off a scramble in the lounge where Ron and Jess were busy re-arranging the sofa. Aware of the commotion Scott coughed in the kitchen before slowly stepping into the lounge.

"Good evening all, how are we?"

"Yes fine."

"Good evening, inspector."

"You don't need to be so formal in my lounge, Bartlett, sorry Jess." Said Scott trying to look all around his lounge at everything except the two people he was addressing. "Ron could I see you for a minute in the kitchen, please."

Scott turned back and disappeared while Ron and Jess exchanged looks of foreboding.

"What's up Scott?"

"I'm sorry to say this and it's my fault I should have said this when you moved in, but I don't want you entertaining people while you're staying here."

"What?"

Scott sighed heavily. "I don't want Jess staying the night here with you."

"I thought you told me to make myself at home."

"I did, and I want you to be comfortable here."

"This is what makes me comfortable."

"I'm sorry I'm afraid that's too much."

Ron walked across the kitchen with his head down, reached the sink and turned back to face Scott who had himself moved across the room.

"I'm giving up a lot here to support the chief, I thought I made that clear to you. But there are some things I can't accept."

Ron shook his head then went for the jugular. "You wouldn't be so uptight if you were getting some."

Scott took a step back. "There's no need to take that approach."

"But it's true."

"I'm not going to respond to that."

"We can't all live like Trappist monks. Life goes on, covid or not."

"This has got nothing to do with covid."

Ron raised his head and stared directly at Scott.

"I told you on Saturday I like to have my own space and that it was difficult for me to have you here, but that I would try because I appreciate things are difficult for you too."

"They are. It's no bloody picnic living out of a suitcase

day after day."

"No, I'm sure it's not. But nonetheless there are some things I can't accept."

JESS TIPTOED INTO the kitchen her eyes darting between the two men.

"It's okay Ron, I'll go, I don't want to make trouble."

Scott nodded towards her and walked back into the lounge closing the door behind him and leaving Jess and Ron together.

Jess wrapped an arm around Ron "Don't worry, it wouldn't feel right with the inspector next door."

Ron nodded. "Boring old goat that he is."

"I'll speak to my aunt and you can come over to her place on Saturday."

Ron pulled her close and kissed her. "That would be fabulous."

Jess kissed him back, blew softly in his ear, "Thanks for a great night. Saturday will be even better."

Ron's grin stretched from ear to ear.

TWENTY-SEVEN

"THANKS!"

"I'm sorry, but I had to speak."

"Did you? Most of the time you don't say anything."

"This was different."

"Really? Because I was enjoying myself and you can't stand to have anyone enjoy themselves."

"That's not fair at all. I'm always pleased to see the world happy."

This exchange was taking place across the island in Scott's kitchen.

"Everyone except me!" yelled Ron leaning across the unit. "You're not my mum you know!"

Scott held up his right hand and retreated towards the lounge but stopped at the door for one more shot. "I've given up a lot to allow you to stay here and remain on this investigation. More than you'll ever know. Can we file this under poor timing?"

Ron dropped his shoulders and sighed heavily. "I'm sorry, I didn't mean to sound off so much. But I really like Jess. I want to spend as much time with her as I can."

"I noticed." Scott bowed his head and made to walk off into the lounge but turned back. "I know you hate talking shop and it's no substitute for what you were planning, but we've had some interesting developments today on the Dawson case. I'd be grateful if you'd give me five minutes to update you and then I'd welcome your thoughts."

Ron looked around the kitchen, the debris of his evening meal needed attention. He blew out his cheeks. "Sure, why not."

"Great. You sort out this mess and I'll fix us a couple of scotches."

Ron slumped onto the sofa where three hours earlier he'd been looking forward to a night of hot passion and picked up the substitute – a generous glass of whisky. "Yippeedy-do. Come on then let's hear it."

Scott began to relay his adventure at the King's School and was building to a crescendo when Ron interrupted.

"Who did you say?"

"Gary Buckley. He's the head of the sixth form there and on my list of six staff members with knowledge of the CCTV system to be interviewed."

"No way. I was chasing a Gary Buckley today. His wife said he was a teacher but I didn't ask about the school."

Scott sent a disappointed look across the sofa, but soon regretted it.

"I know, I know, you would've asked the extra question. But it didn't seem crucial at the time."

"But now."

"Buckley goes to the top of the list."

The tempo of the conversation accelerated as the two detectives shared details of how Gary Buckley had been central to their respective days.

"We have to interview Mr. Buckley tomorrow and get a search warrant for his house."

"Busy day on the horizon."

Scott got up from his seat and headed for the door, then stopped.

"I nearly forgot. Guess who I saw walking together through the town, looking delighted to be in each other's company?"

"Harry Kane and Lily James"

"What?"

Ron shrugged his shoulders, "I don't know. I hardly know anyone in this town."

"Two people connected to the case."

Ron rubbed his chin while he thought, "No still don't know. Phil Church and his number two."

Bee scowled back. "No, Tina Dawson and Greg Savage."

"That's an interesting couple. I wonder how they know each other?"

"We'll ask that question tomorrow."

THE DAWSON CASE had been sucking Bee dry until he felt he'd become a camel, now he was refreshed, revved up and ready to go. He stood impatiently outside the chief's door at 7:45am on Friday morning with his warrant request neatly typed in his hand.

It was approaching 9 o'clock before he was joined in the ops room by McTierney and Bartlett.

"Come on you two, we have an important day ahead of us. I expected better of you."

Bartlett and McTierney exchanged guilty glances but said nothing. Russell Dawson's photo had previously sat alone in the centre of the investigation pictogram on the board of the ops room. For several days no one had dared look at it. But now it had been joined by 9 other faces, one of them his wife and in no time he'd acquired a gang. Dawson was the leader of the pack, albeit a pack of blood-thirsty wolves. Bee had been busy; where he had indulged McTierney's cheeky positioning of a Euro 20 football wallchart following the progress of the England team in the ops room, now that had gone and an ordnance survey map of the town had replaced it. On the map Bee had marked all the key incidents, and the home addresses of the gang members. The geography of the case was tight. McTierney stopped to admire Bee's handiwork but the inspector was eager to press on.

"The headmaster has provided me with a list of the names and addresses of the people he believes to have knowledge of the CCTV system at the school. It's too much of a co-incidence for the video footage from the security cameras to disappear on the night when we believe our victim met a school teacher. I've added to this list the head of the sixth form Buckley, so these become our priority, and Buckley is number one. In addition we should re-interview Savage and Tina Dawson to understand how come they are now friends when there is every reason for them to dislike one another. We should check their phone records going back before the murder to ascertain if there was any contact between them."

"So that's what, three each?" asked McTierney.

"Your maths is correct, but not your assumption. I want you and me to visit Buckley. Bartlett you start with the other teachers and we'll call you when we've done and re-assess. I'm expecting the court will approve the search warrant soon so we could all be back at Buckley's house this afternoon."

Bee handed out a sheet of paper to each of them, Bartlett took hers without a word, nodded at McTierney and left the room.

McTierney offered to drive since he knew the exact location of the Buckley house. Despite a ray of bright sunshine shooting across the front façade the Buckley house appeared as cold as it had yesterday. The knocker boomed into the empty hallway to announce the arrival of the police.

"I enjoy this part of the game," said McTierney, "when the noose is beginning to tighten and you start to see the fear in the eyes of the villain as they realise you're onto them."

Bee lowered his gaze and peered at McTierney over his glasses. "It's not a game."

"Oh it is. You have to separate yourself from the reality of these crimes. If you don't you'll go crazy. Imagine if you took all this crap home with you every night."

Bee opened his mouth to reply but was distracted by a heavy footstep approaching the door. It was heaved opened by a tall thick set man, with short black hair surrounding a high forehead but low dark eyebrows sheltering a pair of green eyes. He boasted two days of stubble. Both Bee and McTierney took a step back, before Bee recovered himself and asked, "Mr Gary Buckley?"

"What of it?"

"We're the police, I'm Detective Inspector Bee and this is Detective Sergeant McTierney, we'd like to ask you some questions." Bee fumbled with his badge and presented it to Buckley. Buckley took it rolled it around in his hand, held it up in the air as if checking the authenticity, then handed it back.

"So you are. I'm busy. Go away." He stepped back and moved to close the door, but Bee lent forward to block it.

"I'm sorry sir, it's important that we speak to you. Could you grant us a few minutes?"

"No sod off." Buckley pushed back against the door.

"If you refuse, you will be providing us with grounds for an arrest."

The pushing match continued.

"Sir, if you grant us a few minutes you could save yourself a lot of time in the long run."

Buckley relented and stepped back into his house allowing the door to open and Bee to stumble into the hallway. Bee stood up, dressed himself down and drilled his eyes into Buckley.

"I think we'll conduct the interview down at the station."

Buckley stepped forward into the personal space of Bee, drew himself up to his full height. Still holding eye contact he flexed his fingers and rolled them into a fist. He moved his line of sight around Bee as if analysing him for a weak spot, then returned to the stare and said coldly, "As you like inspector."

BEE STATIONED BUCKLEY in interview room 2 and left him to stew for forty minutes on the pretence of fetching a cup of coffee. He popped into his office and retrieved an envelope passed it to McTierney with a nod. Then he went in search of Carol Bishop and extracted her from a zoom meeting. He briefed her quickly and she nodded her understanding. Buckley had accepted the offer of a solicitor and Bee expected a protracted and difficult interview. "He's going to play hardball, refuse to answer, no comment that sort of stuff. I need you to watch his every move, look for any twitch of insecurity or fear."

Bishop smiled "I can do that."

"For the guilty the seconds go by like hours and they squirm, so we'll give him plenty of time to get uncomfortable."

"Sounds like you're enjoying this inspector."

"Not at all, it's my job."

They entered the interview room and Bee delivered the cup of coffee. "Your solicitor is taking his time."

"He's a busy man," Buckley replied in a measured tone, "but you can start without him if you wish."

Bee and Bishop exchanged puzzled looks. "I've nothing to hide. George is a formality to keep you on your toes inspector."

"In that case, I assume you'll be willing to allow us to take your fingerprints and DNA – merely procedure but it will allow us to rule you out once we can confirm your prints don't match those we are seeking."

Buckley grunted his acceptance.

Ten minutes later Bee and Bishop re-took their seats opposite Buckley, who's mood had darkened. "There's a lot of abuse of procedure by the police." Buckley continued with his steady rhythm.

"Thank you Mr Buckley. We'll ask the questions from here."

"Am I allowed to know why I'm being questioned? I'm sure my solicitor would expect that if he were present."

"It's in connection with the murder of Russell Dawson,

the tennis coach at the Reigate club on Thursday June 10th."

THE INTERVIEW BEGAN and Bee set the tape player running. "Are you happy with us calling you Mr Buckley, or would you prefer Gary?

"Whatever."

Bee continued speaking directly into the microphone "You do not have to say anything. But it may harm your defence if you do not mention when questioned something which you later rely on in court. Anything you do say may be given in evidence. Is that clear?"

Buckley produced one of his I'm smarter than you smiles, then leaned forward imitating Bee and said into the microphone "I'm perfectly happy to answer every one of your questions." His eyes then added the words you ignorant little man.

Bee passed the baton of interrogation to Bishop for the routine stuff, Buckley's address, his dates of employment at the school, his job performance, knowledge of Dawson, school policy towards to drugs.

Buckley answered the first few questions about names and addresses and occupational records with disdain, but with an underlying vigilance, and then got bored and started batting away questions with a wave of his hand as if swatting a fly.

Bee purses his lips like they have never been pursued before and a silence engulfed the room. He resumed the questioning and immediately the tone changed, Buckley slowed down and became more circumspect.

"Could you tell us where you were on the night of

Thursday June 10th?"

"May I check my phone; it'll show my appointments."

Bee nodded.

Buckley flicked a phone from his jacket pocket and tapped on the screen for a few seconds. "My phone isn't showing a meeting, so I'd guess I was either working late at the school; it's exam time you know inspector, or perhaps I was at home."

"Exams? I thought the government had withdrawn the requirement for pupils to sit exams."

Buckley shook his head and lent forward to explain the situation to the inspector. "That's the headline that you'll see in the press, but the reality is quite different. The exams regulator has proposed that grades for this year will be determined by teachers, that's the easy part. The difficult part is that the school is expected to justify these grades through a series of measures, test papers, course work, ongoing individual assessments that sort of thing. The exam board requires reassurance of the quality of our recommendations. For a school of our standing it's paramount that we are seen to excel, and to excel without question. As head of the sixth form the responsibility for this process rests with me. It's a considerable personal investment." Buckley lent back in his chair with a self-satisfying smile.

Bee allowed the moment to pass, and Buckley picked up his coffee. As he took a sip, Bee threw his first dart at him.

"When did you replace the knife in Emma Garnett's block?"

Buckley's facial muscles didn't flicker as he lingered over his coffee, then replaced the cup on the table. "I don't know what you mean."

Bee let the answer hang, but Buckley wasn't biting.

"I mean, that a knife was taken from Emma Garnett's block and used to kill Russell Dawson and latterly replaced with a replica, but she noticed that it was new, and not worn like the others." Bee paused. "Your office at the school is close to her kitchen classroom; you would have the perfect opportunity to take it and then replace it."

"Myself, and at least a thousand other people who enter the school on a daily basis."

"So you've never touched it?"

"I think you've seen too many Mel Gibson films, inspector."

Bee pursed his lips, "do you ever use drugs Mr Buckley?"

"Frequently, inspector."

Bee turned his head.

"I drink more coffee than my doctor recommends, I'm partial to a glass of Malbec and I succumb to the occasional cigar."

Bee scowled across the table.

"Do you mean illegal drugs? You should be more precise inspector. No I don't use them."

Bee lent back in his chair and pondered his next question but before he could ask it a smartly dressed man in a dark suit knocked on the door and entered the room, a police constable was trailing in his wake.

"George Rowe, inspector, I'm here to look after my client, Mr Buckley. I trust you haven't taken advantage of my absence and begun without me."

"Mr Buckley indicated a willingness to talk to speed the process along."

Rowe frowned but Buckley waved it away, "The inspector was enjoying a little fun at my expense; accusing me of murder and drug abuse all in the space of two minutes."

Rowe took a seat next to Buckley and placed a briefcase on the table, flipped it open and removed a notebook and stylish silver pen. He looked across the desk and addressed Bee. "Such strong accusations inspector, I trust you have significant evidence to support these, a witness statement, a blood-stained item of clothing, a smoking gun perhaps?"

Bee winced and snatched a look at the large white clock up on the wall.

Rowe sensed his moment, "Can you share these with us?"

"There is no evidence of the type you're describing; these are exploratory discussions."

"Exploratory? Accusations of murder sound a long way from a preliminary chat. It seems to me that everything you have is superficial. My client has entertained your whim for long enough. I demand his release. You have no witnesses, no physical evidence, only a desperate theory from an inept police force."

Rowe stood up ready to leave and crossed his arms over his chest, shaking his head at everything going on around him. Buckley stopped at the door, and turned back to smile at the inspector, "Now I think of it, I was at the school on the night you asked about; – it was submissions week. Everything had to be with the exam board so I was burning the midnight oil. Goodbye inspector."

Bee waved him out of the door and hoped that he'd given McTierney enough time.

TWENTY-EIGHT

"WHAT DID YOU find?"

Bee, McTierney, and Bartlett were crowded around the table in the ops room; a hastily grabbed set of sandwiches spread across the table in front of them.

"Not a lot, I'm afraid." McTierney stopped to stuff an egg and bacon sandwich in his mouth.

Bee looked dismayed. "Nothing at all?"

McTierney chewed on, raised his hand to cover his mouth, but his eyes told the inspector that the news would not be good. Bee sighed heavily.

"We searched all the rooms; nothing to suggest he's a killer or even a drug dealer. Perhaps the highlight was a single blood stain in the kitchen near the back door. Forensics are analysing it but unless it came from Dawson, it's not going to take us anywhere."

"I guess he's had long enough to clean up any mess, burn any contaminated clothing."

"Without doubt."

Bee shook his head, "I think we'll file that under disappointing."

McTierney raised his hand and swallowed the last piece of bread. "Not a complete disaster though; Buckley has a study – not unlike yours as it happens."

Bee dismissed the anecdote with a wave of his hand, "and..."

"It contained a large wooden desk with two locked compartments."

"Couldn't you get it opened?"

"We did ask Mrs Buckley, but she claimed not to have the key, or even to go into her husband's study." McTierney shrugged his shoulders. "I tend to believe her. It didn't appear to have a woman's touch."

"Ha, as if you'd be able to tell," interjected Bartlett.

McTierney shot her a cold look and refocused on Bee. "Even if we get the desk open I don't think it's going to tell us much, although we didn't find a lap top that belonged to Buckley, so the chances are it's in that drawer."

An invisible cloud of discontent hung over the trio.

McTierney added to the fog "I developed the impression that there was a lot about her husband that Mrs Buckley didn't know or didn't want to know. Too much time has passed between the killing and now. If Buckley had any compromising evidence to dispose of, he's had plenty of time."

"That's undeniable."

"I took advantage of the occasion to ask Mrs Buckley if her husband was at home on the evening of the 10th. She suggested he'd worked late at the school that week but did come home. Although I would expect her to say whatever she thought would help her husband."

"No surprise there."

"But I did establish that their daughter plays tennis at the Reigate club and that she knew Dawson and that Buckley himself used to take his daughter there for lessons. So he would most likely have known Dawson."

Bee nodded. "Yeah he admitted as much to us here." Bee rubbed his left hand across his forehead as if trying to inspire a genie to appear from his thoughts. Then dropped his hand to the table. "The little bit of video footage we have from the school shows Buckley's car parked in the centre of the staff car park. Almost as if he's playing to the cameras. But of course there's no footage of him parking the car and his home is easily within walking distance so the presence of his car means nothing."

Bartlett joined the debate "Since he knows the locations of the other school cameras, it would be child's play for him to slip out unseen and meet Dawson at 10pm."

"Easily," added the inspector, "but perhaps something happened which was unplanned and that caused Buckley to need to remove the CCTV footage of that later event"

"Like Dawson parking his car in the wrong place?" added Bartlett.

"Exactly, that could be it."

"Or Buckley carrying Dawson's dead body to his car," offered McTierney.

"Yes that too. I fear the list is too long to contemplate," Bee hesitated, "it seems easy to imagine a scenario which implicates Buckley, but we are struggling to find a compelling motive."

Bee's comment brought the debate to a halt. The three detectives exchanged empty expressions. Bee took a slow drink of sparkling water and turned his attention to Bartlett. "How did you get on with the other teachers?"

Bartlett reached into her bag and pulled out her yellow notebook, she flicked over a few pages, found the one she wanted and made herself comfortable in her seat.

"Pinkerton gave us six names of school staff with the potential to have access to the security system, interestingly Buckley wasn't on the list. But that doesn't necessarily rule him out."

"Quite. But let's leave Buckley for a few minutes and see who else pops up."

Bartlett bowed her head and read from her book. "So six names; in the order that I spoke to them we have; number one Will Childs. He's the head porter at the school, been there for 35 years, man and boy, now nearing retirement, he lives alone so has no alibi for the 10th. But I'd be amazed if he could kill anyone." Bartlett paused, and Bee waved her on.

"Number two Nigel Bailey, he's one of Childs' deputies, robust and muscular, some might say fit. He matches the general description, no obvious connection with Dawson or the tennis club. He says he was at home with his wife on the 10th, which as yet I haven't checked.

"Fit is he?" asked McTierney.

"Ooh yes," said Bartlett "with a tight t-shirt over bulging muscles."

"Next," said Bee.

"Number three is Sarah Williams, another of the deputy porters, not been at the school for long. New to the area having moved here from Southampton, no obvious connection with Dawson or the tennis club. She lives alone, so doesn't have an alibi for the evening in question, but I can't see it being her."

Bee waved his hand in the air.

"Number four is Gerard Hannay; he's a teacher at the school, probably an English teacher, there's a delicacy to his movement, and he chooses his words carefully but still struggles with a slight stammer. I can imagine him being taunted by the kids, but I can't see him as a killer. Although as he too lives alone and doesn't have an alibi for the 10th."

There was another wave from Bee.

"Number five Anton Jackson, a large West Indian with an infectious laugh. He provides technical maintenance to the school for anything beyond the range of the porters. So he set up the system in the first place and holds a contract for the upkeep. He lives in Guildford and claims he hasn't been to the school since May and that's supported by their visitor log. It won't be him."

"Are you saving the best to last?"

"Perhaps, lastly is number six Spencer Lewis; the senior deputy to Pinkerton, so he knows the school inside-out."

McTierney raised his hand, "do I know this guy?"

"Maybe, you've heard his name before; he played with Dawson in the tennis team on the night of the murder, so he has opportunity, and he's tall so he fits the general description."

"A tennis playing school teacher, that's a step forward," said McTierney.

"And his wife was away on the night in question so he doesn't have an alibi for the 10th after 9pm when he says he left the tennis club."

"What's your feel with him?" asked Bee.

"He was straight, perhaps too straight. Didn't strike me as a murderer but I wouldn't rule him out. The interview was strange a bit like a tennis match with question and rebuff whizzing across the table. He was ready to smash every question back at me and go for a winner." Bartlett emphasised the point with as swoosh of her arm across the table.

Bee frowned, "You met him in person then?"

"Yes he lives in central Reigate, up on the hill with the posh houses."

"He's thriving on a teacher's salary."

"He said his wife has a city job, and interestingly she has the same car as Dawson."

"So he'd have no difficulty driving Dawson's Nissan."

"No, but all modern cars are easy to drive these days."

"I guess so, but interesting all the same." Bee had become a nodding dog.

"Right do some digging on his past, check his phone records for the tenth, nose about in his bank account, see what you can find."

Bartlett jotted a note in her book.

"Oh and do the same for Buckley while you're at it and check each of their transactions for that day, let's see if we can place one of them somewhere near Dawson on that evening."

"Where do we go from here?" asked McTierney.

"I'm going to ask the chief to fund some surveillance. Buckley and now maybe Lewis are interesting prospects; now we've rattled their cages a bit let's see how they behave."

Bartlett and McTierney nodded their approval.

"Then I'm going to drop in on Savage and ask him about his new best friend."

"GOOD AFTERNOON MR Savage, I'd like to check a couple of points from the interview you gave my colleague, Detective McTierney on the 23rd of June. I'm Detective Inspector

Scott Bee."

"Cock it up did he?" Savage didn't lift his head from the pinball machine he was working on.

"Not at all."

"No? He seemed more interested in scrounging a cup of tea and a free game of pinball than anything else."

"I'm sure he was trying to put you at ease."

"And why wouldn't I be at ease?"

"Most people tense up when they meet a police officer."

Savage pulled his head out of the table and looked Bee up and down. "Nothing scary about you is there?"

"Not if you've nothing to hide." Bee held his gaze and Savage stared back.

"Nothing here to keep you long inspector."

"Good. Now let's start with Spencer Lewis, do you know him?"

"I know a Spencer Lewis; tall bloke from the tennis club, thinks he's a bit special. Is that the one?"

"It is. How well do you know him?"

"A bit, I know his face, he'll know mine. Don't like him. That's about it."

Bee tutted and looked around the unit and counted 15 pinball machines. "You've got a lot of machines here. That must be a lot of working capital for your business."

"I get by."

Bee wandered over to the Indiana Jones machine which stood closest to the door and ran his hand along the glass cover, "Where do these come from?"

"All over really." Savage pointed to a racing car design table in the corner, "that came from Leeds, this one from Croydon, the Batman one over there came from Holland."

"An international businessman."

"Something like that."

"But able to take yesterday afternoon off and spend time with Tina Dawson."

Savage screwed his face up.

"I saw the pair of you walking by the King's School. What were you doing?"

"You've answered your own question; we were out walking."

"How did you get to know Mrs Dawson?"

"I meet her at the tennis club; she's alright. Easier to get along with than that stiff of her husband."

"What is the nature of your relationship with Mrs Dawson?"

"Ha! Are you asking me if I'm sleeping with Dawson's widow ten minutes after he's died?"

"No, you can answer the question however you see fit."

"Well I'm not. You police have no morality."

"It's a luxury we can't afford when investigating a murder. Now there's one important element Sergeant McTierney did forget; would you accompany down to the station, so we can take your fingerprints and eliminate you from our investigation."

"If it gets you off the premises."

AS BEE RETURNED from escorting Savage off the premises he found Bartlett waiting in the corridor outside his office.

"I seem to have adopted the role of your secretary this afternoon."

"How so?"

"People keep giving me messages for you."

"Sorry about that, Dawn's off this week, what have you got?"

"In the order that you'll appreciate them. The chief says that your surveillance programme will be operational from 9pm tonight."

"That's excellent."

"I discovered that Buckley's mobile was turned off from 9pm on Thursday June 10th, through to 7am the next morning, but whenever it was on, it shows him, or at least the phone to be in Reigate."

"Damn. It's incriminating but it's not evidence we can use. But good work."

"Finally Sergeant McTierney asked me to remind you to meet him in The Bell pub tonight for a feast of beer and football."

"Oh joy, an evening with the laughing policeman. I don't know if I can stand that, but thanks for the message."

TWENTY-NINE

BEE SLIPPED BACK to his office and immersed himself in paperwork for the next two hours. He didn't venture out to the coffee machine until he was certain everyone would have disappeared from the main floor. He took his plastic cup back to his office and made a call to both surveillance teams to ensure that they were in place and understood the importance of this particular operation. As the clock ticked round towards 8pm he couldn't think of any reason to remain in the office, but rather than go straight home he stopped at the fish and chip shop by the leisure centre in Redhill, but even this dalliance only bought him fifteen minutes. The sun was approaching the horizon as Bee arrived at the turning for his house; he took a deep breath and raced down the drive. McTierney was nowhere to be seen. He breathed out with relief; he could look forward to a peaceful evening at least until the pub closed.

SCOTT COULD HEAR Ron approaching, the cacophony grew and it sounded to him that Ron was talking to someone outside the door. He opened it and found Ron standing there with two other men.

"Do you know what time it is?" Scott growled at Ron.

Ron wavered and then looked past Scott at the barometer which hung on the wall beside the door. He squinted and then said, "a quarter past cloudy!" The three drunks burst into laughter.

Scott stood alone and stony-faced.

Ron recovered himself and slapped Scott on the shoulder, "How are you doing? I brought a couple of friends back from the pub for a bit of extra time. This is Stuart and behind him is Mick."

Ron turned back to face his new friends; "Guys, this is my landlord, Scott, he's a top bloke. Come in grab a seat and I'll get you a beer."

Ron turned back to Scott, "What happened to you then? Did Jess give you the message that I was going to watch the football in the pub? You missed a great game; the Italians sneaked passed the Spanish on penalties. But boy if the Spanish had a striker they'd have killed them."

Scott followed Ron into the kitchen, he closed the door behind him and watched Ron's new friends make their way into the lounge. He tapped Ron on the shoulder.

"What do you think you're doing?"

"Getting a beer from the fridge, do you want one?"

"No I don't." Scott strode across the kitchen and slammed the fridge door.

"I mean, what do you think you're doing bringing people back to my house?"

"Oh, those guys, you'll love 'em. Stuart's a salesman; he's got dozens of stories, bit blue some of them, but he's a hoot."

"I don't care what he does. I don't want him here in my house."

Ron stared back at Scott as if had spoken Chinese.

"Did you hear me? Get them out. You've no right to invite Tom, Dick, and Stuart here for a party. This is my home, not a hotel for your convenience."

Ron's brain took a few seconds to comprehend the message, then in a quieter tone he replied, "Oh right, yes sure. I thought you'd be happy with a bit of company. You never…" He stopped mid-sentence and returned to the lounge to make an excuse to his new friends.

Once he'd shown the others out, Ron returned to the kitchen where Scott was standing by the sink looking aggrieved. Ron threw him a glance and followed it with a quick, "Sorry, I didn't think it'd be a big thing."

"But it is, so please don't invite people here again."

Ron mumbled, "No. Sure."

"But since we're talking, there's a couple of other things I want to share with you."

Ron pulled out a chair and sat down at the table.

"Do you remember me asking you to put the bins out today for the refuse collection?"

Ron raised his hand, opened his mouth, and closed it again before saying, "yes, sorry, forgot."

Scott stepped aside from the sink and pointed at a mug and cereal dish loitering in the bowl, "and it would be nice if you did the washing up once in a while."

"Sorry."

"Or at least drop them in the dishwasher," Scott pulled the door open, "it's sitting next to the damn sink."

"Yeah, right, will do."

"These things aren't difficult, – a three-year-old could do them!"

Ron smiled, "there's never a three-year-old around when you need one."

Scott slammed his hand down on the kitchen table "It's not fucking funny you know!"

Ron hung his head and a silence developed between the two men; the tick of the kitchen clock became audible.

"I'm sorry to say this but I don't know if I can continue this."

Ron looked up.

"We're so different, it feels like it's too difficult. The way you live, the way you work. Everything."

"What's wrong with the way I work?"

Scott gave him a look before replying, then stood up and started to pace, "Everything. There's no structure, no organisation, no logic, it's guesswork and crazy theories. The police only works if everyone follows a common process and you never do. I was in the office last night re-reading case material to see if we've missed something and you haven't logged a report for your interview with Hammond."

"It was only yesterday." Ron stood up and the two men began stomping around the island, snarling across it like two aged rhinos.

"Or the interview with Savage from June 23rd. You've written two lines; fixes pinball machines and weak alibi for 10th."

"I've got a brilliant memory. I could sit and write down every word that was said in that interview."

"Yes but that's no good for anyone else in the team. They can't read your mind. It's just hunches and humour with you."

Ron fell silent and stopped walking.

"You're either brilliant or terrible and I think it's the latter."

Ron had been stung and sunk back into a chair but came back with fire, as he reached across the table and flung his words. "Look at you, no-one in the station wants to work with you. You plod along sifting data, asking questions, writing reports, taking statements, spending hundreds of hours and taking thousands of steps but never getting anywhere. You're too busy crossing T's and dotting I's to get out there and catch any criminals."

Scott looked hurt by the accusation but Ron continued to strike while his man was down. "I had an exemplary clear up rate back in Norfolk. Don't forget it was your chief who dragged me in to help you."

"What happened did farmer Giles lose his chickens again?"

"Ha. Telling jokes are you, that'd be a first."

"I can't rest while there's a killer on the loose on my patch. You could do worse that show a little reverence around the topic yourself."

"I've told you before, you need to switch off when you come home or you'll go crazy. Like you're doing now."

"I don't need your advice."

"Oh but you do. You try to do everything by the book, like your hero Sherlock Holmes, but you need to wake up. Some of the bad guys have read the same book; they know what you're going to do."

Scott sat up straight. "Don't you dare criticise Sherlock, you're not fit to fill his pipe."

"He's nothing more than a bloody character in a book, a cartoon. Join the real world. Get out there and talk to people."

Scott was aghast but took a breath, then folded his hands on the table, "I find it easier to avoid people in social situations because most of them want to talk about their jobs, or worse, my job. And that's the problem. What do I say? I saw this grizzly body today with seventeen stab wounds scattered across her torso, where once there was hope and life now there's just a listless corpse. Or I popped round to tell a father today that I'd discovered his daughter had been raped and tortured. That would be a cheery conversation opener. No, so I don't say much. If people think I'm grumpy that's fine with me."

Ron waved his hand, "there's no point talking to you. I'm going to bed."

As Ron left the room, Scott shouted after him "Someone should tell Copernicus he got it wrong; it's not the sun at the centre of the universe, its DS Ron McTierney!"

WHEN RON STUMBLED in the kitchen the following morning, the place had been tidied and Scott was nowhere to be seen. Ron pulled a hand-written sheet from under the muesli box on the table. "Gone running!" Ron smiled, picked up the pen and turned the page over and wrote his own reply.

'Sorry for last night. I know it's your house, I was trying to let off a bit of steam and one thing led to another. But I'll make it up to you. This will be the week when I catch your killer! I'll give you a break for a couple of days and see you in the station on Monday. Cheers, Ron.'

SCOTT RETURNED TO his house as the clock approached

noon; he'd run an extra five miles to avoid the possibility of a shared late morning coffee with Ron. As he sprinted the last 100 yards he noticed the absence of Ron's Jaguar and felt a sudden pang of disappointment that his diminutive new colleague wasn't going to be making a noise in the kitchen or be sprawled across the sofa watching sport. He stopped at the door and panted as he searched for his key and analysed his thoughts; this wasn't logical. He didn't like Ron; he was a pain; he did everything the wrong way. Scott entered his kitchen and picked up Ron's note from the table. "Huh. Typical McTierney, run away from the issue." Scott threw the note in the bin and cursed. "The one occasion when I'm thinking I might like to sit down and watch an England game with him and the useless donkey isn't going to be here."

Scott flopped down into a chair at the table. With no playmate available he defaulted to his work persona and called into the station to check on the surveillance teams. Both Buckley and Lewis had ventured out on the Friday evening. Both were spotted watching the football on pub televisions and nothing suspicious had been reported. Buckley had made a couple of phone calls that were not on his registered mobile which raised the possibility of a burner phone. "Nothing suspicious!" yelled Bee down the phone – "you think our murder suspect has an unmarked phone and yet you don't think it's suspicious."

Bee's mood didn't improve when he heard the test results of the blood found in Buckley's house – they didn't match Dawson's blood type. Bee slammed the phone down and stomped around his kitchen. "He's playing with us. He left it there for us to find. You might be laughing now Mr Buckley, but I'm going to nail you!"

THIRTY

RUTH HAD INVITED Jess to watch the Raducanu match on a big screen at the tennis club, where she anticipated there would be an exciting atmosphere. Jess had jumped at the chance since the alternative was to bring Ron around to her aunt's house before lunch and although she thought the meeting would be okay, she wasn't convinced Ron could sustain good behaviour all afternoon.

Ruth met Jess at the door and bumped elbows with her and Ron, "So glad you could make it, this should be a scintillating game, I truly believe we are watching the future of British tennis."

"I hope so," replied Jess.

"For much too long we've been reliant on Andy Murray as our home-grown interest."

"And he's Scottish," chipped in Ron.

Jess dug him in the ribs and turned to Ruth. "This is my … friend Ron, he'll buy you a drink to make amends for his ignorance."

Ron disappeared off to the bar and left the two girls to talk. Ruth took Jess to one side.

"I've another reason to be pleased you're here."

Jess brushed her hair back behind her ear and bent down to listen as Ruth lowered her voice. "It's about Sophie."

"Your star player?"

"Yes. She's not herself. There's something bothering her," Ruth looked back across the clubhouse to check they weren't being watched. She turned back and cupped her hand around her mouth. "I think it's connected to the club, but she won't tell me what it is."

"What makes you think that?"

"She seldom comes down here to play anymore and if she does, she doesn't talk to anyone and leaves as soon as she can."

"You'd think that now her A-levels were finished she'd be down here all the time."

"Exactly, and she didn't have to sit the papers. Their results will be based on teacher assessments submitted by the school."

"Isn't that's going to make them easier?"

Ruth shrugged your shoulders. "You'd think."

"Hmm strange."

"It's more than strange. She used to live down here and she was bright, chatty, always had a smile on her face. But something's happened to her and the more I think about it, I think it happened about the time of Russell's demise."

"Here you go ladies, two wines." Ron broke up the conversation and both girls fell silent.

"Don't stop on my account. I love a bit of gossip."

"No it's nothing," said Ruth, "come on let's go watch the match, it should start at 1pm.

Although she started nervously Raducanu didn't disappointing her growing army of fans, neither the thousands packed around court number 1 at Wimbledon, nor the three-dozen jumping and squealing in the Reigate Priory clubhouse. From 3-0 down she stormed back to take the first set with a majestic lob to the baseline, a shot greeted by a loud cheer in the club.

Ruth lead the praise, "You have to admire this young lady. She is composed and brave at the same time. She's demonstrated some tremendous power hitting; I can see her being a great success and a fantastic mentor to many young people."

As the ladies settled down to watch the second set Ron felt the experience would be more enjoyable with a beer in his hand and he slipped off to the bar where a large, bearded man had taken station. Once equipped with a tin of Stella he started to chat to the barman and they toured the realms of holidays and viruses before returning to sport and tennis in Reigate. It didn't take Ron long to discover that in April of this year Spencer Lewis had terminated Russell Dawson's contract to provide tennis coaching at the King's School and that this had started a rift between them which led to Dawson dropping Lewis from the club first team.

Feeling pleased with himself, Ron slipped back onto the sofa next to Jess and whispered in her ear. She slapped him down, "Watch properly or go to the bar."

Tension grew in the second set as Raducanu allowed an early lead to slip but hung on to beat her third-round opponent 6-3 7-5. The tennis club erupted as a long running duel ending with Cristea hitting the ball into the net.

"When's the next game?"

"Monday I think. Now we have a new tennis celebrity she'll be given the best time so I guess that's early evening."

"That's cool, there's no football on Monday."

"Is that all you ever think about?"

"No," said Ron as he allowed his eyes to slide down Jess's body.

"Stop it, you've got to come and meet Aunt Claire first. I hope you haven't drunk too much. She's virtually tee-total."

JESS MADE RON stop at the top of Park Lane to visit the florist and buy a bouquet for Aunt Claire. He jumped back into the car with a bunch of sunflowers wrapped in pink tissue paper.

"Are you nervous?"

"Yes a little. How about you?"

"I'm shitting myself. I can't believe I'm doing this. I've never brought a boyfriend home to meet anyone before."

Aunt Claire lived on the top of Batts Hill in a large yet quirky detached house with bright blue woodwork and matching front door. The house was on a private road littered with potholes and Ron decided to park on the first flat bit of road he encountered. As they stepped from the car their senses were assailed by the smell and chatter from an illicit garden barbeque party. They exchanged glances and Ron said, "Good job Bee isn't with us, he'd be over the fence running amuck with his handcuffs."

Jess laughed. "I think people are desperate to let off a little steam and say good riddance to covid."

Aunt Claire had been keeping an eye out for their arrival and opened the door before Jess could find her key. She welcomed Jess with a hug and then stood to inspect Ron.

"You must be Ron; I've heard a lot about you."

"That's me."

"I thought you'd be taller, but no matter. You'd better come in."

Jess and Ron exchanged uncomfortable glances and followed Aunt Claire into the house. The hallway led into a sitting room and beyond that there was a large kitchen come dining room. Claire was a tall lady with a sharp intellect and a fashion sense of someone half her age. Her timid blue eyes suggested a gentle nature but she had no time for fools; despite many suitors she had chosen to never marry.

Claire took hold of the conversation. "I guess these are for me, thank you, let me put them in some water. You two grab a seat and I'll go and make us all a cup of tea."

Claire returned a few minutes later and brought with her a new cake that she had bought especially that morning from Marks and Spencer to accompany the tea. The three unlikely companions enjoyed a pleasant afternoon discussing topics from Emma Raducanu to the erosion of global democracy to whether Joe Biden could revive the Paris Climate Agreement in time to save the world from an environmental disaster. At 5 o'clock Claire got up to take the crockery out to the kitchen and Jess nudged Ron to help her.

"Ah thank you; you wash and I'll dry." Ron set the hot tap running.

"I must say I've been looking forward to meeting you. The man who has stolen Jess's heart. In all the time I've known her I've never seen Jess so happy." Ron smiled but kept his mouth closed and his hands in the water.

"You are all she talks about, so woe betide you if you ever hurt her. I can't have children and now with the demise of her mother, I've taken her under my wing, unofficially at least, so if you do anything against, you'll have me to answer to young sir." Claire brandished a cake slice in her hand as she spoke.

Ron gulped nervously and placed a small plate on the draining board.

Claire continued "Jess hasn't known many men in her life and they always let her down so she was wary of you. For a time, I know she was worried that you would return to Norwich. Hence at first I cautioned her against you, but to no avail, Jess seems to adore you and I must confess there's something charming about you."

"If I may speak? I'd like to say I love your niece. She's wonderful. There's nothing I wouldn't do to make her and keep her happy. She's the sunshine of my day."

"That's heartening to hear."

Ron left Aunt Claire in the kitchen and wandered up the stairs in search of Jess, he found her on the landing staring out at a view across the Surrey Hills. He came up behind her, wrapped his arms around her waist, inhaled the scent of her hair and rested his chin on her shoulder, "Whatcha looking at?"

"Wondering what is coming over the hill at me? I like to stand here and think about the future. It's scary but compelling at the same time."

"I don't see anything scary."

"You can't see a road back to Norwich then?"

Ron kissed her cheek. "No, you'd need a mega-telescope to see Norwich from here."

Jess's body slumped a couple of inches. "That's not what I meant."

"No I know you didn't. But I've no plans to go back to Norwich. I don't know where the black and white introversion of Inspector Bee will lead when this case is over but I want to stay here with you."

Jess relaxed and wriggled up against Ron. "It's a marvellous view, all those trees and plants, nature at her finest."

"Hmm. I want to enjoy you like a plant does, what's it called photosynthesis?"

Jess turned around to face Ron. "What?

"Yes I want to absorb you into every one of my cells. To have you touch every one of my sensitive glands."

"Ha! But you've only got two. You're mouth and your friend down there."

"Harsh."

"I know you – you're just trying to be poetic because you want to have sex."

"If you insist!"

RON DIDN'T THINK his evening could get any better and then England beat Ukraine 4-0 in the European Championship quarter-final.

"Damn," he muttered I should've played the lottery today, my luck's never been this good and never will be again.

THIRTY-ONE

BEE HAD SPENT his Sunday in the ops room reading though every report and witness statement he could find and had re-arranged the whiteboard display to feature the three people he considered potential suspects. He was pacing the room on Monday morning when Bartlett and McTierney arrived giggling at some joke. Bee scowled across the room and brought their humour to a sharp end. A line of used white plastic cups suggested Bee had been waiting several hours.

"I've gone back to basics in an effort to crack this case. The chief has invested heavily in this surveillance programme and he's going to be expecting some quick results. We need to pursue these three suspects with everything at our disposal."

Bartlett and McTierney sat and watched Bee present in stunned silence.

"I've re-drawn the board this morning with a three-step approach; motive, means and opportunity for each of Buckley, Lewis, and Savage. Starting with Savage. We know he has a hatred for Dawson; he doesn't have a reliable alibi for the night of the tenth and it's possible Dawson drove to his workshop on the evening, where Savage killed him before moving the body back to the tennis club later that night."

"Sounds plausible," said McTierney, "but there's no evidence for any of that."

"Bear with me, we'll come to that."

"Next Lewis. He hasn't offered any alibi for that evening; he too could've meet Dawson away from the club and then taken him back there. But I don't feel he has a strong motive."

McTierney raised his hand. "I might be able to help there. I was talking to the barman at the tennis club on Saturday afternoon and he mentioned that there had been a falling out between the two and as a result Lewis had terminated Dawson's contract to coach at the King's School and in return Dawson had demoted Lewis from the first team at the club. They were far from good friends."

"How come we've only just discovered that Lewis had stopped Dawson from coaching at the school?"

An uncomfortable silence fell across the room as Bartlett and McTierney looked at their hands.

Bartlett raised her head. "I think because there's over 600 members sir, it's not possible to interview everyone with only three of us."

Bee nodded, "Yeah I guess. All the more reason for us to be focused. So it sounds like Lewis could be a dark horse. McTierney can you focus on him for the next 24 hours. I want to know everything about Spencer Lewis; his hobbies, his friends, his favourite foods, where he holidays, where he gets his money from, and how often he takes a shit. Get on it. And get his prints too!"

McTierney looked stunned but said nothing.

"Last on our list, but certainly not least is Gary Buckley. Here we are light on motive, but he doesn't have a reliable alibi for the night of the tenth and again it's possible Dawson drove to meet him at the school that evening, where Buckley killed him before moving the body back to the tennis club later that night."

"Again it sounds plausible," said McTierney "but there's no evidence for any of that either, it's this idea that drugs are involved and Buckley could be the local drug dealer."

"We did find a stash of drugs in Dawson's car and to date we've no reason to believe that Dawson ever touched drugs so it suggests that the killer put them there for some reason."

"To distract us perhaps?" said McTierney scratching his nose.

"Unlikely. Either way if we could find who left them there it would be a step forward."

Bartlett and McTierney exchanged nods of the head.

"So Buckley remains on our list."

"Fair enough," said McTierney, "What did the surveillance programme reveal over the weekend?"

"Nothing conclusive from any of our three suspects although all three were out and about late on Saturday night and mixing with some unsavoury people. The team took photos of some of those they met." Bee passed a series of images across the table. "And Buckley appears to have a burner phone."

McTierney picked up one of the photos. "I guess he could have had the phone locked away in his drawer at home."

"That was my thinking." Bee issued some more photos. "Plus I've prepared photos of all three of our suspects for us to take with us. I'd like us to concentrate on finding witnesses who can place them, somewhere, anywhere on the night of

June 10th."

Bartlett flicked through the images in front of her. "I know you don't think she's a suspect and I agree that she's not, but I do think that Sophie Carr is involved in this case somehow. We should find time to talk to her."

"She can't be a priority. I want us to focus on these three for the next two days. We'll take one each, concentrate on them and review progress tomorrow."

Bartlett bowed her head.

"Can I suggest one other element?" McTierney looked between his two colleagues. "We've been working on the idea that there is a single killer out there, but perhaps two of these are working together. They all seem to know each other, if nothing else they've met up at the tennis club."

"And two of them work at the same school," added Bartlett.

"Interesting thought. Keep your minds alive to that. Now Bartlett, why don't you take the lead on Savage, you've not had much to do with him before, McTierney you track Lewis and I'm going back to talk to Buckley and his wife."

Despite the optimism of Inspector Bee and the investment of Chief Superintendent Beck and countless steps by Bartlett, Bee and McTierney nobody recognised any of the characters in the photos that were presented around the town. Few people had been out of their houses on June 10th, fewer still in the darkness of 10pm and no one could remember seeing anything suspicious anywhere near either the King's School, Savage's workshop, or Lewis's house. The day would have been a complete blank apart from one small confession. When Bee brought Mrs Buckley into the station she did admit that her husband had been home late that night and that she was already asleep in bed by the time he returned. But then she poured water on the revelation by admitting that she went to bed close to 9pm.

RON AND JESS had arranged to meet up at the tennis club to watch the latest instalment in the sporting drama of Emma Raducana who had raced from unknown to British sporting sweetheart in the matter of days. Her journey was mirrored by the number of club members who had turned out to watch the match. On Saturday the club was busy but comfortable. But by Monday night all the seats had gone and it was standing room only. Ron and Jess squeezed in and stood at the bar.

"What's going to happen if she makes the final?" asked Ron.

"Someone will be selling tickets," suggested Jess.

But sadly the question was never asked, Raducanu's epic journey ended abruptly at the hands of the experienced Croat Aija Tomljanovic when the British starlet had to withdraw suffering from breathing difficulties.

"That didn't take long," said Ron.

"Such a shame."

"Still at least we know she's definitely British,"

Jess turned to face Ron with her nose wrinkled.

"Only a true Brit can snatch defeat from victory in such style!"

"Ha! You cynic."

"Isn't life bizarre. Saturday was such a beautiful day; everything fell into place and then today has been one big pile of crap. And talking of crap, has Sting bent your ear with his Greek philosophy?"

"No."

"Lucky you, keep it that way. He was telling me some story about Cyclops who spends his life pushing some boulder up a mountain but each time he gets to the top, the boulder comes rolling back down the hill."

"Oh yeah I know the story – it's Sisyphus."

"Whoever. I think today is the day when that boulder has reached the top again, and now it's on the way back down again."

THIRTY-TWO

THE TEAM ASSEMBLED in the ops room to review progress from the previous day. The atmosphere was downbeat and movement was slow. Bee pushed his papers aside and looked across the table at his team to draw their attention, but before he could speak Carol Bishop popped her head around the door, an excited grin on her face.

"We've had a call from the surveillance team watching Savage".

Bee raised his head.

"It seems that there was some suspicious activity at his workshop last night."

"Go on."

"A little after five this morning a white van pulled up at the workshop, twenty minutes later Savage appeared and they unloaded three pinball machines. The van is registered in Holland and carries Dutch plates. It sped off at six and we've got a call out to the Channel ports to pick it up if it tries to head back to the continent."

The ops room burst into life; electric glances bounced around the room.

"It's kick-off time," said McTierney.

Bishop lowered her head to check the notes she had on a piece of paper in her hand. "The team maintained the surveillance. Savage left the property immediately after the van and hasn't been back since. When he left he didn't appear to be carrying anything extra, so we believe that if there's anything illegal in the delivery, then it's still at the lock-up. Knowles is watching the unit."

"You're thinking it was a drugs drop off?"

"Looks like it."

"Thanks Carol, that's excellent. Where's Church?"

"Not sure, we're trying to get through to him at the moment. If you want to move on this, I'd say you can. We need somebody down there that's for sure."

"Right. We're on it."

Carol Bishop left the room and Bee seized the moment. "McTierney can you go to Savage's house and pick him up, take a couple of officers with you if you need, Bartlett and I will meet you at his workshop."

Thirty minutes later the group re-assembled outside Savage's workshop. McTierney had taken the precaution of handcuffing Savage who was threatening retribution on anyone who came within shouting distance.

"Shut up, Savage and get this lock-up open, we'd like to inspect a delivery you had earlier this morning?"

"What's this? Got bored with beating up the wrong guys inspector? Been transferred to the customs division? Can't hack it with the big boys?"

"Thanks for the admission that the delivery was an import. Do you need to catch up on your sleep? That's not like you."

Savage grunted and kicked at the kerb.

Bee turned to McTierney. "Did you get the keys?"

McTierney threw a bunch of keys over to Bee, "He says

it's the one with the red tag."

"How considerate." Bee switched back to Savage "Any alarms we should know about?"

"It's clean."

If the alarm system was clean that was about the only element of the workshop that was clean. As the surveillance team had described there were three pinball machines standing inside the door.

"My guess is there'll be something nasty hidden inside these tables," suggested Bee.

Bartlett bent down and checked the tables, "Nothing obvious down here, sir."

Bee turned to confront Savage, "Simple choice for you. Either you open the tables yourself or we'll open them by force. I don't care which."

"You'll have to take these bracelets off."

McTierney shoved him forward, found the key and released him. Savage looked around, rubbed his fingers around his wrists were the handcuffs had started to mark his skin. "You ought to make those with a velvet inside, those things cutting into my hands must be an infringement of my rights."

"You can tell the judge when you see him, which won't be long. Now where's the key for these tables."

Savage sauntered over to a grey key box positioned on the wall above the solitary desk in the dark unit. He pulled it open and plucked a handful of small keys from one of the hooks. He took two steps back towards McTierney and tossed the keys up in the air, as McTierney moved to catch them, Savage leaped forward and smashed his fist into McTierney's face. It sent McTierney sprawling to the floor.

Savage dashed for the door before Bee could grab him. Savage burst out into the sunlight, blinked at the change in light and met the two constables McTierney had brought with him. Savage sprinted to the left with the pair after him. Bartlett caught up with the inspector, "Do you want me to go after him?"

"No need, Simpson was the school 800 metre champion, Savage won't outrun him."

Bee and Bartlett returned inside to inspect the bruise starting to show on McTierney's right cheek. "You'll survive," said Bee as he helped him up, "now let's get these tables open."

Savage had given them the correct keys and although they had to sift through more than a dozen different keys to find the correct one for each machine, it was worth the wait. Twenty minutes later they had stacked thirty small cellophane bags each sealed with a tiny piece of crimson tape on top of the first table, appropriately one with a gangster backglass.

"As a guess I'd say that red tape is a match for the one we found on the bag in Dawson's car."

"I think you're right Bartlett," said Bee, "and I imagine the drugs will be a match too. Our forensics team are in for a busy afternoon."

IT WAS AN eventful time for all departments at Reigate police station. Despite the athletic prowess of Constable Simpson, Savage had eluded capture and was on the run. Bartlett had been assigned to dig into his contacts and her list of 5

possible close friends who might be persuaded to help him had been shared out across the surveillance team who were watching each premise. In addition all police had been issued with a photo of the suspect and a manhunt was underway.

McTierney had been checked for concussion at the local hospital and been given the all-clear. On his way back to the station he called in to see Darren Fisher, who had refused to confirm Savage as the school-teacher, much to the annoyance of McTierney.

"We caught him with fifty grand's worth of drugs in his lock-up, why won't you accept that this is him? His days are numbered, he won't be able to hurt you."

"That's not the bloke I remember seeing." He screwed up his face. "Maybe it is, but I'm not sure."

McTierney had abandoned his quest and returned to the station eager to be involved in the case now that it was approaching a positive conclusion.

While McTierney was out, Bee had briefed Chief Beck.

"What do you mean you let him escape? How many of you were there?"

"Five sir."

"Five, for Christ's sake! How can one man evade five of you?" The door on the chief's office rattled in its hinges.

"It's only a matter of time until we get him sir, he can't run for ever."

"I bloody hope not!"

"Once we've got him back in custody, we can charge him with possession with intent to supply and that should lead to a murder charge."

"It better had."

Bee walked slowly back down the stairs and slumped into

the chair behind his desk. He pulled a blister pack of paracetamol from his drawer, took two and swallowed hard. He was sitting staring out of the window, when McTierney and Bartlett came back up from lunch. They both put their heads around the door. "You okay sir?" asked Bartlett.

"Not really. Tell me how can it be that we make a major break through this morning and now I feel further removed from the resolution?"

Bartlett and McTierney moved into the office and each took a seat opposite the inspector as he recounted the meeting he had endured with the chief. Bartlett's phone rang and she quickly pushed the call through to voicemail. McTierney picked up the debate.

"I hate to pour cold water on this, but even if we can prove Savage is importing drugs into the county and potentially supplying them around the town, and he is in fact the school-teacher."

"I think we can be sure that he is the school-teacher." Bee pointed across the desk.

"Okay, let's say he is the school-teacher. That doesn't mean he killed Dawson."

Bee grimaced. "I know."

"All we've really done is make life easy for Church and his team."

Bartlett's phone continued to ring. She noticed it was Ruth ringing her each time. "I think I'd better take this sir, it's the same person ringing over and over."

Bee waved her out of the room.

RUTH JONES WAS waiting at the tennis club when Bartlett arrived. She looked pale and her make-up had run suggesting she'd been crying.

"Thanks so much for coming, I've been so worried I don't know what to do."

"Let's grab a seat and maybe a cup of tea and you can tell me what's been happening."

No sooner had they sat down than Ruth's resolve broke and her fears burst forth. Tears and words jumbled together and Bartlett couldn't understand a thing but knew everything.

"Calm down." She grabbed her friend by the shoulders and shook her. "Stop. Take a tissue, wipe your eyes and start at the beginning I'll stay with you for as long as it takes."

Ruth stopped babbling, looked up at Bartlett, brushed away her tears and flung her arms around her neck. Bartlett let her hang there until she was ready to move. When Ruth was able to compose herself she gave Bartlett a succinct summary.

Ruth hadn't seen Sophie for 5 days, which was unprecedented. The last time she had seen her they had discussed Sophie exam results and her plans to go to university, Exeter was her first choice. Sophie seemed unduly stressed about the results and wouldn't tell Ruth why. Ruth was convinced there was something else distracting her, she clearly wasn't herself and Ruth hadn't seen her hit a tennis ball for two weeks which was unprecedented.

"I decided that today I would get to the bottom of it, but I couldn't find her anywhere, and she's not picking up her phone. I spoke to her mother and she said she wasn't at home either."

"I can follow up on that and make it a bit more official."

Ruth squeezed Bartlett's hand, "Would you, that would be great. I hope there's a simple explanation here but I'm worried that it's something more sinister."

SINCE BARTLETT HAD returned she'd been buried in her notes, McTierney had rarely seen her so occupied. He sauntered over to her desk. "Busy?"

"Yes,"

"Can I help?"

"No." Bartlett retained her focus on her laptop.

"Sure?"

"Yes."

"Whatcha working on?"

Bartlett slowly put her pen down and turned around to face McTierney. "Ruth Jones, who you met on Saturday, called me today to share her fears about Sophie Carr the young starlet at the club. I'm doing some background checks."

"Hmm interesting." McTierney tilted his head towards Bartlett to check she was paying attention, "more importantly what do you fancy doing tonight? I've got a suspicion it's time for another McTierney cookery masterclass."

Bartlett sighed but smiled back at him. "But since you've been in the wars today, maybe nurse Bartlett should take care of her brave soldier."

McTierney offered her his best puppy-dog eyes. "That would be great. How about I pop over to yours at eight?"

"Fine, but for now leave me in peace."

"Unconditionally."

BEE WALKED DOWN to the canteen, picked up a large coffee and muesli bar and ambled back up the stairs to his office. He could see a long evening ahead of himself as he sat and tortured himself over the case. He fell back into his chair as his desk phone rang. He pulled a face, who could be calling him at this time of night, gently he lifted the receiver. It was his old friend Chief Inspector Forbes from Norwich CID with some disturbing news. Bee put the phone down and inhaled deeply. He wouldn't be spending the night worrying about the Dawson case, now he had something more important to ponder.

THIRTY-THREE

On Wednesday morning the ops room at the station resembled a 6th form common room with noise and activity everywhere – the hallmarks of an exciting investigation. Beck had granted Bee's request and four new officers had joined the team. The inspector had set all four to work on different aspects; primary amongst them was handling the flurry of calls purporting to have seen the fugitive Greg Savage somewhere across the county.

McTierney stood in amazement at the industry before him. Bee popped into the room behind him. "Have you heard the latest?"

"Tell me."

"We have six sightings of Savage. It won't be long before we have him in custody."

Bee took McTierney over to a map of the Surrey area and showed him the six mini red flags pinned on to the map. They were spread far and wide and ranged from Priory Park in Reigate to Morrison's supermarket, across to the King's School, to Barclays Bank in Redhill, the train station and as far north as Croydon.

"They're a bit scattered" said McTierney.

"We'd expect that. They won't all be right, can't be. When the phones calm down I'll send a couple of these boys out to interview the witnesses and that will start to sort the wheat from the chaff."

McTierney turned and looked around the room at the willing crop of new recruits, "Sounds reasonable."

"Interestingly Savage withdrew £300 from the bank at 4am this morning."

"He's going to find that hard to spend, with most people worried about covid and everyone using credit card payments. It's plastic or nothing in most places."

Bee nodded, "Indeed. Although the people he mixes with might not be too worried about current business protocol."

The two men chuckled and Bee continued. "He's probably aware that we can track any use of his credit card, so it's cash or nothing."

"Or theft?"

"Yeah, wouldn't surprise me. In fact I think I'll send one of our team around the open market in Redhill precinct to warn the traders to be on their guard." Bee stopped to write himself a note.

"He's lucky it was warm last night, as I recall he was only wearing a plain cotton shirt. I wonder where he slept last night?"

"Probably some farm building. If he slept at all."

McTierney's eyes lit up. "Maybe he slept in the barn down the road from your place."

Bee tilted his head. "I doubt it. More important though is the certainty that he's getting tired and likely to make a mistake soon and we'll be there to capture him."

McTierney nodded in agreement.

"By the way, do you know where Jess Bartlett is?"

"She said she was going to track down this teenager from

the tennis club."

Bee rolled his eyes. "What? We could do with her being here. Can you give her a call and get her in?"

WHILE BEE AND McTierney were revelling in the immediate demise of Greg Savage, Bartlett had visited Sophie's home address and after speaking to her mother had set out to find Sophie. Her mother had offered two possible locations for Sophie but didn't have the time to join Bartlett; 'I've twins under five to take care of, Miss fancy-pants is old enough to look after herself', was all she had to say.

Bartlett tried the small Memorial Park in the centre of Redhill but to no avail. Then she walked into the main precinct, slipped past Sainsbury's superstore and up the steps to the public library. She flashed her badge at the desk and tiptoed around the reading tables that lined the large window looking out over the town. She stopped to sigh and regretted not collecting a photo from either Ruth or Sophie's mother. One circuit of the bookcases and she'd better head back to the station. She walked past the young adult and self-improvement sections and turned the corner into sport. She ran her finger along the long line of football books and wondered how many McTierney had read. Probably none! In the opposite corner from the entrance was a children's section. "I'll go and see if 'Winnie the Pooh' is in the collection," she mumbled to herself. And it was, but it was being read by an oversized child sitting on the floor. Bartlett sat down next to her.

"Hello Sophie. That used to be my favourite book when

I was a child."

Sophie turned her head but didn't speak.

"Can I read it over your shoulder?"

Sophie shuffled around and they sat together with the book across their knees.

Bartlett's phone buzzed, she glanced down and flipped it to silent. Sophie had selected a hybrid Pooh book of the 'Blustery Day' which didn't take long for them to complete.

"Do you know this was only written after Disney made the film?"

Sophie didn't answer.

"And that the film is a compilation of several scenes from two of the original books."

Still no reply.

"But I can't remember which ones."

Bartlett allowed the conversation to lull.

"It's my favourite story," said Sophie, "when I was a little girl my dad used to read it to me. It's my happiest memory of him."

Bartlett reached out and put an arm around her shoulder, "Is your Dad no longer at home?"

"He left when I was 7 and now mum has a new boyfriend. He doesn't have time for me."

"I never knew my dad either."

Sophie turned to face Bartlett as if questioning the words. Bartlett nodded softly and the two young girls embraced. Silent tears trickled down four cheeks.

Bartlett could feel her phone vibrating in her pocket, McTierney wasn't going away. She reached into her pocket and pulled the phone out. "Look I'm going to have to take this call and that will probably mean I've got to return to the station. It's a bit busy there today."

Sophie nodded and wiped her hand across her face.

"But I'd like to talk some more with you, maybe we could read about Eeyore."

Sophie gave a nervous nod.

"How about I fetch my Pooh book and bring it to the park at 5pm this afternoon? Would that be okay? I'll even stretch to a milkshake in Costa."

Sophie grinned and nodded again, "Okay, I'll be on the seat by kiosk in the park at 5pm."

"Deal." Bartlett reached out and gave her a hug.

BARTLETT SCURRIED BACK to the station, keen to brief Bee and McTierney with her suspicions around Sophie and the school teacher. She burst into the station and skipped across to the canteen. Bingo, both detectives were sitting in the canteen; it seemed that the progress on the case had brought them together since their differences at the weekend.

"Hi both, can I talk to you?"

"Sorry Bartlett I have to update the chief at 11am," Bee looked up at the large wall clock which stood above the door in the canteen, "and that's in two minutes, so I'll leave you to talk to McTierney, but come and find me later, say 4:30pm? We can talk then."

"I'll happily talk to you," said McTierney, "What's on your mind?"

Bartlett pulled up a chair and joined McTierney at the table. "It's Sophie Carr. I think she could be our missing witness."

Bartlett recounted her conversations with Ruth and Sophie and her theory that something nasty had occurred at the tennis club to upset Sophie and that this could be linked to whatever had happened to Russell Dawson.

"Bit fanciful," said McTierney, "you teenage girls get upset about all manner of things. Perhaps she lost a couple of games of tennis."

"You dolt! Tennis is her escape from the real world, it's her go-to when there's a problem elsewhere. This is like you giving up football or beer!"

"What? I'd never do that."

"That's my point!" Bartlett swung a frustrated arm at him.

McTierney rubbed his arm, grimaced and thought for a second.

"Even if I might believe you, Sting certainly won't, he's wrapped up in his pursuit of Savage. He feels salvation is at hand."

"Hmm. I'll have to talk to him later."

With a lull in the conversation, McTierney took the opportunity to change tact. "Moving on to social matters," McTierney tilted his head towards Bartlett to check she was paying attention, "what do you fancy doing tonight?"

Bartlett shrugged her shoulders.

"Only it's the England semi-final tonight. Kick-off at 8pm. I'd be delighted to see you, but I also want to watch the match, you know how I can't give up football?"

Bartlett lowered her gaze and stared at him. "I know, apparently these England semi-finals don't come around all that often."

"No, about one per lifetime, although our manager seems

to be improving the ratio; this is our second big semi in three years."

"Yippee."

McTierney feigned dismay. "But I've still got to watch it because it might be the last one for twenty years."

"Ha! You football fans live life on the edge."

McTierney smiled.

"Look I don't think I could complete with that level of excitement, so why don't you watch it with your landlord tonight and I'll see you tomorrow."

"Okay."

McTierney looked around the canteen and seeing that it had emptied out he reached across and kissed Bartlett on the cheek. They pushed back their chairs and headed towards the door. Before they reached it, one of Bee's new recruits came bounding into the canteen.

"Sergeant McTierney sir, sorry to bother you but Inspector Bee told me that the police at Harwich have stopped the white van trying to board a ferry to the Hook of Holland. He wants you to go there and interview the driver. Here's the name of the officer up there."

The constable thrust a piece of paper into McTierney's hand.

"Looks like you might have to work fast to watch your beloved football team," smirked Bartlett as she stepped through the open door.

BARTLETT WAS ON edge all afternoon waiting for her conversation with the inspector. But his afternoon had been punctuated with visits from the chief and his new team; good news was arriving from every angle. There were several more sightings of Savage and the forensics team had confirmed that the drugs found in Savage's workshop were a match for those discovered in Dawson's car.

Bartlett paced up and down the corridor checking her watch every other minute. As the second hand ticked inexorably up to the number twelve the sweat bubbles multiplied on her back and she cursed the fact that she hadn't taken Sophie's number, she couldn't contact her and now she was going to be late. She feared that Sophie wouldn't wait for long and might be hard to find again. She was on the point of abandoning her vigil outside the office, when Bee opened his door and called her in. But McTierney had been right, the inspector had closed his mind to any other possibility and didn't want to hear any theory that didn't subscribe to his view that Savage was guilty and soon to be apprehended. Bartlett sighed and got up to leave. If she escaped now she might get to the park in Redhill only twenty minutes late. But the inspector had other plans.

"Bartlett, could I have a quiet word with you on a different subject? There's something I feel you should know."

"Of course, sir, what is it you want to say?"

"This isn't easy for me, but I want you to know that I've always tried to look out for you and see that you're okay."

"I know and I appreciate that inspector. I've always felt you've looked after me."

Bee looked down at his hands. "I wish I didn't have to be the one to tell you this but sooner or later you were bound to find out," he paused, "it's right you know. McTierney is married."

Bartlett gawped at him.

"I'm sorry to be the one to tell you, I know you think a lot of him."

Bartlett still didn't speak and sat frozen in her chair staring at the wall. Bee got up from his chair walked around the desk and wrapped an arm around her. "I'm sorry, but it's true."

Bartlett mumbled "No."

Once he had started it seemed the inspector rallied to his task.

"I know this will be painful but I think you can do a lot better than McTierney, definitely somebody younger. I'm afraid that his social and moral compass all point south. He's like a midnight kebab. It seems like a good idea when you've drunk a little too much but you will regret it next morning, when you look inside the pitta bread pouch all you will see is contents that do not live up to the promise on the poster outside the shop. It will leave a horrible after-taste."

But Bartlett wasn't listening, she shrugged off his arm got up and ran out of the office. She grabbed her bag and stumbled down the back stairs avoiding eye-contact with everyone around her, it was only her concern for Sophie that kept her going. It was pushing 6pm as she pulled into the Gloucester Road car park, she didn't bother with a parking ticket and ran across the junction and into the park.

No Sophie.

Damn!

Jess dropped to her knees and screamed. It was a release of everything that had been going wrong that day. Every turn, every decision, every conversation had made the day a little bit worse, now she was at the bottom. She trudged to a bench and flopped down. Bollocks! How could Ron do this to her? She'd wring his neck when she next saw him. Except she didn't want to see him. She didn't want to listen to any charm offensive from him. No more lies. She wasn't going to give him the satisfaction of seeing her hurt. She didn't want to allow herself to cry. She wiped her sleeve across her eyes and stared across the park. What a mess the day had become. She bent forward put her elbows on her knees and ran her hands up and across her forehead and looked at the ground.

Jess had no idea how long she had sat there, minutes, hours, days – time didn't matter to her anymore. She would have stayed longer if a stranger hadn't parked herself at the other end of the bench. Jess pulled herself up, blew out her cheeks and made ready to move, she glanced towards the stranger.

"Hi, I thought it was you."

"Sophie! What are you doing here?"

"I think I should be asking you that question."

"I, er we, er I don't know." Jess's face crumbled.

Sophie shuffled along the bench and wrapped her arms around Jess. She pulled her so tight Jess coughed and struggled for breath. The girls broke apart and looked at each other.

"What happened?"

"I found out my boyfriend is married." The tears started again but Jess tried to fight them and pawed them away.

"Why do men have to be bastards?"

"I don't know, but never fall in love; it's too painful."

The girls embraced one another again. "I won't" said Sophie maintaining the hug. Jess started to sniff and pulled back to clean her face. Sophie held her gaze, "What are you going to do?"

"I don't know, it doesn't make sense, I can't believe it."

"You need some time and some distance."

Jess sniffed in agreement.

"And a friend," Sophie reached out and took Jess's hand, Jess let it stay there.

The sun was setting and long shadows extended across the grass from the trees behind them; the chatter of the birds grew to a cacophony as they prepared for nightfall. Sophie shifted to face Jess and gently wiped away her tears with her index finger. Jess' eyes found Sophie's and asked her to be gentle. Sophie lent forward and softly kissed Jess, before pulling her into a tight embrace. Jess squirmed and then whispered, "Can you tell me what happened at the tennis club to change things. I know you've seen something or experienced something. If you tell me, I can help you, I can fix it,"

"I can't, he'll kill me." Sophie buried her head in Bartlett's arms.

THIRTY-FOUR

BEE COULDN'T THINK about anything else. He knew he'd handled it badly, but he was convinced that Bartlett had to be told and he was the only person who could tell her. He cursed the day that McTierney had walked into their lives. He stomped down the stairs but stopped as he left the station, he ought to go after Bartlett and see that she was okay, but what would be say? He was more likely than not to make it worse. He'd be better off going home and leaving this sort of thing to one of her girlfriends. But what if something happened to her, – he'd never forgive himself for not trying. He opened his car door and sat there contemplating his options. There was no debate he'd have to do something. He flicked through his phone and found an address for Aunt Claire, which would be a start.

But Bartlett wasn't there.

The only other place he could imagine her being was at the tennis club. He turned his car around and headed for the club, bumping his head again on the sleeping policeman at the top of the lane.

But Bartlett wasn't there either.

He was out of options; he'd have to go home. He drove up the lane and arrived at the speed hump and slowed his car to roll over the ridge but still bumped his head. He was about to curse but stopped, reached over for his mobile and punched in Dr Kelly's number.

THIRTY-FIVE

BARTLETT HAD BEEN in a quandary in the park, she didn't want to abandon Sophie and she didn't want to be alone, but she didn't want to get intimate with a young girl. In the end she had allowed fate to take the decision for her. Sophie had asked her if they could 'go somewhere' that night; Bartlett had offered her a bed at Aunt Claire's but on the strict understanding that all they did was sleep. Bartlett was relieved to discover that they were so late arriving home that Claire was in bed and no introductions were required. As they tiptoed around the lounge Sophie had spotted a bottle of peach schnapps and the rest of the night became a blur.

Morning came too soon for her because she knew she would have to deal with the shit Bee had delivered yesterday. She lay in bed fiddling with her phone listening to Aunt Claire potter around the kitchen waiting for her to leave. Once she heard the front door close, she lifted Sophie's sleeping arm off from her waist and sent a text into the station and then another to McTierney. She put her phone on the bedside unit and rolled over to face Sophie, who stirred, smiled, groaned, and then dashed to the bathroom.

McTierney had endured a laborious day in Harwich. The local police had taken the van driver into custody and held him until McTierney arrived. The driver, Leo Smulders was a Dutch national, who refused to say anything, but his name was on the documents bringing the van into the country and it was his name on the ticket back to Holland. A brief conversation with the Dutch police had confirmed that the vehicle was registered to him in Amsterdam. As far as McTierney was concerned he didn't have a leg to stand on, and his refusal to speak irritated the detective immensely. From his perspective it was clear that the pinball business was a front for drug smuggling. Smulders was known to the Dutch authorities and one of their detectives was on his way to Harwich. McTierney expected that the Dutch would want to charge him in their own country and that was fine with him, the sooner he could sign him over the better. He knew only too well that the English jails were over-full already.

By the time he had finished all the admin, it was approaching 8pm and McTierney was struggling to find a pub where he could watch the football. In the end he had listened to the game on his car radio and then crashed in the cheapest of cheap hotels while he waited for his Dutch counterpart to arrive on the morning ferry. Hence he was not in the best of moods when at 8:45am his phone pinged to tell him he had a new text message. He was sitting in his car parked outside the ferry terminal waiting for Detective van Sleumer. He lent across to the passenger seat and picked up his phone.

"What does that idiot Bee want now?"

He glanced at the screen; it was a text from Jess. He gawped at the first line; 'You bastard!'

He pushed the button to open the full message. 'You

bastard! You low-lying scum. How could you do it to me? Bee told me you're married. You lying little shit. I never want to see or hear from you again. Crawl back to your wife in Norwich.'

"What the hell?"

McTierney threw his phone down on the seat and scrabbled to pick it up again. What was happening? He pressed the number to call Jess, but the phone rang through to her voicemail.

"Damn!"

He pushed the buttons again. Same result.

"What the hell has Bee done? I'm gonna kill him."

Ron called Bee on his mobile.

"Inspector Bee of Reigate CID, how can I help?"

"You fucking arsehole!"

"What? McTierney is that you?"

"Bloody right it's me. What the fuck are you doing telling Jess I'm married?"

"Ah well, it's not right for you to lead her on. I was..."

"Shut up, you arse. I'm not married and never have been."

There was a pause on the line.

"The Norfolk constabulary seem to think you are. I spoke to Chief Inspector Forbes and he assured me you're married to a woman called Angela. Angela Watson I think her name was."

"Bullshit. I used to live with Angela but we were never married; that's some fantasy she invented."

"Ah."

"Call yourself a detective. You're fucking useless. Did you never think to check your source?"

"I'm sorry McTierney, I'll see if I can sort out this misunderstanding."

"Don't bother, you'd only make it worse!"

McTierney gave Detective van Sleumer the quickest hand over in the history of international police co-operation, signed every piece of paper thrust in front of him and stormed out of Harwich police station. He pushed his way through to the staff car park, yelled at a young constable who dallied when parking his patrol car, jumped into his Jaguar, and hurtled down the A120 towards Colchester and ultimately the M25.

The 90-minute journey hadn't calmed him at all, he screeched into the car park at the back of the Reigate station, dumped his car and sprinted up the stairs in search of Jess Bartlett. But she was nowhere to be seen. He sped from room to room looking for her until he bumped into Carol Bishop.

"Have you seen Jess?" he bellowed.

Bishop frowned back at him.

"Jess. Bartlett. You know, have you seen her?"

"No, I think she's off sick today."

"What?" The answer confused McTierney and he stopped in his tracks.

"The inspector was looking for you earlier, he asked all of us to send you in his direction if we saw you."

"Sod the inspector!"

McTierney turned and headed off in the other direction, got to the stairs and then stopped. Rather than heading down and back to his car, he galloped up the stairs and burst into Bee's office. Bee had been on the phone but ended the call abruptly, "Ah McTierney good to have back here."

"Stuff it, where's Jess?" McTierney lent on the desk and

shouted into Bee's face.

Bee backed away. "I don't know. I'll help you find her tonight, but now we need to capture Savage. He's still in hiding, I think someone must be helping him."

"Bollocks to finding Savage, I need to find Jess."

"Get a grip McTierney."

"I'll give you a grip." McTierney lunged across the desk to grab the lapel on Bee's jacket but missed and fell forward onto the papers spread across the bureau. "Shit!" He pulled himself up, placed two hands on the files and flung them all off the desk.

"Fuck you! I quit."

JESS AND SOPHIE spent all morning in Aunt Claire's house. Peach schnapps was replaced by strong coffee but the easy conversation flowed. Jess suggested stepping outside for some fresh air to blow away the last of the hangover. She picked up her watch, thinking it would be mid-morning and was shocked to find the time had gone passed 2pm.

"Do you know what the time is? It's after 2pm," she said answering her own question.

Sophie shrugged and stretched out on the sofa inviting Jess to join her. "Time doesn't matter today."

"Maybe not for you, but don't you think you should tell your mother where you are?"

"She won't care. I'll send a text."

"Come on, it's a fabulous day, let's go catch some sunshine and stomp around Priory Park."

Sophie grimaced at the prospect, so Jess sugar coated the

option with a promise of dinner at Wagamama's after their walk. As they stepped out from the front door, Jess popped her phone into her light jacket and noticed a dozen missed calls. They would have to wait.

RON PULLED UP outside Aunt Claire's house and looked at the forbidding front door; where once he had seen bright welcoming colours now they were transposed into a sinister mix of eccentric shapes and shades. His natural confidence deserted him and he stepped slowly towards the door, wondering what Aunt Claire might have been told. He knocked timidly and stepped back sucking his breath in across his lips. He waited a few seconds and surmised that his knock had been too quiet, he leaned forward to knock again as Claire opened the door. He narrowly avoided falling into her.

"Hello Claire, I wonder if Jess is here and if I could speak with her."

"Hi Ron, No she's out, I assume she's at work." Claire stepped back to allow McTierney to enter but sensed a change in tone and stopped in mid-turn. "Is everything alright with you two?"

"Oh yes, nothing to worry about. I had to go to Harwich last night so was hoping to see her before I went back to work, but I guess she's busy somewhere."

"I guess."

JESS AND SOPHIE wandered aimlessly around Priory Park sharing stories from their past, laughing and giggling most of the afternoon. Jess felt so removed from her regular day that she stopped noticing her phone vibrating as McTierney maintained his barrage of attempted calls. After a long circuit of the perimeter of the park they settled on a bench in the central area and sat for a while people watching. It didn't take them long to spot three 'Eeyores,' two 'Piglets', and a 'Pooh', but 'Tigger' was by far the most bountiful character in the park. When the temperature dropped a few degrees, Jess suggested they grab something to eat.

"Could we find something to smoke?" asked Sophie.

"I get the feeling you're not talking cigarettes?" said Jess.

Sophie shook her head.

"You do know I'm a police officer," said Jess.

"I thought you'd know where to get some good stuff."

RON WAS RUNNING low on options. He had hung around at the end of the road keeping an eye on Aunt Claire's house but to no avail. The relief he had felt when he concluded that Jess hadn't told Claire about Bee's news was short-lived and as the clouds massed to block out the sun, he felt his optimism disappearing too. He rolled the dice again and headed down to the tennis club.

"Hi Ruth, I know we haven't always seen eye to eye, but I need your help. Jess and I had a big fight yesterday and I need to find her."

"Oh yeah? And why should I help you?" Ruth looked down her nose at McTierney.

"Because it was a mis-understanding and the sooner we clear it up, the better for everyone."

Ruth held her stare.

"So in reality, you'd be helping her as much as me."

"Hmm."

"All I'm asking is, have you've seen her?"

"No, I haven't but if I had to guess I'd say she was either searching for Sophie or maybe she's found her. Jess is convinced she knows something about the killing of Russell."

"I remember her mentioning Sophie." Ron wore his most earnest face. "Any idea where I might find Sophie?"

"I think she lives somewhere at the top end of Frenches Road in Redhill, but to tell you the truth, I don't know the exact address."

"No worries, you've been a great help."

JESS DALLIED OVER the meal and proposed a long route back to her aunt's house. She determined that this was the moment to push Sophie for a full disclosure of the Russell story, but she didn't want the moment to be interrupted by any questions from Aunt Claire. This evening her timing was good, as she put her finger to her lips and silently opened the front door. Sophie giggled at the signal, her vibrant dark eyes enjoying the conspiracy. They tiptoed into the lounge and Jess picked up a note from her aunt. Sophie peered over her shoulder to read that Ron had been looking for Jess. Jess screwed the paper up and threw it into the bin, "Come on let's sneak upstairs but you need to be discreet, I'm not sure my aunt is asleep yet and she'd have a fit if she knew we were going to smoke some pot."

Jess opened the windows while Sophie sat on the bed and rolled a couple of joints.

"I make them clean, no tobacco so there's no risk of developing a nicotine craving."

"Oh good, heaven forbid we should start a bad habit."

Jess found herself relaxing more than she had expected. Up to this point all she could think about was Inspector Bee peering over his glasses and tutting but the sweet smell was lifting those concerns up and out of the window. She looked across at Sophie who seemed to be in another world.

"Chilled?"

Sophie nodded her understanding, budged up beside Jess and pulled Jess's arm around her.

"Tell me about your tennis success."

"Is that what you want to hear?"

"Yes, I want to know everything about you."

"Wouldn't you rather I told you about Russell?"

"Only if you're ready."

"Russell was my friend he tried to help me, and that's what got him killed. I don't want the same to happen to you."

"But if you don't tell me, Russell will have died in vain trying to help you; there's nothing sadder than that."

Sophie lay there silent and Jess imagined her weighing up the argument.

"I didn't see who killed Russell but I'm guessing it was Mr Buckley." Jess felt Sophie's body tense as she mentioned his name.

"The teacher at your school."

"The pig at my school."

Jess bit her tongue and waited for Sophie to continue.

"Since the school announced that we wouldn't be sitting our exams, but instead the school would determine our grades, he's been threatening all the girls with bad grades if we don't do nice things for him."

"Like what?" Jess wanted to scream but kept her tone level.

"Mostly he wanted us to buy his drugs, but there's a couple of rumours that he asked a couple of girls to toss him off. It wouldn't surprise me."

Jess inhaled deeply and a shiver went down her spine.

"Thankfully he only ever made me take his drugs. He wanted to get me to persuade all the girls at the tennis club to take them. He said a bit of whizz would help our game and maybe I might get to play at Wimbledon. He even said I'd thank him one day when I won something."

"I see why you call him the pig." Jess's body stiffened in shock.

"Anyway, I played a Wimbledon qualifier tournament over at Guildford recently and I was truly dreadful, my timing was out and I couldn't serve. Russell was upset and a bit pissed off because he'd taken me over there. So on the way home he asked me what was going on, and I told him. I thought he was going to crash the car; he was so mad."

"I bet he was."

"But five days later, Russell was dead."

Jess's eyes were on stalks, suddenly she was back on duty and focused on apprehending Buckley. Sophie interrupted her thoughts.

"I'm scared you might die too. I don't have many friends; I couldn't bear to lose you."

"I promise you I won't die. I've got lots of friends who can help me."

As Jess said the words she thought of her two colleagues; Bee didn't believe a word she'd said about the school conspiracy and she never wanted to see McTierney's miserable face again.

THERE WAS NO such comfort for McTierney; his companion for the night was a take-away bag of fish and chips and several pints of beer in the pubs of Reigate. He hadn't really expected to bump into Jess in any of them but he didn't know where else to go. On Saturday afternoon he had felt like this town could be a fresh start for him with friends galore, four days later and the landscape had transformed. He was a stranger in a strange place and one without a bed for the night. He staggered back up Reigate Hill at midnight, pulled a blanket out of the boot of his car and settled down for a rough night staking out Aunt Claire's house.

THIRTY-SIX

JESS WAITED FOR Aunt Claire to leave the house, then tiptoed out of the door herself. She walked past the car of McTierney but an odious attraction forced her to glance inside. He was sprawled across the reclined passenger seat with a blanket over his legs; Coke bottles and Costa cups littered the dashboard and a half-eaten bag of crisps lay discarded on the driver's seat. Jess shuddered and turned her nose up at the smell she could imagine would be in the car. McTierney stirred in his sleep and Jess jumped; not wanting to be spotted, she intensified her pace and walked on down the hill into central Reigate, and Buckley's school office.

THE SOUND OF morning acted as an alarm clock for McTierney. He yawned, stretched, and scratched the stubble on his chin. He told himself that he must find a proper bed tonight. He took a slurp of flat Coke and a mouthful of stale crisps. His stomach needed a decent meal. He rubbed his eyes and searched for his phone, no missed calls. Most of all he needed a plan. Perhaps a new plan. He still had a key for Bee's house and he was sure that by now the place would be empty and the fridge full; if he wanted to make a good impression with Jess he would need to freshen up. He had convinced himself of this plan as he noticed a strange young girl leaving Claire's house. The opportunity was too good to miss; he jumped out of his car and ran along the road to meet her.

"Hi, I'm Ron, a friend of Jess, can you tell me if she's at home?"

Sophie looked shocked by Ron's direct approach and started to panic. "Err."

Quickly he blocked her exit; with no key to the house, she had nowhere to turn. She spun around looking for an escape and McTierney sensed something was wrong and changed his tactic.

"I'm with the police, can you tell me what you're doing at this property, I know you're not the owner."

Sophie burst into tears and slumped to the ground. Ron knelt down beside her.

"What are you doing here?"

Sophie brushed her hair away from her eyes, and a streak of defiance ran through her body.

"I was visiting my friend – not that it's any of your business."

Her reply knocked Ron back. "Your friend? You mean Claire?"

"No – durr, Jess."

"What? How do you know Jess?"

"We were smoking joints last night. What do you know?"

Ron shook his head, what was happening. This millennial was talking a different language and making no sense at all. He went back to basics.

"Do you know where Jess Bartlett is right now?" He moved into her personal space.

"She's on her way to arrest Gary Buckley."

"Buckley?" Ron retreated as horizontal wrinkles spread across his forehead.

"Yes, the pig who abused everyone at the King's School."

"Why?"

Sophie recounted the same story to Ron, who sat aghast as the details spilled from her mouth.

BEE WAS SITTING behind his desk reading through a page of alleged sightings of Greg Savage when Dr Kelly called him.

"Inspector, I have some good news for you."

"Excellent, let's have it."

"We have a match. As you suggested I went back to re-test Dawson's car and I made sure to swab the roof of the car above the driver's seat. I discovered new DNA and we have a match."

"Good work. Who?"

"It's Gary Buckley. He's driven that car and in all probability he was the last one to drive it. But the roof is the only place I could find any of his DNA."

"That's because he was wearing one of Savage's coveralls. But they don't have a hood so when he bounced over the speed humps he bumped his head on the roof.

"Possibly."

"Definitely. And a careless move by Savage that makes him an accomplice to murder."

"Have you found him yet?"

"No, but we will. For now I have to arrest a school-teacher."

BARTLETT ARRIVED AT the school fuelled by rage and indignation, but as she walked around to the side car park and the science block her fire started to wane, perhaps she should call the inspector first. She turned the corner and there was the red Range Rover belonging to Buckley, she walked passed it, grimaced at the smoked glass windows, and wondered what misdeeds had taken place behind the tinted glass. She had to act and act now. She retraced her steps from the previous week and creeped along the top corridor. As she approached Buckley's office she could her a commotion. Unsure of what to do she called out, "Is anyone there?" Her voice echoed slightly in the passageway and the noise abated. She stopped and noticed her hands turning clammy. Buckley stepped out of his office; his look of morbid fascination quickly morphed into a malicious smile.

"Why if it isn't Detective Bambi, out on her own, and if I'm not much mistaken she's unarmed and shitting herself."

"Gary Buckley, I'm placing you under arrest for the murder of Russell Dawson."

Buckley waved his arm in the air, "be serious detective, you're not arresting anyone."

"Yes I am." Bartlett's confidence started to return.

Buckley pulled a gun from behind his back. "No you're not! Now step inside my office, while I decide what to do with you." Buckley stepped aside and waved Bartlett in with his gun. As she advanced passed him Buckley shoved her in the back knocking her to the floor. "Ha! How dare you come here alone and think you can arrest me. You stupid girl!"

Bartlett sucked the blood from her lip where she had cut it in the fall and turned to face Buckley. "The game's up you know. Sophie told me everything. The police will be here shortly. You're going to jail."

"I don't think so. If the police were coming there'd be sirens. This is just you, trying to impress the big boss and biting off more than you can chew."

Buckley walked towards her and kicked her hard in the stomach. "That's for telling lies. Did your parents never tell you not to tell lies?"

Bartlett groaned and rolled over. "I never knew my father, but whoever he was, he was more of a man than you'll ever be."

"Shut it." Buckley spat at Bartlett.

"Now I've been dying to tell someone how I outsmarted the police, how I've had them running around looking like bloody idiots. I had hoped it would be someone more significant than a mere constable, but needs must, so you'll do."

Bartlett propped herself up on her elbows. "Another bid from a lunatic who thinks he's a master criminal."

Buckley scowled at her jibe but started his story.

"Yes I did kill Dawson, but ironically I didn't mean too, – the meddling do-gooder kept sticking his nose in my business. I'd warned him off a couple of times but he threatened to report me to your mob, so I invited him here for a late-night discussion. I had planned to frighten him with one of these." Buckley waved the gun at Bartlett. "I figured once I'd told him that I knew where his kids went to nursery school, he'd back off. But he kept arguing, telling me that drugs and tennis didn't mix; that I was ruining Sophie's chances of making a career in tennis. As if I cared about that."

The mention of Sophie stirred Jess into a response, "She's a decent girl, you're supposed to be her teacher, she deserved better than you!"

Buckley pushed his gun into Bartlett's face. "Enough!" Buckley pulled up one of the chairs in his office and made himself comfortable for his next instalment.

"So Dawson turns up here at 10 o'clock and I slip outside to meet him. He doesn't want to listen to my point of view and starts to push me. Can you believe it? He's pushing me. Who the hell does he think he is? So I punched him, not hard, more of a warning punch, but he loses his balance, falls over and hits his head on the kerb down there." Buckley pointed out of the window with his gun. "The silly sod has killed himself."

"No. You killed him when you punched him."

"Whatever. I couldn't have the body discovered here, or even his car, so I shoved his body in the bushes, dashed up here to grab one of Savage's clean suits and a pair of gloves, then took the knife from old Garnett's kitchen. I knew she was off sick so no one would be using her kitchen for a few days. I put the body back in Dawson's car and drove him back to the tennis club and dumped the body on the tennis court. Then I stabbed him and that time I meant it. He'd been a fucking pain in the arse and he got what was coming to him."

"Just like you'll get what's coming to you."

Buckley bent down and slapped Bartlett hard across the face with the gun, knocking her flat across the floor. "Stop fucking interrupting bitch!"

"I liked Dawson but he wouldn't let go. He caused me a few problems, I had to replace that knife of Garnett's and jiggle about with the school video cameras, but nothing I couldn't handle." Buckley stopped to brush an imaginary fleck of dust from his shoulder. "Dawson didn't understand that it's not easy in the drug business. All this covid has changed everything, the easy weekend trade has dried up, people aren't coming out anymore, the soft punter is staying indoors. But the Dutch won't listen to that, they say they've made commitments and we have to take our share. The tennis club filled a gap and conning some of these dumb bitches into taking some tabs to ensure I gave them the right grades for university all helped but it wasn't enough. It's never enough."

Bartlett rolled over and spat out a tooth, "my heart bleeds for you."

Buckley stopped and looked down at her. "Now I have a different problem, what to do with you? I can't let you walk away; you know too much."

Bartlett shrank back against the desk, her mouth stretched and drawn back.

BEE STUCK HIS head into the ops room and rounded up a couple of deputies for his mission, next stop was the floor below where he enlisted Carol Bishop. Five minutes later his makeshift army rolled out of the station and made its way up to Buckley's house. He sent the two new recruits to the rear of the property and marched to the door with Bishop. At the door he glanced across to his new partner. “Ready? This could get nasty.”

“You don’t need to worry about me sir. I won’t let you down.” She drew her taser to back up her words.

Once again the door was opened by a bemused Mrs Buckley and once again she told the police that her husband was at work. But this time Bee insisted on checking the facts for himself. This thoroughness delayed his operation by ten minutes. But soon the cavalcade swept down Cockshot Hill and sped off to the King’s School.

ADRENALINE WAS SURGING through McTierney’s veins as he raced down Croydon Road and into the small car park at the back of the school. He spotted Buckley’s Range Rover and pulled over a few metres away from it, strode up to it and peered through the windows – the tinted glass obscured his view. He pulled back and cursed. What to do? There was no sign of any police activity here. If he bounded in and ruined the case, Bee would be livid. Technically he was no longer a serving detective with the protection and rights of the police force. Damn! Bartlett didn’t appear to be here and certainly not in danger. He grabbed his mobile and pressed the button to call Bee but the call went through to voice mail. Typical. His thoughts were interrupted by the double doors at the front of the building bursting open. It was Buckley carrying someone over his shoulder. Time stood still for both men.

“Keep out of my way or she dies.”

McTierney stepped back and lifted his arms indicating that he was unarmed.

Buckley strode to his car and flung Bartlett's body across the bonnet. McTierney could see tape across her mouth, her hands were tied and there was a look of terror on her face. Buckley clicked the doors opened and dragged Bartlett's limp body to the back door. He pulled his gun from his waistband and pointed it at McTierney. "You make any attempt to stop me and she's dead. Now fuck off out of the way."

McTierney kept his eyes on Bartlett but stepped slowly back away from Buckley and towards his own car. As the two men circled around, Bee's old Mercedes roared down the narrow drive and burst into the car park. Buckley spun round to confront the noise and fired wildly at the car. One bullet smashed the passenger window another tore into the rear door. The car screeched to a halt. Buckley turned to shoot at McTierney but he was nowhere to be seen. He swung back to face the Mercedes but Bee had rolled out of the driver's seat and was behind the car. McTierney edged around the front of Buckley's car until he was within ten yards. Suddenly Buckley was exposed; four bullets left, two police detectives on either side of him and no cover. He reached for Bartlett and pulled her close to him.

"Give up now Buckley," shouted Bee. "Throw down that gun and nobody needs to get hurt."

"Fuck off!" yelled Buckley and he fired at Bee's car shattering the windscreen; Carol Bishop, trapped in the passenger seat of the car, screamed.

Then it all happened at once. McTierney leapt forward onto Buckley and the pair tumbled to the ground, knocking Bartlett over at the same time. Bee took his opportunity to raise his head and fired at Buckley. McTierney and Buckley collapsed to the ground. Buckley swung a fist at the back of

McTierney's head and his hand scrabbled around for his gun, but McTierney's rugby tackle had caught Buckley across the thighs and taken the teacher three yards from the weapon. McTierney buried his head in Buckley's neck and pressed him to the ground with all his might. The big man tried to wrestle him over but couldn't get the momentum, Bee grabbed his right hand and twisted it backwards. "That'll do Mr Buckley."

With Buckley in handcuffs, and McTierney dusting himself down, Bee bent down to help Bartlett. He turned her head over but her vacant eyes told him everything and he collapsed to the ground. "My God, what have I done?"

THIRTY-SEVEN

RON OPENED SCOTT'S fridge, it was a hot Saturday morning and he needed a cool drink. It was a choice between beer, orange juice and oat milk. He picked up the milk out of curiosity and read the small print on the grey pack. 'What the fuck have you been putting in your body, Scott? No wonder you're such a tight arse!'

He put the carton back and took a beer. The cold beer soothed his thirst but sparked his hunger. He looked around for something to eat. He pulled open a cupboard and spotted a tube of cheese and onion Pringles. That was more like it. And Scott had already started the packet so he wouldn't miss a few. Ron tilted the tube and a dozen or more perfect crisp circles tumbled on to his open palm. A few quickly became the whole tube, a pang of guilt ran up his spine and he tipped the last three back into the pack and returned it to the cupboard.

Scott had been out running across the county to take his mind off the tragedy that had unfolded the day before, but no matter how far or how fast he ran he could only think of Jess. His mood didn't improve when he approached his house and saw Ron's car on the drive.

"Couldn't you have waited until I returned?"

"Didn't know how long you'd be?"

"You could've called?"

"Didn't think you'd want to see me!"

"Ha, you got that one right. I see you've made yourself at home."

"Don't worry I only came to collect my things; I'll be out of here within the hour."

Scott nodded at the response and took the orange juice from the fridge, flopped down at the kitchen table, and drank half the bottle. Ron watched him. Scott put the bottle on the table.

"What? You weren't thinking of having a juice chaser were you?"

Ron shook his head and a stillness fell on the kitchen, both men let their eyes drop to the floor. The radio DJ offered some banal advice about covid safety before playing a Springsteen track. Scott maintained his radio silence. Eventually it was Ron who spoke.

"What happened to Buckley?"

"The chief brought in DI Miller from Guildford to wrap it up. I believe he's been charged and they've picked up Savage. He was hiding in Buckley's shed at the bottom of his garden. Beck's been decent about it, he understood that I didn't want to pick up the pieces after Jess's death."

"Fair enough."

"Of course there'll be a major enquiry. Bishop told me she'd had to give a statement. You'll get called back I'm sure."

"Already said my piece, but Beck knows where to find me if he needs me."

Scott nodded his acceptance and fell silent again. The radio DJ was back but the music choice deteriorated.

"I'm sorry the way things turned out with Jess." Ron put

an olive branch on the table but Scott wasn't about to pick it up.

"I should never have allowed you to date her. What was I thinking?"

"It wasn't up to you. It was Jess's choice – she's not your puppet. She had her own life And I loved her for that."

"Don't tell me you loved her; you barely knew her. What was it? Four weeks since you met her. You can't love someone in that short space of time, not truly love them. You might have fancied her a bit, you might have been in lust with her, but you didn't love her."

Ron slammed his fist down on the table. "Don't tell me what I felt. You don't bloody know. You've only known me for four weeks!"

Scott jumped up from his seat. "Get out. Get out of my sight. Get out of my house."

Ron disappeared to pack up his things, dropped them by the door and stepped back into the kitchen for one last time. He found Scott slumped over the kitchen table crying. Ron stopped and put his arm around Scott's shoulder. "Come on now Scott."

"I can't. You see Jess is my daughter, was my daughter, and I never got to tell her. I never got to tell her how proud I was of what she's achieved, of who she'd become."

Ron pulled up the chair and sat in front of Scott. "Your daughter! Why didn't you say?"

Scott wiped some tears from his face, sniffed and stared at Ron.

"Her mother didn't want me to be any part of her life. She gave me a choice when she discovered she was pregnant and I was too scared to accept it. So from that day on, we made a deal. I would silently support them and she would send me details of her growing up, but I would stay out of her life." Scott pointed to the photo on the table, "that's Jess in the photo when she was three months old, her mother had taken her to Stockholm."

Ron turned to look at it and saw the resemblance.

"For the most part she's been out of my life, and then when she turned eighteen she joined the police and all at once I had a small window on her life."

"That must have been good."

Scott looked up and gave a weak smile. "It got better; she applied to join the detective branch and Beck asked me if I'd take her under my wing and show her the ropes. Of course he didn't know the relationship, but all at once I was getting to learn so much about her. At last I was watching her blossom. It was perfect, as perfect as anything can be in this shitty world. I got to see her every day, it was like fate was making up for all those early years. The price I had to pay was not telling her she was my daughter. I should have known it would go wrong."

"It wasn't your fault. We were arresting a violent criminal who was shooting at us."

"But I'm the one that fired the bullet that killed her."

Scott hung his head and Ron's hand dropped across his shoulder.

The silence grew.

"Nobody knows she's your daughter."

Scott shook his head.

"No. If they did I would have been in trouble. I'd thought about how I wanted to tell her, how to share my joy with her, I hadn't worked it out yet but it was most certainly not via the minutes of a police disciplinary review."

Ron took a moment to digest the revelation. "What are you going to do now?"

"Take some leave and get away from this place, and you?"

"Clear up my mess in Norwich and look for something new, but don't worry your secret is safe with me."

THE END

If you've enjoyed reading this story,
then sign up for more stories by Phil Hall.

VISIT

www.philhallauthor.com

★★★★★

ACKNOWLEDGEMENTS

In the past whenever I reached the end of a book, I've either been excited about the story and keen to tell someone about it or let down by the conclusion and tossed the book aside. Rarely, have I stayed to read the acknowledgements. I hope your approach is more mature than mine. I hope you enjoyed the story and have a few minutes spare, I think two will suffice to read my thank-you speech.

I'd like to start at home and thank my wife Andrea and daughter Lauren for not complaining about my regular fights with our home printer.

No writer can succeed without a small army of beta readers willing to plough through early copies of their work. My battalion of unpaid warriors are Andrea B, Anne H, Andy G, Andy L, Dave B, Frank B, Gary S, Karen S, Katie B, Mary I, Pauline F, Russell D, Stuart M and Tom G. All were generous beyond what I had any right to expect. Especially those blessed with reading the first draft, a tortuous process at any time.

I can't ignore the one professional involved in this process, especially as he kindly returned to fight again after the first book – and he really should've known better. Patrick Knowles – a first rate cover designer and great sounding board.

My eternal thanks to you, one and all. It's been a slice.

Whilst I have casually killed off a tennis coach and heaped the blame on a school teacher in this story, I would like to point out that I have tremendous respect for both professions. Additionally the Russell in the book is alive and well and available for coaching sessions most days of the week. As final proof my daughter is both a tennis coach and has been educated in two Reigate schools.

Finally, all the crime related stats that I quote in the book are genuine, or at least they were when I copied them from the internet, most relate to 2019. I have nothing against Redhill or Croydon – they were simply stats to add colour to a story.

Printed in Great Britain
by Amazon

81746901R00190